To Ride the Wild Wind

To Ride the Wild Wind

Ian Whyte

FOR BARBARA BULL.

Pearl Press

First published in Great Britain by Pearl Press Limited
ISBN 978-0-9566518-3-9

Printed and bound by Good News, Ongar, England.

To Jen and Kim for their patience and encouragement

*Thanks to Joy Young for her advice and constructive
criticism. To 'Jumper Gee' and my other English teachers
for nurturing my love for words.
To Chris and Jessica Hart for the book on their shelf
containing the photograph which sparked off
the original idea for this novel.
To John Heaton for his kind words and for pointing
me in the right direction.
To Wendy Mellor for endless typing and for making sense
of my hieroglyphics.
To all at Pearl Press for guiding me so thoroughly
through the whole publishing process.*

All characters and events in this book are fictitious; however, the situation with the shingle banks is based on a factual occurrence at Hallsands, Devon, 1917

Contents

Introduction

I ran. Like a crazed animal trying to escape a predator: aimlessly, despairingly, agonisingly. I tripped, falling headlong, tearing the flesh from my hands and knees and my eyes, half-blinded by sweat and tears, glanced down at the blood on my hands and I cried out with a bellowing roar of anguish. I dragged myself up by the branch of a tree, my mind wrestling with the consequences of the awful thing I'd just done.

My aching legs carried me on the tortuous path down the hill through the olive groves, stumbling and falling numerous times in the semi-darkness until eventually I could lift myself no more and I lay where I landed, in a pit of rubbish in a deserted farmyard on the outskirts of Vietri town.

That was where they found me two days later; staring up into the sky with dark, swollen eyes my body buried in filth, my arms limp by my side, my legs folded under me, twisted and contorted yet not feeling pain, my brain too numb to register anything as simple as physical affliction.

The nightmare which I had dreaded for so long had only just begun.

Chapter 1

'What's done is done, boy…..you can't turn back the clock.'

He always called me boy. I was never referred to as Alexander… always, boy.

Every day, without fail, there would come the time when I would be compelled to describe the activities of the last twenty-four hours in minute detail. The closing comment from my father would invariably be: 'Well, what's done is done, boy…..you can't turn back the clock.'

There were no words of encouragement if I had done well and a swipe from his belt if I had done wrong. My mother said nothing.

She showed no affection, no emotion. There were no kisses, no cuddles, not even a pat on the head or a touch of the hand. I would go to my room at night and climb into a cold bed, but no one ever came in to tuck me up and wish me goodnight. I would blow out the candle and lie awake in the darkness making wishes that the next day they would love me.

Birthdays were different. In the morning, I would be showered with expensive presents. They were never wrapped up, but expensive nonetheless. In the evening we always went to St James's park to feed the ducks with pieces of stale bread which I had saved over the previous week. Mother and father would laugh and joke, and for an hour I felt like any other well loved son. On the way home, they reverted to their normal, disagreeable selves, leaving me feeling cheated and confused. I longed for that one hour of the year in the park, but loathed the journey home and the way my father continually mumbled the himself: 'What's done is done.....we can't turn back the clock.'

My tenth birthday was the same as all the others, that is, until we were nearly home. I sensed that something was different during the final walk from the station when my mother uncharacteristically strode out in front of my father and me. She always walked just behind, and if necessary, held the umbrella keeping us dry, but allowing herself to get soaking wet. This time she stayed dry and we were the ones to get drenched.

We were only a few steps away from the front gate when he uttered the words which would alter my whole life, 'Boy.....you're not our real son. You were adopted when you were a baby.'

He didn't even break his stride or offer a single word of explanation.

My mother, as usual, said nothing.

They left me in the street in my little gabardine coat while the rain mingled with my tears and dripped off the end of my nose. An hour later, cold and shivering, I pushed open the front door and entered a house that felt as lonely as the grave.

From that day forward I hated them above anything else, and my young scheming mind would continually be devising ways in which I could hurt them. Every night when I blew out the candle, I would verbalise my thoughts in harsh, obscene whispers until I fell asleep and dreamt of them dying.

4

The subject of my adoption was never brought up again, but the sense of rejection ran deep. In a forlorn attempt to gain their affection I devoted all my time and effort to school and sports; but no matter how I excelled, no praise was ever forthcoming. The remotest laxity on my part however, was greeted with a shake of the head and the admonishment that I wasn't trying hard enough, followed by a sound beating.

As I grew older, the continual striving conjured up in me a morbid fear of failure. Outwardly, I was still the boy who ran faster, worked longer and punched harder than anyone else. I was described by my form master in my school report as 'extremely tenacious' but the more observant headmaster was much closer when he used the word 'ruthless.' Inwardly, however, the pain and hurt ran so deep and so intense that I knew that one day I would lose the fight to disguise my true feelings and it was this thought alone which filled me with unmitigated dread.

The charade on my birthday continued until I joined the army. We tried it once more a few years later while I was home on leave, but I felt a fool standing there: tall, dark and lean with officer's pips on my shoulder, feeding the ducks, and I told them so on the way home.

I left early the next day to return to my regiment and they were both killed that same night as the first of Hitler's bombers arrived over London.

I got drunk to celebrate their demise, but when I sobered up, the hurts and fears were not only still there, but even more so. I was granted a week's compassionate leave so I could stand alone by their graves and mourn the loss of nothing.

*****

5

As the strictest of disciplinarians and the maintainer of seemingly impossible standards, I quickly rose to the rank of Major. My reputation soon spread as the one to whom the dirty jobs were given. I had an almost indifferent attitude to pain and death and expected any men under me to be of like manner. I drilled them remorselessly and the ones who couldn't take it branded me a bully and a sadist, but I was beyond caring. The collection of medal ribbons was sufficient evidence that I was doing what my superiors wanted of me, even if they had to occasionally turn a blind eye to the hard line I took with some of my methods.

In the busy hubbub of war certain things go unnoticed that otherwise would be of an extremely serious nature. I was a loner by nature anyway and I had no friends as such. My men acknowledged me, but didn't like me and I mixed socially with no one. Consequently, nobody noticed the toll that was being exacted on my mind as I constantly struggled to keep above my fear of failure. Each time I was given a new mission I drove my men even harder, but the fears were growing more intense day by day as I descended the slippery slope towards inevitable disaster.

*****

I was eventually posted to North Africa where I spent two months as one of a select group of six section officers, each in charge of thirty men. We had been given no clues as to what it was we were training for other than the fact that it was classified as top secret. There was great friendship, but also great rivalry between each section. This had been cultivated deliberately by the Colonel in Chief, the aim being, so he said, to get us razor sharp for the job to come. My section had come through in top place.

The camp had been alive with rumours for almost a week before notification had eventually been given that a full briefing would be forthcoming the following day. I slept little during the night and when I shaved and dressed in the morning there were dark rings under my eyes. There was to be a joint meeting of all section officers at 0800 hours followed by individual briefings from the C.O. Finally, all the ranks were to be brought together and we would each fill in our units on the final details.

'Today is September 5th 1943,' began the Colonel, 'The next few days will go down in history as the largest amphibious invasion of all time!' He paused for effect, raising his closely cropped head from the typewritten script, then carried on reading, his voice a staccato monotone. 'Very soon, Operation Avalanche will take place on the beaches of Salerno! A vast armada is converging in the Mediterranean ready for the assault on Italy. There are hundreds of craft, and thousands of men. The enemy know we are there, but they don't know where we're going to hit them.

There will be no preliminary bombing, instead, to maintain surprise, your units will be parachuted in with the soul purpose of destroying selected targets and consequently destroy their communications network.'

He stopped speaking for a few seconds and removed his glasses while surveying the room. A wry smile crossed his lips as he said slowly, 'The maximum confusion..... with the minimum of fuss!' He replaced his glasses as he once again turned his attention to the paper in front of him. 'You will rendezvous with the main invasion force before being moved further forward in the advance on Naples where, again, specific targets will be designated to you. Needless to say, those targets won't be made known to you until you regroup. Security is vital, so at present, you will only be told what you need to know, we don't want the enemy to learn too much should you fail in your objective and be captured.'

He seemed to look directly at me when he mentioned the word 'fail' as if reading the very thoughts I wanted to keep from him. The rest of the briefing continued for an hour before we were given the details of our specific targets individually from the Colonel.

I was first in and was handed a sealed envelope with my name, rank and unit number on it.

He let out a deep breath as I marched in and stood at attention in front of his desk. 'Your objective, Major, is the Villa Angrisani outside of Salerno itself. Our reports say that it's being used as a temporary headquarters for the area. It's a crucial target! It has command of the most northerly beaches where the U.S. Rangers and the 46th Infantry will land. You will be relieved by the Commandos landing in Salerno town who are, in turn, relying on you to knock out the command post. The 15 Panzergrenadier Division will be snapping at your heels from the Vietri Pass which is a narrow road through into the hills above your target.

Map references, dates and times are detailed with your instructions. Get it right, Major Kinsey. You have the most important target!.....Any questions?'

'No. Sir.' I replied.

'Then go, and good luck.'

I saluted and left. I never saw him again.

Afterwards came the long briefing to my unit. We had done the practicing again and again, but this was the real thing. They were tense yet excited. They were all battle hardened but for most of them, this was their first experience of being dropped behind enemy lines. I, too, was apprehensive but I hid it by being deliberately matter of fact about the whole operation.

Kit had already been allocated to us, and all there remained for us to do was to eat and try and get some sleep before we were flown out to Sicily where we would spend the best part of the next day with the Eighth Army. From there, it was about two hundred miles to our dropping zone north of Salerno and a short trip to our objective.

*****

The interior of the plane was dark and unfriendly. The creaks and rattles that were everyday noises to aircrew were foreign to us and did nothing to ease my disquiet. I could scarcely make out the blackened faces of those with whom I had worked so intimately over the last two months. I knew their names of course, and their skills, but no camaraderie had developed between them and myself. They worked mechanically and efficiently for the glory of their country, but they didn't work for me. I knew they despised me for the bullying tactics I used and they hated me even more for my lack of compassion.

The steady drone of the engines hypnotised me into fitful sleep and I dreamt of rows of smoking chimney pots in a street full of endless, grey houses and a frightened little boy in a gabardine coat.

The dropping zone was upon us sooner than expected and hardly before I knew it, I felt the buffeting of the wind and the pull of the chute opening. Thirty dangling mushrooms suspended under a canopy of camouflaging cloud, seemingly motionless in the blindness of night, and then the abrupt hard fall to the ground. I lay slightly dazed in the ensuing silence, listening intently for any sound that might betray our presence, but all was still. I quickly unclipped the chute and buried it hastily under some loose soil; my movements were rapid and effective but my hands were shaking. By now my eyes were well accustomed to the darkness and my ears were sharp. I heard a distant owl hoot and another in reply and within a few minutes quiet footsteps approached in the gloom. I hid behind a tree, just in case, but it was only one of my unit joined, soon afterwards by two more.

Within half an hour, twenty-eight of us had congregated, but there was no sign of the other two. We waited for another fifteen minutes before I ordered the unit to break into small groups and go looking for them. I glanced at my watch; it was already one o'clock and we still had to find the villa.

It was another hour before a young corporal reported back that he had found both of the men in a small wood about half a mile away, so I followed him, leaving my Second-in-Command to regroup the rest of the unit. One chute had not opened properly and the soldier had come down too quickly breaking both his legs and probably causing internal injuries as well. The other had landed in the trees but had managed to release himself and climb down to assist the man on the ground.

'Why didn't you come to the rendezvous point Private Oliver?' I hissed at him in the dark.

'But I didn't want to leave him Sir. He's badly hurt.'

'And are you the medic on this trip, Oliver?' I asked, with considerable agitation.

'No Sir.'

'Then you should bloody well have come to the rendezvous point as you were ordered. We're more than an hour behind schedule now because of you, now let's get going!'

He looked at me, dumbfounded. 'But what about Jimmy, Sir?'

'You'll have to pull him into the undergrowth and leave him, we'll pick him up later.'

I had never been a paragon of tender, loving kindness, but even I was shocked at my own lack of compassion.

'Move it, soldier!' I barked, trying to cover up a sudden tinge of conscience; so he got on with his job then followed me back to where the rest of the unit had assembled.

There was a two mile walk south down the edge of the Vietri Pass, and as we had to avoid the road, our progress was slow. Broad, low branched olive trees hampered both our movements and our visibility and we almost stumbled into a heavily manned road block. We stood like statues and watched them as they talked and smoked and I tried to suppress an almost irresistible urge to make some sort of noise to attract their attention. A prison camp for the rest of the war seemed like a pleasant alternative, but the temptation passed and we melted into the shadows and carried on our way.

I kept looking at my watch as the minutes ticked by. It would be dawn in two hours and we would lose the cover of darkness. My whole body was aching with the cumulative effects of the tension and lack of sleep. I knew that the enemy must have realised by now that an invasion was imminent, I just hoped that they were looking out to sea and not inland from where we were now approaching.

We descended the steps of some vineyards, eventually seeing the Mediterranean beneath our position as we looked down on Vietri. I was very worried now. I had heard one or two muffled explosions in the distance and wondered if it was the other units already destroying their targets and alerting everybody else in the vicinity. We hadn't even arrived at our target yet, never mind the task of actually destroying it and I could sense the mounting tension in the men around me.

Uncannily, I had the feeling that the day of reckoning , which I had so earnestly dreaded, had finally arrived. I had fought too hard and for too long and could feel myself weakening rapidly. A voice inside me willed me not to fail, but it sounded more feeble by the minute.

I wiped the back of my hand across my mouth tasting a mixture of sweat and mud. We were close to the road which led down to the crossroads where the villa lay, but we still had to creep slowly for another mile before we dared approach directly on the road. Over the cliffs of Vietri the sea was still dark but to the east there was the ghostly silhouette of a myriad trees against the background colours of a hazy dawn. Not long now and our shapes would no longer be able to disappear into the darkness. I tried desperately to dictate caution to my legs so as to maintain cover for as long as possible, but for some reason they wouldn't do as I bade them.

When I finally caught sight of the crossroads and the buildings around about it, I broke in to a cold sweat. A wave of my hand was enough to send the unit into concealment in the nearby, dewy, wet undergrowth. I circled round, slithering silently in the grass like a snake ready to strike and finally lay prone at a safe vantage point above the location of our target.

As I reached down for my binoculars, my eyes alighted on a spider as it scuttled across a web saturated with fine droplets of water. It left a jigsaw pattern of footprints over its perfectly constructed home while an unfortunate fly struggled in vain as the spider weaved unbreakable, suffocating chains around it. Silent....but deadly! I looked around at the human shapes hidden in the long grass and had the same thought. For a brief moment my worries subsided and were replaced by the faint glow of pride.

As expected, there were no lights from any of the small collection of villas that lay nestled in the hillside, but neither were there any signs of life whatsoever. I couldn't understand it. I focussed the glasses on the Villa Angrisani where there should at least have been guards and vehicles, but there wasn't even a moving shadow to betray the presence of a restless sentry. I looked up and down each of the neat dwellings set back from the road, but there was no sign of movement anywhere.

A voice whispered in my ear, 'See anything, Sir?'

My Second-in-Command, a boyish looking Lieutenant fresh from officer training with too much enthusiasm for his own good, was the one to ask the question.

'Nothing....Nothing at all.' I muttered in reply, trying to hide my mounting concern.

'Perhaps they've all gone home , Sir?' He said, half laughing, but I could detect the nervousness in his humour.

'No..... I don't think they've gone home, Lieutenant.' I replied, slowly, shaking my head, and as an afterthought I added: 'But where have they gone? .....I think they're just playing hide and seek.'

I stopped. The glasses alighted on a villa half surrounded with olive trees, the faint glow of an illicit cigarette giving away the position of a sentry. Eventually two moving shadows congregated with a third then separated by strolling around the far side of the villa.

'They've moved their H.Q.' I stated emphatically to the Lieutenant.

13

'Damned inconvenient if you ask me, Sir! Why would they do that? Are you sure you're looking at the right villa?'

'Are you questioning my judgement?' I snapped, instinctively.

He looked at me with a glint of defiance in his eyes, then remembered his rank. 'No, Sir,' he replied, defensively, 'It's just that the villa is supposed to be on one side of the road and you're looking at the other.'

I felt strangely intimidated by his questions, sensing that despite his youth, he was beginning to discern my unstable mind.

I checked again through the glasses, but the villa we were supposed to target was totally lifeless whereas the one opposite had at least four guards in operation.

'Then perhaps they got the intelligence wrong, Lieutenant!' I barked. 'Our supposed target is uninhabited, it's all boarded up and no one there!'

I suddenly realised that it was getting lighter and already I could see things much clearer, but that, in turn, also meant that the enemy could see us more clearly as well.

'Shouldn't we do a recce first, Sir, just to check things out?' He said, with some insistence.

'What! And risk losing our surprise! There's no other possible explanation. There's only one building here being guarded, so it has to be that one!

'But what if it's not?' came the stubborn reply. 'What if we hit the wrong target?'

I retaliated. 'There is no other target! Look.....!' I argued, in a quieter tone. 'It's getting light, we're behind schedule, and our lads will be landing on those beaches soon. We have to take that villa out and be away before they can get any reinforcements from that roadblock further up the pass.'

I knew I couldn't wait any longer. He was about to reply when a distant explosion and a faint flash of light a few miles south signified another target being destroyed by one of the other units. I lifted my binoculars and saw two of the sentries run round the side of the building and look in the direction of the explosion. They would be alert now and know that they would very likely be a prospective target themselves.

I rolled onto my back and looked around me at the blackened faces partly concealed in the undergrowth and whispered sharply in command. 'Sergeants Harper and Gould! Corporals Serridge and Tudor!' Four men shuffled towards me with barely a sound. 'Harper and Serridge take the north and east sides of the villa. Gould and Tudor move around to the west and south sides. There are at least four guards. Silent approach, silent dispatch until we penetrate the main building. The rest of us will advance through the front entrance. There's no time for explosives; grenades and machine guns will suffice.

Watch the crossfire. Our record in north Africa was out in two minutes after initial penetration. They won't know what hit them.

We have a change of target. They've moved their H.Q. to the villa across the road.'

There were puzzled glances on their faces when I made the last statement.

'Is there a problem, Harper?' I snapped.

Harper was a sergeant of the old school: hard as nails, obdurate and with a tongue almost as sharp as mine. The difference was that the men under him worshipped the ground he walked on!

'How do we know they've switched, Sir?' he growled.

I laughed almost hysterically, 'Do you want to knock on the door and see if they want to come out and play, sergeant? Our original target is deserted, the only inhabited villa is the one we're going for!' I glared at him in the semi-darkness and he shrugged his broad shoulders and kept silent.

'Brief your groups. We move out in five minutes. We'll rendezvous in the woods back up beyond the vineyards. We should be safely out before anyone arrives.'

They moved silently away and a few minutes later gave the thumbs up that they were ready to go. I could feel the panic rising in me and only just managed to stop myself from being sick.

'Are you alright, Sir ?' came the voice of my lieutenant beside me.

'Go to hell, Pillington!' I rasped into the night air. 'Of course I'm alright!' But he didn't look convinced.

'Let's go.' I hissed and we set off down the last two hundred yards towards the villa. We crossed the road under the shadow of a cloud and fanned out into five groups as we reached the wall surrounding the villa. The building itself was large and square and any areas which weren't decorated with ornate brickwork were painted white to reflect the main heat of the midday sun. New vines had recently been planted around the walls and were already reaching towards the lower shuttered windows and in different circumstances it would have been a place to delight in and aspire to. The gardens around it were flat and full of fairly dense vegetation which helped us in our approach, but we would have to rush the main entrance as it was the most exposed area.

My mouth was dry and I tried to lick my lips to work up some saliva. Countless times during training in north Africa we had done this sort of exercise, and every time it had been successful, but this time someone would be firing back at us and they wouldn't be firing blanks!

I looked at the second hand on my watch as it moved round unbearably slowly to the minute position. I must not fail, but I gave no thought to the importance of the mission; the fear of failure was the only motivation at the forefront of my brain. It seemed as if all my memories of continually struggling towards higher goals resurrected themselves in my mind during those final seconds. I didn't even know who I was; just some nameless orphan with adoptive parents who cared nothing for me. Nothing I had done had ever generated any feelings from them, and even now, with both of them dead, they still haunted me. I had continued in my upward spiral of achieving until I knew that one day it was inevitable that I would fail.

The second hand reached twelve and exactly on cue, we attacked the building from all four sides. The four breakdown groups secured the four sides while the fifth group, led by myself, carried out the frontal attack. The front door collapsed with the first grenade, and we raced in with my group splitting to right and left, running fast and low, firing at anything in our path. I heard shouts from beyond the large door which led into the room directly in front of the main entrance. Pulling a pin from a grenade I ran full pelt at the door, crashing through it and throwing the grenade at the same time. I dived for the floor while simultaneously spraying the whole room systematically with machine gun fire, silencing the dying screams of the occupants. I was yelling at the top of my voice as the explosion deafened my ears, the exhilaration and blood lust sending me over the boundaries of sanity while my finger cramped on the trigger.

No sooner had it started than it was over, the crumbling of masonry the only sound in the stillness, any other noises being blanketed by the fog and dust that gently settled on the room. I slowly pushed myself to my feet and looked around me as the fine particles from the air collected on the furniture and the lifeless bodies that littered the room.

The walls were covered with a mosaic of bullet holes none more than four feet above the ground, exactly as I had been trained to do. During the ensuing hush, a ghostly ray of light began to glisten through a broken window pointing a finger of accusation as realisation dawned on me. I suddenly felt my heart pounding in my chest, not with exertion but with the growing significance of what I had done.

Lieutenant Pillington stood shakily at the door and let out the worst string of obscenities I had ever heard. He would have killed me there and then had he not had to pause to throw up on the floor. I heard footsteps behind which stopped momentarily at the door then continued past me. Sergeant Harper surveyed the room, then slowly pivoted round. The expression on his face was a mixture of horror and agonising despair and his body shook with barely suppressed rage. He stepped clumsily over the piles of rubble, his eyes never leaving mine.

'I'll......I'll......' he tried to speak, but the words wouldn't come. I was vaguely aware of other sounds as the rest of the unit assembled in the room, but I was totally transfixed by the penetrating stare of the man before me.

'I'll.....I'll..... see you rot in hell!' he finally sobbed before hitting me so hard in the stomach that I careered backwards and crashed violently against the wall. Pillington, who had recovered by now, dragged him off me.

'Leave him, Harper!' He yelled. 'Don't waste your energy on an animal like him, let's get the hell out of here!'

I heard them all go; leaving me pitifully isolated in the graveyard that I had created through my own folly.

'Don't leave me.' I whimpered after them. 'For God's sake, don't leave me!'

I pulled myself to my feet, trying to blot out the slaughter. My stomach was wracked with pain as I stumbled to the door, falling over bricks and mortar that had dislodged with the grenades.

'Don't leave me!' I shouted again, 'I'm your commanding officer.' My cry was pathetic and the disappearing men didn't even acknowledge my presence.

I reached the main door pleading with them not to leave me behind, but they ignored me. I peered after them and saw the villa opposite which should have been our target. I watched in horror as two of the windows opened revealing the dark shapes of enemy soldiers.

It only lasted a few seconds.

The staccato sound of repetitive machine gun fire cut through the early morning atmosphere like a razor sharp knife. It was like a macabre dance; almost graceful in its movements as my men threw their arms up in death while the bullets ripped into their flesh. They slumped to the ground, one by one as if the massacre was some perfectly choreographed finale to a West End show and they would soon all leap up again for the encore. But no one responded to the silent applause.

I crept back into the shadows of the villa muttering words of disbelief, my mind completely unhinged by the events of the last few minutes.

'What's done is done, boy. You can't turn back the clock.'

I heard my father's words echoing round my head, uttered without love or understanding. I saw a little boy in a cold bedroom with a single candle to dispel the gloom. I saw a young child feeding the ducks, longing to be loved, but destined only for loneliness. I saw a dishevelled creature in a gabardine coat standing in the rain outside a locked door.

'You're not our real son.....'

I had failed at last.

*****

I couldn't face returning to the room, neither could I face going out through the front, not even to surrender. Instead, I crept down a long passage and out through the window at the far end, hearing as I left, the first, cautious entry into the villa followed by shouts of dismay as they witnessed the room and its contents.

I didn't know where to go. I didn't know what to do. I didn't know what to think. So I ran. Like a crazed animal trying to escape a predator: aimlessly, despairingly, agonisingly. I tripped, falling headlong, tearing the flesh from my hands and knees, and my eyes, half blinded by sweat and tears, glanced down at the blood on my hands and I cried out with a billowing roar of anguish. I dragged myself up by the branch of a tree, my mind wrestling with the consequences of the awful thing I had just done.

My aching legs carried me on the tortuous path down the hill through the olive groves, stumbling and falling numerous times in the semi darkness until eventually I could lift myself no more and I lay where I landed in a pit of rubbish in a deserted farmyard on the outskirts of Vietri town.

And that was where they found me two days later, staring up into the sky with dark, swollen eyes, my body buried in filth, my arms limp by my sides, my legs folded up under me, twisted and contorted yet not feeling the pain, my brain too numb to register anything so simple as physical affliction.

'Where the hell have you come from, mate?' the U.S. Ranger said to me in puzzled surprise.

I didn't speak.

'Who is this guy?' he said to the two others with him. 'Looks like he's been through hell and back!'

He knelt down beside me. 'Who are you with, mate?.....How long've you been here?'

I didn't speak.

I didn't speak for six months.

Chapter 2

'Time is what you need, young man.....Time...and some good, wholesome food and fresh air.... lots of it ....fresh air that is. The seaside or the hills. Sit by a river with a fly rod and have a couple of pints for lunch.'

The doctor sucked on his pen and stared longingly up at the ceiling. 'I wish this Godawful war was over,' he mused, 'and I could retire with a fishing rod and a cool pint.'

He put my medical notes down on his desk and looked at me. 'You could be out of here tomorrow if you wanted, Major. What do you say?'

I said nothing.

He looked at my case notes again and pointed his pen at me while he leaned forward in his chair. 'You're a strange man, Kinsey, but there again, it's my job to deal with strange men. War does peculiar things to people....More than that, it does peculiar things to people who were peculiar already....' he paused for effect. 'You were peculiar already.'

A silence descended on the room.

'So what if I was.' I replied, my voice shaky after so long with no speech.

The doctor raised his eyebrows and breathed deeply. 'So, the Major has a tongue after all does he? How come you didn't speak before?'

'I had nothing to say before.'

'And you have something to say now?'

'Not really, but if it'll get me out of this hole I'll say anything you want!'

He looked at me then with no comment and eventually started to slowly nod his head. 'I've watched you over these last few months, Major Kinsey. As a psychiatrist, I learn as much from observing how people behave as I do from listening to what they say, and as you never said anything, I had to be content purely with watching.' He got up and walked towards the door, signifying that the interview was over. He placed his hand on the doorknob, but didn't turn it. 'Major Kinsey,' he said, quietly, 'I meant it. when I said that you could leave here soon, but I am a doctor and I am supposed to make people better .... but I cannot cure someone who goes around with a great big chip on his shoulder!'

I glared at him, but he wouldn't respond to any intimidation.

'Do me a favour, Major.... on second thoughts, do yourself a favour.... arrogance is a poor bedfellow....destroy it before it destroys you.'

I pushed past him and heard him muttering to himself about fly fishing and a cool pint. I closed the door. I knew he was right, but the habits of a lifetime are hard to break let alone habits hardened by the pressures of war.

Twenty five thousand men and civilians dead or wounded during twenty one days of carnage at Salerno. My mind juggled with the unreality of the numbers. By day, they were insignificant numbers, but by night I knew their names, everyone of them; their names, their faces, their families, their friends. I knew everything about them. Every night their imaginary faces would flash before me in an unrelenting ritual of repetition. Inevitably, I would wake up screaming as my tortured mind returned to the villa where I had made that first, fatal mistake. I no longer feared failure .... the burden of guilt hung over me far worse than any fears I had ever had before.

'Emotionally unfit for service.' it said on my medical discharge papers, but I knew no other life. A profitable career in the army with a comfortable pension had been my only idea for the future, and now I had nothing even remotely to look forward to. What little money I had was soon flittered away on drinking, coupled with a series of disastrous relationships which left me physically and mentally bankrupt.

In a fit of despair and depression, I signed the pledge at the feet of a soapbox orator in Hyde Park and joined the church. I broke the pledge the same day but stayed with the church as I had nowhere else to go. It was an odd liaison but one with which I was not totally unhappy. No-one knew of my background, and when asked, I would casually change the subject. I even developed some superficial friendships with other students; nothing deep and nothing lasting, but friendships nonetheless. The hostel had been bombed in an air raid so we each had had to find our own accommodation. I eventually ended up in the attic room of a house owned by a deaf spinster who couldn't hear my night-time cries as I dreamt of Salerno and Vietri Pass. She cooked me dinner on Sundays and called me Reverend and insisted on taking confession behind the living room curtains even though I was at an Anglican theological college and not a Catholic one.

The terms passed quickly with a mixture of study, preaching and sport. The holidays were spent in the same attic room or running across Hampstead Heath until I was exhausted. This was followed by a single pint to replenish some fluid while I sat in the corner of a quiet pub near Swiss Cottage. I drank alone. I invited the landlord to my ordination and asked him if I could call him Uncle Charles for the day as a joke. It didn't take him long to realise that I was the only new clergyman with no relatives present, and that night we got drunk together at his expense. The Reverend Kinsey and his Uncle Charles spent the night being sick into a vase on the landing. He was the closest to a friend I had ever had and I didn't even know his surname. The old lady didn't hear a thing.

I was sent as a curate to a remote parish in the Derbyshire Peak District and got the distinct impression that I had been sent there to be kept out of the way. The place was pleasant enough: a few streets, a church and two pubs, and that was it. After the noise and bustle of London, it somehow felt too quiet.

I got off the bus and soon found the vicarage which was sited, as was so often the case, next to the church. The house was large and inhabited solely by the Reverend John McNulty and his wife, Isobella. Their family had long since grown up and left the fold and they were due to retire within a few years' time.

There was a bell pull which I noticed only after I had knocked, but before I could ring it, the door was opened. I was greeted by a condescending smile between rosy cheeks on a face with two days growth of grey beard. He was corpulent and clad in a threadbare suit that might once have been expensive. I had always expected my men to be smartly turned out, so I felt immediate antagonism towards this unkempt man who was to be my senior.

'You'll be Alexander Kinsey, I presume.' he said, with the faint trace of an Irish accent.

I nodded.

'Now, what do we call you, my boy? .... Come in....Come in....' he beckoned me into the hall. 'Everyone knows me as Father John ... Now, is it Alex or Alexander?'

'Alexander!' I said, stiffly. His use of the word 'boy' brought back all sorts of unpleasant memories of my father.

'Then Alexander it is, my boy, though the locals will call you what they wish, but I'll tell them it's Alexander, and they can make up their own minds.'

He led me along the hall and into the kitchen at the far end.

'Put your case down, my boy,' he ordered, 'This is your home now, no need to stand on ceremony.'

He smiled at me as I tried to restrain my mounting anger as he continued to patronise me by referring to me as 'my boy.' He gestured across the room before I had time to make any remarks. A dignified looking woman sat perched upright in a chair by the stove, her gnarled hands wound round an intricate array of crochet spread over her lap.

'Isobella, my dear, this is Alexander.'

She looked at me with eyes that threatened to look right through me, yet not without gentleness. I swallowed involuntarily to hide my sudden embarrassment. Here was a woman who commanded respect and authority, but without the need to shout it from the rooftops.

'Good afternoon,' I said, and bowed slightly; it somehow seemed appropriate.

'I must go across to the church,' Father John interrupted, 'I'll leave you two to get acquainted. Sit down, my boy, make yourself at home, I'll be back a few minutes.'

I sat awkwardly as he left the room. There was just the faint hiss of burning coals in the stove and the muted ticking of a clock elsewhere

27

in the house.

'That's a nice shawl.' I ventured.

'It's for my grand-daughter....her christening is in three weeks time.' She shuffled a little to get more comfortable. 'It will soon be time for tea. John will be back soon .... I expect you're tired after your journey.'

I nodded my head. I couldn't place her accent; it was certainly not local, and certainly not Irish. Father John appeared a few minutes later and he and Isobella proceeded with an afternoon ritual with which I was to get very familiar over the next year. Bone china crockery was laid out on the table with a knife and cake fork by the side of each plate. Local produce had obviously managed to circumvent post war rationing as there was always home baked bread and a selection of cheese and fresh cream cakes, meanwhile, the teapot was left brewing on the hot stove.

'Well, my boy,' he said, wiping his lips with his napkin. 'I expect you'll be wanting to know what you'll be doing in this beautiful part of God's earth.'

'Just one moment,' I said, sharply, 'before we go any further! My name is Alexander! '... I object to being referred to as 'my boy' at the end of every sentence! Is that clear....? During my military career I was called 'Sir' or I was referred to according to my rank! I was never..... I repeat .... I was never called 'boy!'"

I thumped the table for emphasis and knocked the teaspoon out of my saucer. It clattered onto the stone floor, reverberating in the tense silence that followed my outburst.

Isobella nonchalantly carried on eating as if nothing had happened, washing down the cake with a mouthful of tea. 'He calls the

Bishop 'my boy.' she said, quietly. 'Don't you John?'

Her eyes met mine, and again, I was aware of her penetrating stare.

'I don't give a damn what he calls the Bishop,' I responded defensively. 'I don't give a damn what he calls Jesus Christ himself as long as he does not call me 'boy! .... Which is my room?' I said, sharply as I rose from the table.

Father John led the way up the stairs in stony silence to my room on the first floor. He opened the curtains which had kept out the heat of the afternoon sun and a hazy glow filled the nooks and crannies of the old-fashioned bedroom.

'Supper is at nine, my boy.' he said as he left the room.

If he had been a younger man, I would have hit him.

*****

I dreamt again that night. The same faces on the beaches; the same faces of my men; the same faces in the villa in Vietri. I shouted at them all to come alive again. I repeated the futile command for their resurrection and shouted louder and louder when they didn't respond. I woke with a start, aware that the door to my room was open as I could se the light from the landing. I was drenched in sweat and shaking all over, especially my arms which were throbbing violently up and down on the bed clothes.

A figure appeared in the doorway and quietly moved towards the bed. An arthritic hand was laid gently on my throbbing arm and a cold flannel placed across my hot forehead. I relaxed onto the pillow feeling the panic subside and my body go limp. Isobella leaned over me and kissed me lightly on the cheek. 'I'll leave your door open,' she whispered, 'so you can see the light....Goodnight, my child....sleep well.'

She floated to the door like a guardian angel, turning to smile at me in the dim light. I couldn't see her eyes but I knew that they didn't look on in judgement but rather, somehow, in understanding. I smiled back as an unuttered thank you and closed my eyes in the hope of untroubled sleep.

*****

In the following weeks I was aware that the sermons I preached were inadequate. Father John had oversight over four small churches so that we had to preach in rotation at each one. Congregations were small, so any hymn -singing was poor and, as I was not blessed with a marvellous voice, that part of the service tended to fall flat before I even started preaching. I found it easier to read my sermons rather than try to exude any sort of feeling or passion for the subject and after arriving back at the vicarage I often felt despondent and disillusioned.

I once asked Father John why he was known as Father and not simply 'John' or Vicar or Reverend. He had laughed at the question initially, then paused for a moments private reflection before he replied.

'I came from a staunch Catholic part of Dublin, my boy, where anyone wearing a clerical collar was called 'Father.' My first job as a curate was in a high Anglican Church, more Anglo-Catholic really.' He paused again and smiled at the recollection of it all. 'I was called Father there and the name stuck. I don't think twice about it now. At each church where I've been vicar I've been introduced as Father John; a few raised eyebrows until I explained that it was more of a nickname than a theological statement.'

Occasionally, we would preside over a service together and I had to admit that as the months passed, I developed a grudging respect for the way the man handled the congregations. His command was so different from the way I had led my army unit. I had led by fear; he led by example.

I had often shouted, he let his quiet influence do the leading. I realised then that when they called him 'Father John' it was much more than a nickname; it was a term of great endearment. Isobella was his constant supporter and tireless assistant and, although we never talked deeply or personally, I sensed a depth of love between them that was far, far beyond my level of experience or understanding.

Almost a year after my arrival, I received a letter which threw me into a state of confusion. My nightmares had continued and I had taken to going for long runs into the hills to hide my depression. I would run until I almost dropped in the hope of tiring myself so much that I would sleep that night. It was after one such exhausting run that I discovered the letter. I opened it in my room not knowing who it could possibly be from as I never wrote, and apart from an odd letter from a college acquaintance, I never usually received anything either. The letter was from a firm of solicitors in London and was signed by the senior partner.

Dear Major Kinsey
I write on behalf of your late father, Mr Thomas Bradbury.
It was his express wish that his identity should be kept secret until

after his death so as not to compromise in any way your adoption by Mr and Mrs Ebenezer Kinsey.

As sole beneficiary of the estate of Mr Thomas Bradbury, may I suggest that you contact me forthwith for an appointment at our mutual convenience.

Yours sincerely.

J. P. Gallimore.

Two days later, I found myself on the train down to London wondering what was going to happen at the interview with my real father's solicitors. I had never before experienced any desire to know about my past, so my mind was a jumble of conflicting thoughts tinged with suppressed anticipation.

Situated along the Edgeware Road, ironically, not far from Hyde Park where I had made the momentous decision to follow the path of religion, the offices of Gallimore and Reynold were shoddy and old fashioned. I was shown in half an hour late to be received by a grey haired, wizened, little man who looked at me frowningly over half framed spectacles.

'Good afternoon, Major Kinsey. My apologies for keeping you waiting; alas, the pressures of modern business do not always follow the timetable to which they were assigned.'

He gave a limp handshake and offered me a seat on the opposite side to his desk. He juggled with a pile of papers, pushing some to one side. 'Ah, yes! Here we have it, the last Will and Testament of Thomas Bradbury.....'

'Just hold it a moment,' I interrupted. 'I've come this far through life with the name of Kinsey and now find that I am really Bradbury ….. Before we go any further, don't you think that I deserve at least some sort of explanation as to what's been going on all this time.'

He coughed nervously, 'There is nothing in the will that says you should be told anything.'

'Come on!' I said, impatiently, 'I'm going to find out one way or another, so it may as well be from you.'

'Very well,' He replied, 'but this is strictly off the record you understand.'

I nodded and gestured for him to continue.

'Your father approached the firm of Gallimore and Reynolds thirty-six years ago, my father, in fact, was the solicitor in attendance. There is no longer a Reynolds in the partnership, and I am afraid that I will probably be the last Gallimore.' He shuffled his papers again, as if too embarrassed to continue. 'Mr Bradbury, I believe, had entered into a liaison of an extra-marital nature, the result of which was the birth of a boy.'

'Me!' I said, emphatically.

'Quite!' he replied, then cleared his throat, nervously. 'Mr Bradbury was a man of some standing in the community, so to avoid embarrassment to the family name, the mother of the child gave birth in a private nursing home here in London and the child was then sent for adoption.'

'Mr Gallimore,' I said, raising my eyebrows, 'I would be obliged if you would, perhaps refer to this child, as you say, with his proper name and not as if he does not exist!'

'Very well,' he continued, looking somewhat sheepish. 'The boy…..'

I coughed.

'You.....were born in a private nursing home as I said, and adopted by Mr and Mrs Kinsey soon afterwards.'

'Could they not have children of their own? I mean, why were they chosen? There must have been some sort of reason?' I questioned.

He looked at me, puzzled. 'Did you never ask your parents...your adoptive parents...why you never had any brothers or sisters?'

'We were never close.' I stated, matter of factly. 'Come to think of it; who was my real mother, anyway?'

'Perhaps, Major Kinsey, if I could continue, you will understand things better.'

I nodded assent.

'It was purely a financial agreement.' he said, and I frowned at the remark, but he was obviously uncomfortable. 'Mr Bradbury paid a regular amount to Mr Kinsey for the purpose of your well being.'

'Well that explains it!' I said, nodding my head, thoughtfully.

'Explains what?'

'Simple really. My father ..... that is ..... Mr Kinsey ..... never seemed to have to work very much. It also explains why there was precious little affection shown towards me ..... but you still haven't answered the question of who my real mother was. If he was so influential in the community, what about her? Was she some sort of local nobility or something? A curse on both our houses perhaps?'

'Nothing so grand, I'm afraid. She was the parlour-maid employed in Mr Bradbury's household and, apparently, very quickly out of a job ..... I believe Mrs Bradbury saw to that! Mrs Bradbury was unaware that her husband had secretly paid for the nursing home and for the ..... for the ..... er ..... financial arrangements since then.'

'And what about Mrs Bradbury now? She won't be pleased to find that there's an heir she thought she'd got rid off.'

'Thankfully, that problem will not arise. Mrs Bradbury passed away all of ten years ago.'

I was beginning to feel angry. 'And no effort was made to contact me?'

'Well ….. no, Major Kinsey ….. Mr Bradbury thought it best that you never met, although each year he would arrange for Mr and Mrs Kinsey to take you somewhere on an outing and he would apparently just…..well…..see you…..but, of course you never knew.'

'St James's Park!' I stated, flatly.

'I beg your pardon.'

'St James's Park! Each year, on my birthday, we went to St James's Park! It was the only time my parents ….. my adoptive parents ….. looked anything like happy! Even as a child it seemed quite false the way they laughed and joked in the park, and then never said a word on the way home. It was all a show just to impress my father!'

'Er ….. Yes ….. Quite. I wouldn't know about that would I, but I suppose it does sound very likely.'

'And so to the parlour-maid,' I continued, 'what became of her?'

'Disappeared without trace. It was Mr Bradbury's instructions that she should never be contacted. She was given a sum of money on the understanding that she was not to be seen again. She was ….. er ….. now how shall I put this tactfully?' he stumbled over his words and paused for a deep breath, 'she was ….. um ….. rather young at the time ….. and ….. and quite grateful to be relieved of the responsibility of bringing up a young child.'

The room fell silent.

'And so to the will.' I said, changing the subject.

He looked relieved.

'Mr Bradbury owned part of a quarrying and dredging company in Devon.'

'Devon?

'All the details, as you will see, are here.' He pointed at the documents on his desk. 'Thirty percent of the company is now in your name as is the family home and a small cash sum. Obviously, on the death of your adoptive parents no more money was paid out, which was probably fortunate as I believe that the funds were rather low at the time.'

'No siblings, I suppose?'

He shook his head.

'No cousins, or second cousins?'

'That, I can't say. You can appreciate that I was only a junior in the firm when all this came about.'

I saw him glance briefly at his watch, an indication that my allotted time was over. He saw my attempts to rise and got up himself, handing me a copy of the will as he walked around the desk. After another limp handshake he removed his spectacles which somehow made him look younger. I opened the door and then as an afterthought said, 'Where is my father buried?'

'I believe he's buried in the village cemetery,' he replied.

'I would have liked to have gone to the funeral. Flowers, a card, something like that. When was it held?' I asked.

He got his spectacles out again. 'About two years ago,' he replied.

'Two years ago!' I exclaimed, slamming the door shut again. 'Two years! .... Why ....? Why now after two years do I get to know?'

'As I said, Major Kinsey,' he said, trying to sound calm, 'an embarrassment to the family. Perhaps he thought that two years might soften the blow? It's written in the Will; two years to elapse.'

I hesitated, thinking about asking more questions then decided against it and opened the door again to leave. 'By the way,' I said, as I walked into the outer office, 'it's not Major Kinsey anymore ..... It's Reverend ..... The Reverend Alexander Kinsey....You should put that on your records for future reference.'

He looked taken aback but not as taken aback as I was feeling after the revelations of the last half hour.

I spent the night in a hotel in the Strand but might just as well have spent it on the platform at the station for all the sleep I got. I took an early train and was back in Derbyshire by mid afternoon.

'You look tired, my boy,' were Fathers John's opening words. I had long since ceased objecting to the use of the term 'my boy,' it didn't do any good objecting anyway, he was just as stubborn as I was, and I had come to the conclusion, after a while that he really meant no offence.

'Tea?' he offered, and busied himself by the stove, 'Isobella is shopping so you'll have to rely on me for lunch today. I presume you'll be wanting some lunch?'

'Yes, please.' I replied.

'Did it go well in London?' he questioned as he poured the tea.

I took some time to answer. 'I suppose so.....if you call finding another identity, another existence, an inheritance even, as going well, then, yes, it did go well in London,'

He waited, silently coaxing me to tell him more, so as my tea went cold I told him all about my trip to London and while I was telling him that, my mind did cartwheels at a subconscious inclination to tell him about Vietri as well.

'Can we go for a walk tomorrow?' I asked, impetuously.

'I'd love to, my boy!' he replied, with great enthusiasm.

'I sometimes run up over the brow to a little stream that dips into the valley past the main road.' I could feel my voice beginning to shake as I knew that tomorrow I would tell him about Vietri; the first person I had even thought about telling. The very thought itself frightened me, and yet there was relief at even suggesting it.

'After breakfast?' I blurted out, as if to confirm the idea in my own mind. 'After breakfast tomorrow? But what …. what if it rains?' I was stuttering as I spoke and I could feel myself trembling again.

I hadn't noticed that Father John had turned away and was washing up at the sink. 'Is tomorrow alright then?' I said, desperate that he might not come.

He put a plate down on the draining board then came to sit by the table. His hands were covered in soap suds but I was shocked to see that there were tears in his eyes.

'My dear boy!' he said, with tears now running unashamedly down his cheeks, 'I have waited for a year to go for a walk with you into the hills.'

My mood suddenly changed. 'But why?' I shouted. 'Why….What do you know?'

He wiped his hands on the tablecloth and reached into his jacket pocket and withdrew a well fingered envelope. He handed it to me and indicated that I should open it. It was addressed to him and had been cut open carefully with a knife. The letter inside was grubby and the ink had run in places. Both my hands were shaking now as I realised that it was probably his tear stains that had caused the ink to blot and I had to spread it out carefully on the table in order to read it. I used the sugar bowl and the butter dish to hold it flat and saw that it was from the Bishop and was dated about eighteen months ago:

Dear John,

I know that life shapes us into what we are and that sometimes life can be cruel. For this reason I am sending you a new curate by the name of Alexander Kinsey, who needs your help. He is a headstrong, arrogant young man whose few redeeming features were generally only manifest on the rugby field! Nevertheless, I believe that there is far more to him than meets the eye.

I realise that this may be painful for you, John, but it will be infinitely more painful for him. He is wrestling with a problem that reminds me very much of a certain story involving the Grand Old Duke of York! You will understand by now I should think John, and so I am giving you time to think it over with Isobella.

I appreciate that you might not want to get involved and I most certainly cannot force you, but should you wish to help, then please contact me as soon as possible. You may be the only hope that this young man has and so I do not make this request lightly.

My love, as always, to Isobella.
James.

I read the letter a second time before I looked at Father John. 'I don't understand ….. ?' I questioned, shaking my head. 'The Grand Old Duke of York ….. What's that all about?'

He reached across and picked up the letter and read it again and my earlier suspicions were confirmed when a tear dropped onto the bottom of the page. 'A story ….. ' he stated, neutrally looking directly at me.

I jumped up, 'Let's go now!' I insisted. 'Let's go now, before it's too late!'

I could see that he was eager, too.

'Alright, my boy.' He said. 'Let's go now! I'll get my coat.'

I heard the sound of the front door and a moment later, Isobella came into the room.

'We're going for a walk, dear,' he said to her, casually.

She saw the letter on the table and looked at us both. 'That's good,' she said, quietly. 'That's very good.'

Although she tried to disguise it, I saw the colour drain from her face.

Chapter 3

We left the house and walked around the church yard and through the gate that led onto the thin track across the meadow beyond. A well worn path sloped upwards, zig-zagging around bramble bushes that might have been placed there purposely to make an authentic assault course. Rabbit droppings littered our way forcing us to tread carefully until we reached the sparser vegetation towards the top of the ridge. As if provoked by an unseen signal, we both stopped to rest at the same time and looked back over the hazy outline of the village below us.

'What's the Grand Old Duke of York got to do with me?' I began.

He kept his gaze on the village and hesitated. 'Alexander, my boy, you must make me a promise,' he turned to look at me and I nodded. 'You must promise that if I open my heart to you, then you must open your heart to me.'

I nodded again.

'That means everything! .... do you understand?'

'Everything,' I confirmed, knowing the turmoil I would face in doing so.

'Then let's walk ..... the beauty of nature can soften the memories like nothing else.'

We walked for a while in silence with the old man stooped in meditation while he thought of the best way to tell me of his past.

'It was the summer of 1914,' he said, rather loudly, then coughed. 'The summer of 1914. Hot and unreal as I remember. I was a sergeant in the Royal Field Artillery newly arrived across the channel. The war was an adventure to us ..... nothing more. We had learnt to fire guns at targets. We hadn't learnt to fire guns at people who lived and breathed like we did. What rank were you, my boy?'

'Major,' I replied.

He raised his eyebrows, impressed. 'Major ..... so here we have a sergeant talking to a Major!'

He stopped to look at the stream which nestled between shallow banks as it wound its way through a gully and down towards the village.

'The war was fun......it seems strange to say that now ...... we had never seen any Germans let alone fired a single round in anger. There was nothing better to do, so our Commander in Chief allowed us to help the local people bring in the harvest. The men had all signed up, so it was left to the women to bring in the grain. We stripped to our waists and showed off to the young girls and at night we had camp fires and told bawdy stories while the French women plied us with home brewed cider.'

He paused, and I tried to imagine this gentle man of the cloth swopping crude jokes and getting drunk.

'Do you find that hard to believe?' he asked, as if reading my thoughts.

'Very ...... Yes! .... But ...... well, stranger things have happened, I suppose.'

'They have indeed, my boy ..... they have indeed ..... Anyway, it was decided to move us to a higher vantage point. The Royal Flying Corps had started bringing news of the approaching German armies and we had heard odd stories of small groups of Germans on horse back having the occasional running battle, but nothing of substance! And then, all too quickly, it was on us and within months the fields we had harvested became a bloody graveyard of mud and barbed wire. It's something I will never forget ...... It's something I don't want to forget!'

'But surely ...... surely you must want to forget all that suffering and waste!' I interrupted.

'Yes, of course,' he said emphatically, continuing, 'there was waste ...... there was horrific waste ...... of life ...... of limb ...... of equipment ...... of land. But there was also sacrifice. When men who had never met, willingly gave of themselves for another ...... No! I never want to forget ...... the waste of life to teach me the lesson that a man's life is sacred ...... and the sacrifice to realise what our Lord went through. To understand also that human nature can produce such amazing examples of care for others in the most appalling of conditions, and for the ultimate cost ...... No, I never want to forget!'

'But I do!' I shouted, 'I want to forget the vileness of it all ...... The stench of the bodies ...... the screams of pain ...... I ...... I ...... I never want to feel pain ever again. Don't you see ...... I can't bear the thoughts any longer!' I stopped, fearful of the memories that I would eventually have to resurrect from my subconscious.

Father John seemed to ignore me and walked on ahead of me leaving me to chase after him so as to catch up. I reached him and pulled him round by the shoulders.

I screamed into his face, 'I tell you, I can't bear the thoughts any longer!'

'I know this is not easy ...... it's not easy for either of us,' he stated, calmly.

'You're damn right, it's not easy!' I yelled back.

After a moment or two I released my grip on his shoulder and let my arms fall to my sides.

'I'm sorry,' I said, meekly.

'I'm sorry too,' he replied. 'I'm sorry that we have to go through this but there's no other way.' He looked at me then, '......is there?'

'No,' I sighed resolutely.

We carried on walking while I breathed deeply, inhaling the fresh air and tangibly calming down. 'So what happened next?' I questioned, restarting the conversation.

'It was the village where the Grand Old Duke of York marched his ten thousand men up and down the hill, back in 1794. It was a good site for keeping an eye on the surrounding area from our gun emplacements. We saw no action at all to start with, then things hotted up. We would take the mobile field guns and go down from Cassel towards Bailleul for forays, supposedly into enemy occupied areas. We were taken by surprise one evening. It was twilight and we'd got complacent with conflicting opinions of enemy positions. We were on our way back to Cassel when a few shells suddenly hit us. The field gun was immediately put out of action and a number of men killed or wounded including the captain, which left me as the next highest rank.

We were scared to death and unsure of where the shell-fire had come from but knew that it must have been fairly close by for it to have been such a direct hit. Visibility was poor, but we were drunk with excitement by then. The impetuosity of youth conquered our fear and without thinking, we moved off in the direction from which we thought the shells had come.

Eventually, we came across a farmhouse in the mist that none of us had seen before and there was a gun carriage in the farmyard. The place was unreal. Like a dream somehow, and deathly silent.'

I saw him falter in his step and sensed that he was coming to the climax of his narrative.

'We launched ourselves at the farmhouse, whooping and shouting like misbehaving school boys. We tossed grenades through the windows and fired at shadows in a fit of unbelievable madness.

I can't remember who first pointed out that there was no return of fire, but we all stopped and stood outside the wreck we had made of the house. There were no flames ...... no fire ...... just a shell of rubble. And that was when we heard the quiet wailing from inside the house ...... On and on it went......

We scrambled through the blown out door and climbed over the fallen brickwork into what was left of the kitchen. I held back because I knew I couldn't face what I suspected we would find.

A soldier ...... I don't remember his name, shouted back, 'Sarge, it's a girl!' I had to go through then and see this poor, teenage girl lying underneath what was left of the kitchen table. She was covered in blood. The plaster from the ceiling and walls was engrained in her hair, and she was surrounded by the bodies of the rest of her family ...... two sisters ..... a four year old boy ...... mother ...... and grandparents.

How she was not more seriously hurt I will never know, but her constant wailing was more disturbing than the sight of death in the room, and in the end, I slapped her face to get her to be quiet.

It wasn't even a gun carriage! A big, unhitched plough had given a false impression in the half light and it all ended up with us making a disastrous mistake.'

He paused, as if to gather his breath after such a long speech. He was obviously upset at the recollection, but still maintained a dignity that I found inconceivable after such revelations.

'Were there repercussions?' I ventured.

'Oh yes! ..... I was fortunate not to face a court martial, but someone was looking after me even then. They hushed it up, but I was never the same again.'

'How do you mean, 'never the same again?' Did you lose your nerve?'

'No! ..... Far from it! I was even more determined then ever and tried to excel at everything I did. I was demobbed in 1919 with a good war record, but I was so burdened with guilt that I couldn't settle into civilian life.'

'So that was when you joined the church?'

'No ...... not then ...... that came later ...... I went back ...... It was harvest time again and I thought that I might be able to help in the fields again and to even help the girl. What was left of the farm had been demolished and a much smaller house rebuilt on the same spot. The girl's father was back from the war and was looking after the place and I managed to get employment for the summer nearby. I saw her a few times, but she didn't recognise me.

I saved everything I had earned that summer in a leather pouch that my father had given me and when the harvest was finished, I went to see the girl and her father ...... It's amazing to think now how naïve I was to offer them money, especially after I explained who I was. He threw the money back at my feet and swore everlasting hatred. All she did was just glare at me in contempt. I bent down to pick up the money and she came and stood over me. I was feeling ashamed at my own stupidity by then and when she spoke it came as a shock as I'd not heard her speak before.

'On n'achete pas le pardon. Il faut qu'il se donne. Librement.' She said.

'Which means?' I asked, urgently.

'I'd picked up a fair bit of French by then, so I did manage to translate it …… It means, 'Forgiveness cannot be bought, it has to be given freely.'

'Then you joined the church?' I interjected.

'Then I joined the church ……Yes …… I didn't know what forgiveness was …… not real forgiveness anyway…… I thought I might find it in the church.

I thought it would be easy, but I went through total anguish of body and soul before I learnt that the secret of forgiveness is repentance …… It took nearly five years before I felt sufficiently at peace, and then, and only then, did I feel it was right that I should go back.

She wasn't a girl any longer, she was a young woman by then … … proud and dignified …… I stood facing her at the door of the farm and, strange though it may seem, I felt no fear. I had worked out in French what I was going to say and rehearsed it until I was word perfect. I simply asked for her forgiveness and explained in simple terms what had happened over the last few years …… I didn't even know her name so I asked her what it was …… she told me she was called Isobella after her grandmother, and we were married a year later.'

I was stunned! Yet, when I thought back, it explained so much: Isobella's slight accent; her seeming understanding of my emotions and her readiness to comfort me when I needed it most.

'And now, my boy?' Father John said, not even looking at me.

'What?' I replied, still recovering.

'I have opened my heart, now you must open yours.'

'No! I can't!' I said, desperately looking for some means of escape now that the time had come. 'I can't ….. perhaps tomorrow…… I'll be better tomorrow …… Just give me some time!'

'Major Kinsey!' he began, firmly, using my rank, 'there is no time! No time to waste, no time to wait …… Unless you start now, you will never find what you are so desperately looking for!'

'I'm going back to the house.' I said, and turned back down the path.

'Stop!' He ordered, loudly.

'No! ….. I can't face it!' I cried back.

'Unless you face it now……' he left the sentence unfinished.

I knew that he was right.

He sat awkwardly on a ledge composed of rocks covered with tufts of moorland grass and looked at me as I stood a few paces down the path.

'I will sit here until you tell me …… if it takes all day and all night …… and tomorrow as well. But I will not move until you have completed your side of the bargain!' He gave me a stubborn look and I waited, agonising as I recalled it all in my mind. Finally and reluctantly, I walked back up the path and sat down close to him.

It was quite some time before I could speak. 'Alright,' I said, with resignation, 'I'll try.'

'Good!' He replied, more gently this time.

'I was at Salerno in Italy ...... Operation Avalanche ...... I was part of select small units of men assigned to do rapid search and destroy missions behind enemy lines.'

I hesitated. Both of us were looking directly ahead, not daring to meet each other's gaze. In the chill of early evening I could feel the presence of the men of my unit and the posthumous accusations of the occupants of the villa.

'No!' I said, firmly. 'It began long before Salerno ...... I've been an arrogant bastard all my life!'

Father John didn't flinch.

'I knew that someday I would make a mistake, but I never dreamed of the consequences. All the way through my army career I pushed people about ...... Ordered! ..... Commanded! ..... Shouted! ..... until everyone was sick of me, yet with complete determination to be the very best ...... No! ..... More than that! ..... To be perfect in the execution of everything I did, yet knowing deep down that I was setting myself a target that was impossible to reach.

By the time we got to Salerno I was at breaking point. I knew that I couldn't tell anyone as it would have been too much of a blow to my pride to admit that I was a failure in what I had set out to do.

Our target was the Panzer Grenadier Headquarters in Vietri Pass, north of the Salerno beaches. We had to knock it out so as to confuse communications to the area. It was the most important target of them all ...... a villa ...... blow it up and go home ...... that's all we had to do ...... We'd practiced such a manoeuvre again and again in north Africa, but I was so pig headed that I wouldn't listen to any of my men about whether it was the right villa or not. We were behind schedule; the villa we were supposed to attack had no obvious indication of being anything other than a villa, but the one over the road had a number of sentries posted …… I didn't check …… What a fool I was.'

I stopped for a minute to recollect. It seemed so unreal to relate the events while looking down onto a peaceful English valley at sunset.

'Before the war, there were obviously British people living in Italy, and once the threat of war was imminent most of them went back to Britain, but of course, some stayed behind, particularly those who had married Italians. When war was declared most of them were thrown out of the country. What was not generally known though, was that a number of them had been influential in the business world. They knew a lot about the way that the Italian mind works and could therefore have a detrimental effect if they confided in the Allied command …… To stop them doing this …… or at least to keep it to a minimum …… the children of the families were kept behind.

The excuse was that moving away would effect their education, but in reality it was a hostage situation. There was, needless to say, a lot of diplomatic 'to-ing' and 'fro-ing,' but relationships were not good, until finally all communications were severed. The parents of the children apparently arrived back in Britain totally distraught and were reluctant to pass on any of their knowledge to the powers that be in case their children were harmed; in other words; the Italians had achieved exactly what they had set out to do.

The eleven children were kept tightly guarded in a convent in Vietri, supposedly out of the way. What they didn't realise was that when the invasion eventually came, it would strike right on their doorstep.

The Germans and Italians knew the invasion would come at some point in time, but they didn't know when or where, but by the 8th of September, they knew alright! The children were sent out of the town away from the beaches and the cliffs. Many people hid in caves or tunnels but the Germans insisted that the children should be safe, but within reach. They put them in a villa across the road from their Communications Headquarters. We ......' I stopped. 'We went ......'

I couldn't continue. The merest thought of it paralysed my speech, so we sat there in silence until the sun went down while I tried to say the words that choked in my throat.

'Tell me, my boy,' Father John said softly in the growing darkness.

'I can't, damn you!' I shouted.

'Say it!... Say the words! .... Tell me what you did!'

'I can't say it.' I whispered.

'You can, you must,' he urged.

'We burst in ......' I faltered again, then it all came out in a rush. 'We burst in ...... grenades, machine guns, the lot! ...... I mowed them down ...... Eleven children ...... four nuns ...... Defenceless. The Italians had surrendered that very day and the children were longing to be reunited with their parents ...... and I murdered them ...... every last one of them.' I halted, breathless with the effort.

'That's not all though, is it?' he questioned.

I jumped to my feet and exclaimed, 'What do you mean: 'that's not all?' You knew all along didn't you? You just wanted to punish me ...... see me suffer even more! It was all a set up wasn't it?...... That letter from the Bishop ...... I bet he told you more?'

He shook his head.

'Don't lie!' I screamed, bitterly.

'Sit down!' he ordered, sharply.

'No!' I shouted back.

'Sit down!' he said, again. 'No one told me anything ...... I can tell there's more.'

'Alright,' I said forcefully. 'There is more …… The whole of my unit was cut down the minute they stepped out of the villa …… The whole bloody lot of them …… There was just me and one other poor sod with two broken legs who survived and I've suffered ever since … … Every time I try to sleep I see those children; those nuns; those soldiers. Every time I close my eyes I see them.'

Father John got stiffly to his feet, shaking his legs after sitting cramped for so long.

'Where are you going?' I asked, crossly.

'Home, of course,' he replied, casually.

I was confused. 'But aren't you going to help me?' I said.

'No!' He answered, shaking his head.

'But …… but what was the point of this stupid exercise if you're not going to help me …… Has this all been a waste of time?……a stupid waste of time?'

He walked on ahead of me and stumbled in the semi-darkness. I raced after him and grabbed his arm to steady him. He made no resistance but there was a barrier between us now. I hurled abuse at him on the one hand yet saved him from falling on the other.

'Why can't you help me?' I shouted over and over again as I half supported, half carried him over the rough ground. 'Tell me why?' I begged.

I knew he couldn't answer because he was panting hard by now, but I pestered him nevertheless all the way down from the ridge.

We eventually reached the churchyard and he paused for breath by leaning his weight on a tall gravestone. The last light had gone from the sun and just a faint glow penetrated through the trees creating haunting statues out of the stone.

'Tell me …… Tell me why you can't help me! …..You've told me what it's like to have a burden of guilt ……You said you wanted to help me …… now you say you can't.'

I waited for his answer, but none came.

'At least tell me what to do?' I tried in desperation.

He steadied himself, then began to walk towards the church and I shouted after him at the top of my voice, not caring who heard. 'You stupid, old man! You don't really care at all …… you don't give a damn …… about me or anybody!'

I followed him, still shouting, until he reached the church door. He pulled the key from his pocket, unlocked and opened it and left it ajar for me to go through after him. I followed him to the far end where the altar sat surrounded by the stained glass windows that tourists came to gloat over. He pointed upwards at the windows.

'What's that?' he asked.

'Windows! Bloody windows!' I mocked.

'And what, pray, is depicted on the windows?' he questioned, with equal derision.

'Bunyan's Pilgrim's Progress,' I said.

'And tell me about Bunyan's Pilgrim's Progress,' he continued.

I sat down in one of the choir stalls and laughed. 'If it wasn't for those windows, and if it wasn't for the money that people put in the box at the back of the church when they came in to see them, I suppose the church would close for lack of funds …… My sermons don't exactly cause a great increase in collections anyway.'

He sat down in the choir stalls opposite me and we faced each other in the dim light of the single bulb over the altar.

'Tell me about the story.'

'Alright ...... Bunyan's in prison, for ten years was it? ...... or twelve, released in 1672 ...... made use of his time to write a book ... ... and sold a few copies since.'

'Now tell me the story, not the history.'

I shrugged my shoulders, not getting the point. 'Christian goes on a journey, meets all sorts of people and eventually loses his burden.' As I said it, I began to understand the line of questioning.

'And? ...... ' he probed.

'And ..... I suppose you're going to tell me that I need to go on a journey to lose my burden of guilt ...... Ha! ...... It was a book! ...... We're talking about real life here, not pages from a book. Do you think I ought to go to darkest Africa and find enlightenment for my guilt there? Rays of light from heaven and all that! Angels singing, doves of peace everywhere! ...... Come off it, Father John, this is real life! ...... I'm a murderer, a real, live murderer who can't sleep...... who can't live because of his burden of guilt! ..... Rubbish! ..... Absolute rubbish!'

Father John got up and walked across to the altar and brushed off a few crumbs of bread left over from communion. He went round the back of the altar, straightened the cloth and looked at me from behind the silver cross. His face had long shadows cast over it from the light bulb above which aged him even more, but gave extra power to the next sentence that he uttered.

'You haven't got a burden of guilt,' he said, quietly.

Suddenly, my attention was riveted with the impact of his words as I pushed myself up slowly. 'What have I got then?' I said, sourly.

He hesitated.

'Tell me! Tell me what then! Tell me what I have got!' I insisted.

'You won't like it.'

'I don't care!' I said, angrily.

'Alright, Alexander Kinsey, if you really want to know......
You're full of self pity and it's completely destroying you!' He spat the
words out with venom. 'You murdered fifteen harmless people, yet in
everything, you've never shown any real remorse for any of them ...
... all you've ever shown is selfish thoughts about yourself and how
you've suffered!' He waved his hands at the windows. 'You're not like
Christian because you haven't even found your burden of guilt to
carry!' He stabbed his finger into the air in my direction, his voice
getting louder all the time. 'For a year I've watched you ...... for a
year and more. I've known there was something wrong ...... but I can't
help you ...... you're one of those who doesn't really want help,
because you'd be too selfish to accept it!'

I jerked myself out of my seat, took three flying leaps and hit him
hard on the side of his face. His head whipped back and he slumped
against the wall and slid to the ground.

I stood in shocked silence for what seemed like an eternity but it
can only have been seconds. I heard the pattering of running steps up
the aisle and Isobella appeared at my side, paused briefly then ran to
her husband's sprawled body.

'What have I done?' I whispered under my breath.

'How dare you desecrate the house of God!' she cried hysterically,
holding his head in her hands. He groaned and sluggishly opened his
eyes and I didn't move ...... I didn't dare move ...... I was held by her
eyes.

'I heard it all,' she said, more calmly, but with no less authority. 'I heard you shouting in the church yard and came over ...... I stood at the back and listened to you ...... You don't know what it cost him to go with you this afternoon ...... and this is how you repay him!'

She looked down at him, stroking his grey hair as he gradually regained consciousness.

'What .... what do I do now?' I stammered. 'I came here for help ... and I can't find it ... and I've ended up hurting the people who took me in ... What more can I do?'

I walked back down the aisle leaving them together and had almost reached the door when she spoke. Her tone was haunting as it echoed round the dark building, but in its firmness, there was no bitterness.

'We could tell you what to do, but you wouldn't listen would you......Admit it, you wouldn't listen.'

I mumbled in agreement.

'John's often said that forgiveness only comes from repentance.'

I mumbled again as she repeated the very words that father John had said only a few hours before out on the hills.

'You don't really feel repentance do you?'

'No ...... not yet.' I said quietly and walked out of the door, closing it behind me.

*****

I spent most of that night trying to gather my thoughts. Finally, in the small hours, I wrote two long letters; one to the Bishop, and one to

Father John and Isobella.

I did my best to explain to the Bishop what had happened. I also asked for his understanding as to why I felt that the only right and proper thing for me to do in the circumstances was to tender my resignation with immediate effect.

The letter to Father John and Isobella was more difficult to compose. I wrote stating that there was no excuse for my disgraceful behaviour and that I no longer felt worthy to accept their hospitality. I had made up my mind to travel down to Devon and, for the time being at least, to stay in the house which had been bequeathed to me by my real father. I wrote down the address and asked them to write to me there if they could find it in their hearts to forgive my behaviour.

I woke early the next morning and packed my bags. I was tired from the relatively sleepless night and from the emotions of the previous day and wanted to be out of the house before anyone else woke up. I trod quietly down the stairs with my bags and almost reached the front door.

'Tea, or coffee?' Isobella asked through the half open kitchen door.

'I ...... er ...... I ...... well ...... coffee ...... coffee, please.' I eyed the front door.

'You'll be wanting some breakfast, no doubt?'

'No ...... No, I'll be alright ...... just coffee.'

'I'll do you some ham and eggs,' she persisted.

'No ...... honestly.' But my protestations were in vain and we made small talk about the weather and the village while I tried my best to eat the food in front of me.

'Where are you going?' she asked, gently, and I had to finish my mouthful before I could reply.

'Devon ...... Devon, I suppose. At least there's a house there. I don't know what it's like, but it's a roof over my head. There was a bit of money in the Will so I won't starve. I ...... I can't stay here, not after what I did yesterday.'

'And what will you do?'

I shrugged. 'I don't know. I'll look for a job, I suppose. I've left a letter ...... two letters ...... my resignation to the Bishop ...... and one to you and Father John. How is he? I didn't hurt him ...... I mean I didn't hurt him badly, did I?'

She played with the wedding ring that sat on her swollen finger. 'He's sleeping. He's tired. He'll have a bruise I expect.'

'I'm sorry,' I said.

'I'm sorry too,' she replied. 'John and I are very happy. We love each other despite what happened in the war ... No! .... We love each other because of what happened......You've never known love, have you?'

I shook my head.

'That's sad,' she commiserated, 'but we'll keep hoping and praying that you will ...... you will tell us, won't you ...... if you do find what you're looking for?'

'What am I looking for?' I asked, confused.

'You'll know when you find it.'

I made as if to answer, but she interrupted me.

'Yes, it's a riddle isn't it. Life is a riddle; that's why we can't tell you. You must find it for yourself, just like John did with me.

'Forgiveness cannot be bought, it has to be given...is that what you mean?' I queried.

'He told you it all then, did he?'

I nodded.

'It took him five years you know,' she said, 'five years before he realised.'

'How long will it take me?' I asked.

'Not long,' she replied.

I raised my eyebrows questioningly. 'Why not long?'

'Because you've already started looking.'

I got up to leave and walked into the hall. Isobella followed me and stopped as I lifted my bags. I paused and put them down again and stretched out a hand to shake hers but she pushed it aside. I was momentarily offended until she came close and embraced me. It was a long, firm embrace and eventually I clumsily put my arms around her. We stood there like mother and son saying farewell for the last time.

She loosened her grip and I hid my embarrassment by bending to pick up my bags. She opened the door for me and I walked out into the fresh, morning air.

'Goodbye, Isobella,' I said.

'Goodbye, Alexander ...... and whatever you find ...... it won't be easy...... and that's a warning.'

I smiled a weak smile and began walking down the road towards the bus stop. I turned round once and she waved a last goodbye.

Whatever you find ... it won't be easy .... that's a warning.

It wasn't just a warning ...... it was a prophecy!

Chapter 4

It was a long, tedious journey which I spent looking out of the window barely noticing the passing countryside. Nothing in my army or theological training could have prepared me for the situation in which I found myself, and for once in my life, I felt distinctly unsure of myself. Episodes of my life flashed before me: words and actions I now regretted accompanied by forlorn wishes of travelling back in time and starting all over again.

The man sitting opposite me talked incessantly about going on holiday to see his grandchildren. I smiled politely, feigning interest, but his words, though audible, didn't register in my brain. He dried up eventually and snored loudly for the rest of the way, in time to the rhythm of wheels on rails.

My mind wandered: a house and a share in a business plus a small sum of money and an uncertain future.

I thought back to the previous day and my shameful actions against Father John, and not for the first time, I marvelled at the way Isobella had expressed no bitterness or anger when she had embraced me on my departure. Inside of me, I longed to experience that depth of love and devotion, but knew that my words and attitudes had driven me in the other direction.

Father John had Isobella. The snoring man had the love of his grandchildren. I had no-one.

I looked out of the window and it began to rain.

I arrived in Dartmouth later that same afternoon feeling cold and wet. It was one of those autumnal days when the normal bronze, foliaged beauty of September was marred by a blanket of torrential rain. I was tired and hungry and my mood was as grey as the skies. I was tempted to go straightaway to the hotel that sat overlooking the small, square quay and get some food and well deserved rest, but I was soaked anyway so I stopped to survey my surroundings.

Small boats nestled in the shelter of the larger vessels of the estuary receiving protection against the spray from the white topped waves. I stood and absorbed the setting while the smell of the sea and the salt air revived my flagging spirits. I had two addresses, one was the house I had inherited at Windle Bridge further down the coast, the other was the central office of Latchley Aggregates which was situated in Dartmouth itself.

I decided to postpone my initial need for refreshment and instead, satisfy my curiosity regarding the firm in which I now had shares. I asked directions and discovered the office to be in a large house at the top of a steep flight of steps. I knocked and felt the door move on its hinges, so I pushed it wide and found myself in the small foyer leading into a larger outer office. It was inhabited by filing cabinets, telephones, a single desk and a very prim looking middle-aged secretary. She took one intolerant look at my wet, bedraggled state and became an immediate barrier to any further progress.

I dropped my bags on the floor and attempted to discover if she had a more sympathetic side to her nature than the one she had demonstrated so far.

'Could I possibly see Mr Latchley?'

'Do you have an appointment, sir?' she asked, with no semblance of welcome.

'No. I had no idea I was coming down here until last night.'

'Well, I'm afraid that Mr Latchley only sees visitors by appointment.'

'Does he have anyone with him at the moment?' I asked, irritably, quickly forgetting any attempts at gaining sympathy.

'No Sir, he doesn't, but he only sees visitors by appointment, I assure you.' she stressed.

'Well......just once......try and see if he will see me without an appointment.'

'I assure you that......'

'Just try, will you!' I interrupted, not allowing her to finish.

She played needlessly with her typewriter. 'I have been given strict instructions not to disturb Mr Latchley,' she said, with determination.

'Perhaps if you tell him that Alexander Kinsey is here, he might change his mind.'

She immediately stopped fiddling with the typewriter and for the first time looked directly at me. 'I beg your pardon,' she questioned, 'what was that name?'

'Alexander Kinsey,' I repeated.

She looked slightly flushed while she lifted up a 'phone, an internal one I presumed, thought better of it, rose from her chair and marched into another office at the far end.

I sat down to rest my tired legs and overheard a heated exchange of words from the other side of the door. I couldn't grasp much of the conversation at all except that, by the sounds of it, I wasn't welcome! She was away for some minutes and when she did return she looked flustered and quite upset.

'Mr Latchley will see you now,' she glared at me as she said it and I guessed that I had probably ruined her day.

'May I leave my bags here?' I asked, as I rose from the chair.

'I suppose so,' she replied, disinterested.

'Thank-you,' I said, with a touch of sarcasm.

I walked across the office and through the connecting door without knocking and into a much more opulent room. The most obvious feature was a large, picture window looking out onto the estuary taking in all the grandeur of the picturesque little town. The other obvious feature was the man sitting behind a desk talking on the telephone and completely ignoring my entry.

'I don't care what they called you!' he bellowed down the mouthpiece, 'Just get it, and by tomorrow or there'll be hell to pay!'

He slammed the phone down and leaned back on his chair. He exhaled loudly and drummed his fingernails on the desk. The hostile look on his face dismissed any thoughts I might have had about a trouble free arrival in Devon. Our eyes met like a clash of Titans, immediate animosity between us, a sixth sense telling me that my arrival was more than just a mere inconvenience.

He looked me up and down before he spoke, making mental adjustments to his initial assessment of me. 'So ......' he sneered. 'You're Tom's bastard are you?'

He was a large man, fat around the face and with a thin moustache that gave him the appearance of having a third lip. His hair was short and greased back exposing a large forehead with eyes that seemed to remain half closed.

'The name's Alexander Kinsey,' I said, sharply, the colour rising to my cheeks.

'That's what I mean ...... you're Tom's bastard!'

I found myself wishing that I'd gone to the hotel after all and come to the offices the next day in dry clothes and with food in my stomach. 'The name's Alexander Kinsey,' I said again, endeavouring to keep calm.

'I don't care what your damn name is, you're Tom's bastard, that's enough! Have you any idea the trouble you've caused over the last three weeks?'

'Now just hold on one minute!' I retorted. 'I didn't even know who I was until a few days ago!'

He got up from his chair and walked over to the window. He was perhaps a year or two older than me, it was difficult to say, he moved well for a man of his size with a forceful bounce to his step.

'There's something you should know Kinsey .....' he said, angrily, addressing the window and the view outside. 'It's a bloody nuisance you coming along! I had notification three weeks ago that Tom Bradbury had a bastard son and, worst of all, that Tom had left him his shares. Now that is a bloody nuisance!

Have you any idea what it's like to run a firm for ten years, drag it up by its heels .... convert it from a second rate, run of the mill, mediocre, dumping ground of a business into something that works, and works damn well I might add; then to be told that there's some illegitimate offspring with a large enough share to mess the whole lot up again! You didn't know your mother, I don't suppose?' he ignored me and went to sit back at his desk.

'No,' I said, quietly.

'Always a bit of a ladies man was Tom. A pretty wench so I'm told, for a servant girl anyway. Goody-goody Tom had to get rid of her pretty damn quickly, pity we didn't realise he'd got her pregnant as well. What does the bastard son of a servant girl do, anyway?'

I glowered at him, distinctly annoyed at his rudeness. I controlled my anger, but only just. 'Army,' I said, simply.

'God almighty! That's all we need! Some former Lance Corporal trained to kill Germans coming down here strutting around as if he owns the place!'

'Major, actually,' I corrected him.

He dismissed it with a wave of his hand. 'Well they were taking almost anyone in the war I suppose.'

'And where did you serve?' I prodded.

He looked taken aback. 'My dear fellow! Right here of course! I'm not cannon fodder to be fed into the sights of some enemy sharpshooter. They thought it prudent for me to do something useful ….. use my organisational skills ….. They wanted my brains intact not splattered over some Godawful battlefield!'

He started tapping the desk with his fingernails again. 'So……?' he said.

'So what?' I replied.

'So …… what are we going to do? You haven't come down here just for the bracing sea air. You must have some plan of action; or doesn't the military believe in that sort of thing?'

It was my turn to go over to the window, mainly to give me time to think. I had no plans, but would never admit that to this bully of a man who had the controlling interest in the firm of Latchley Aggregates.

'Well ...... I have a house here,' I began.

He laughed at the suggestion. 'House! ..... Have you seen it?..... It was a house, but no one's lived there for two years. I doubt you'll find any clean linen!'

'It's four walls nevertheless,' I argued, 'and I have a share in a business. Whether you like it or not I have every, legal right to be here if I so wish.'

He leaned back in his chair and let out a great bellow of mirthless laughter. 'My dear chap! You're a soldier boy!' he mocked, 'I don't suppose you've any experience of business at all, have you? And you wouldn't know the first thing about fishing, and fishing is what they do hereabouts by the way. Take my advice: go and re-enlist, go and shoot people somewhere else in this Godforsaken world of ours. You wouldn't be wanted round here anyway, there's no room for passengers.'

When I made no reply, he tilted forward and rested his chin on his hands closing his eyes even more so that they were mere slits.

'Hmm,' he began, after a little thought. 'I'll buy you out! Here and now! .... Ten thousand pounds ...... Cash if you want! I'll even buy that wreck of a house at Windle Bridge. I don't want some jumped up amateur ruining what I've built up.'

'No thank-you!' I said, and shocked myself with the speed of the decision. Even the very substantial amount of money mentioned didn't deter me. Something about the way in which he had been so quick to make such an offer made me want to stay around out of sheer stubbornness.

'Very well,' he responded, relaxing back into his chair. 'If that's your choice ...... But the offer's still open, and when you find you want it after all, you'll find me a generous man.'

I took a long, hard look at him: he looked about as generous as a starving lion with a pile of raw meat.

He spoke again. 'There are just three rules round here, and you'll do well to remember them: first of all, keep out of my way. I don't like meddlers. You'll get your percentage from company profits as and when.

Second: what I say goes! I own the majority share. If I want to do something, then I do it!

Finally: your house is next along to James Bardell; he's the unofficial leader of the fishermen of Windle Bridge and I am engaged to be married to his daughter, Gwenlyn. Tom was a ladies' man ...... let's hope you're not the same because if you so much as look at Gwenlyn Bardell ...... I'll kill you!'

I felt as if the lion had just taken the first bite of raw meat, and that I was the meat!'

'O.K.' I said, non-commitally. 'How do I get to Windle Bridge?'

'Got a car?' he asked.

I shook my head.

'Bus runs once a day.....and you've just missed it.'

He picked up a pen and began writing, effectively ending any further possibility of conversation. I compared the contrasting welcomes I had received from Father John and the one I had received from Jonathan Latchley and wished I was back with people who at least cared about me.

I walked out of the office and closed the door behind me. The prim secretary looked as if she had overheard everything, so I gave her a sarcastic smile, picked up my bags and left. After standing by the road for twenty minutes, I managed to thumb a lift to Windle Bridge and home, sweet home.

The farmer who picked me up spent most of the short journey dripping spittle from his mouth while he chewed slowly on an unlit pipe. He drove carefully in an old, left hand drive American jeep which he said was good on the hills.

We drove along the road on the narrow piece of land that separated Slapton Sands from the fresh water Ley and then up and through Torcross. I looked back at the beach from the higher vantage point and felt a rekindling of memories. It was this very beach that had been used as a practice ground for the Normandy landings and it reminded me of the beaches of north Africa where I had trained for my ill-fated part in Operation Avalanche. I tried conversation to avoid the memories, but the farmer didn't respond.

He stopped at the junction which led down to Windle Bridge and I thanked him. He grunted, waggled his pipe and drove off, heading further south leaving me to take the short walk down the hill into the village.

I had not walked more than two hundred yards when I passed the cemetery on my left which was set outside the village with no adjacent houses. I stopped briefly to rest my arms and hands from carrying my bags and remembered that the solicitor had said that my father had been buried in the local cemetery. I presumed that this must be the place. A steady drizzle was coming down and as I was wet anyway, I decided to place my bags in the relative shelter of the decaying thatched gate into the graveyard and to attempt to find his grave.

The place was deserted apart from one lone figure dressed in oil-skins tending a grave on the far side of the cemetery closest to the sea. I began walking slowly up and down the rows of gravestones looking for the newest stones. The dates were almost worn away on some of them with erosion from wind and rain and it wasn't until I was at the farthest row that I realised that the dates there were the most recent.

The oil-skinned figure was kneeling down placing flowers in a small, metal vase and, obviously, hadn't seen me because of the hood which almost totally concealed the face. My foot made a crunching sound on the shingle path and the figure whirled round with a start of surprise.

'I'm sorry,' I said. 'I didn't mean to startle you......I was looking for ......'

I glanced down at the gravestone and read the words: 'Thomas Bradbury, Born: September 2nd 1870. Died September 2nd 1948. Rest in peace.'

'I was going to say that I was looking for my father's grave ...... but I've found it! At least he died on his birthday anyway.'

'You're Alexander Bradbury!' came the excited voice.

It was my turn to be startled, not so much from someone knowing my identity but that fact that when she looked up at me, she had the most captivating face I had ever set eyes on!

I stood there, fascinated, as the rain came down and soaked right through my clothes. A lock of dark hair lay plastered down the side of her face, moulding round the fine cheek bones, framing her deep brown eyes into an exquisite sculpture of beauty and emotion. Her face was dark from exposure to the elements, but unnaturally smooth and I wanted to stroke it to feel its softness.

I thought of the women I had had after my discharge from the army. They had all been attractive in one way or another, but none so bewitchingly beautiful as this young woman. What I couldn't understand was the feeling that it was as if she had been expecting me, even though I hadn't known until the previous day that I was going to travel down to Devon. The sensation was uncanny and at the same time, unnerving.

'So,' I began, hesitantly, trying unsuccessfully to avert my gaze, 'why are you tending to my father's grave?'

'Why am I tending his grave?' she said, echoing my question. 'Because I loved him, I suppose. Is that a good enough reason?' Her voice was strong and assured without being overpowering, and again with that sensation of knowing I was coming.

I looked at the dates again. 'But if he's been dead for two years, why do you still do it?'

'Why?' she stated, sounding shocked. 'But surely you should know that! He's dead but not forgotten; not by me, not by others either.'

She looked at the stone and I lost sight of her face. She leaned forwards and lifted a flower from the vase and pushed herself more upright with her other hand. She turned to face me again and handed me the flower. 'You're not like him are you?'

'I......well.....I don't know.....I never met him,' I responded, taken aback by her forthrightness.

'That flower,' she continued, and I looked at it held gently in her hand, 'that flower is dead; cut off from what gives it life, but it's still beautiful, it still gives pleasure, it's still appreciated.'

I countered, 'Well ......yes ...... but that flower will wither and fade. It won't last forever. I mean ...... two years!'

'Memories don't fade,' she replied, matter of factly. 'Memories last forever.'

I nodded my head. 'I know only too well how memories last, but why memories of the dead, why not of the living?'

She took the flower from me and replaced it carefully in the vase. She mumbled something under her breath and I didn't quite catch it.

'Pardon?' I tried.

'You've never loved, have you?' she said, with amazing perception.

It seemed ironic that it had only been yesterday when Isobella had asked me the same question.

'What's that supposed to mean?' I asked, defensively, unused to such a direct approach from someone I'd never met before. 'Were you lovers or something?'

I regretted it as soon as the words came out.

She had a hurt look in her eyes as she stood up and pulled the oil skins tighter around her body. She walked over to the boundary fence beyond the row of gravestones and I let a few seconds elapse before I went to join her.

'I'm sorry,' I said with genuine feeling. 'I meant no offence. I never knew him. I never knew what he was like or what …… or what he did, or anything like that. For all I know he might have been a real lady's man.' It was Latchley's description of him and not mine, but I was beginning to get very interested in the father I'd never met.

'I'd hoped …… I had hoped you'd be more like him …… but you're not …… you're different,' she observed, with a tinge of sadness in her tone.

She had a habit of tilting her head slightly to one side when she spoke which I found both disarming and sensuous at the same time. 'So you weren't ...... you weren't .....?

'No! Of course not!' she said, emphatically. 'He seemed old even from the day I first remember him. A sort of grandfather figure. My real grandparents died long before I was born, so Tom was a ...... well, a sort of substitute, and with my father and mother involved with fishing, we spent a lot of time together.'

'And he told you about me?'

'Yes, of course.'

'And what did he tell you.'

She looked out to sea, avoiding the question.

'What did he tell you?' I asked again, with a firmer tone. 'It's important for me to know what he told you.'

She still kept quiet.

I probed further. 'What's the matter? I need to know.....!'

The initial excitement of discovering who I was seemed to have evaporated to be replaced by a mood of disappointment.

'All right!' she said bitterly. 'I'll tell you what he told me ..... He told me nothing but empty lies!'

I opened my mouth to speak, then thought better of it. She was obviously resentful over something but of what, I had no idea.

We both looked out over the darkening sea, watching the slanting pillars of rain slicing into the white, turbulent wave crests. I was feeling a strange mixture of emotions, the main one of which was confusion. I was still recoiling from the rude confrontation with Jonathan Latchley and now I had unwittingly upset someone who had been very close to my father. Something within me wanted to comfort her, but I didn't know how. In my whole life I had never given or received genuine compassion. Even while working with Father John, any display of sympathy towards needy parishioners had been entirely superficial.

'What lies did he tell you then?' I asked, tentatively.

She gripped the fence with her hands and took a deep breath and tilted her head. 'He said …… he told me …… he told me you were coming to see him……but always at the last minute, you couldn't come. There was always an excuse. You were doing something kind for someone else he would say…… but you never came.'

'How could I come!' I remonstrated. 'I never knew anything about him, so how could I come and see him!'

'He said you were kind, thoughtful……a gentleman. And I believed him …… When I was a little girl anyway, then as I grew older I doubted that you ever existed …… so I told him …… I told him I didn't think there was an Alexander Bradbury at all. Then he showed me a photograph of someone in the army…… someone who looked like him, but somehow different. I believed him then, but you still didn't come …… and now, now that he's gone …… two years …… now you come.'

I was exasperated. 'Look, How could I come! I didn't even know who my father was!' I threw my arms up in the air. 'I can't read people's minds! I was brought up as Alexander Kinsey; adoptive parents, all that sort of thing. It's only a few days since I discovered who I really was. So how could I come?'

She gripped the fence again. 'And are you kind, thoughtful …… a gentleman?'

'I……'

'Well……are you?'

'That depends on what being kind ...... being thoughtful ...... being a gentleman means.'

'So he was lying!'

She looked even more disappointed.

'O.K.' I responded. 'So, maybe I am different ..... I'm his son but I never knew it ...... Maybe I am like him ..... but underneath ...... disguised. Maybe I'm like my mother, whoever she was; I never met her either. Maybe I'm just like me! Maybe I'm a product of life and not just a product of two people who fleetingly met and regretted it: no happy ever after. Maybe I'm not the knight in shining armour who's going to come out of the sunset and be the younger version of a pretend grandfather! Maybe ...... Maybe I'm just human!'

She rubbed her hands across her eyes. 'It's peaceful here.' She said, trying to avoid further discussions. It was obvious that I hadn't matched up to her expectations.

'What's peaceful?..... The graveyard?'

'No ... the place ... Windle Bridge. Peaceful. Simple. Uncomplicated.'

'You've always lived here?' I asked.

'Born ... lived ... and die I suppose,' she said dreamily.

'But don't you want to see the world ...... travel ...... see people ...... different people?'

'Why?' she questioned.

'Because ...... because you see other things, other places, other simple, uncomplicated places.'

'But I'd also see places ...... and people, that are not so pleasant, not so nice as here.'

'You really are a dreamer aren't you,' I said, trying not to sound unkind. 'And dreamers can't confront reality even when it hits them in the face. You can't acknowledge the fact that I'm not perfect, that I'm not the picture of the perfect gentleman that my father painted … you can't face that, can you?'

She shook her head.

I looked down in the direction of the village where the road went over a narrow bridge before winding towards the houses that leaned against the side of the rocks. There was undoubtedly a peaceful unreality about the whole area, as if it had been dropped into place from a bygone era.

'Is that the bridge that gives the village its name?' I queried, pointing at an unruly collection of stones that carried the road.

She sounded relieved that I had changed the subject. 'Yes. There's been a bridge there for centuries.'

'Does the river Windle go underneath?'

'No, there's just a split in the rock and a small spring. A windle is a bird …… a redstart ……you're a city person aren't you?'

'Most of my life, yes,' I replied, 'But I've lived in the country for the last year or so.'

I thought of Father John and Isobella. I'd only seen the countryside while running myself to exhaustion and consequently missed out on any real appreciation of the beauties of nature.

'Which is my house?' I asked, looking down at the village.

She gave me a mystified look.

'It's my house now,' I stated. 'Left in the Will, plus a thirty percent holding in Latchley Aggregates, though what I'll do with the house or the shares, I've no idea.'

'It's Uncle Tom's Cabin.' she said.

'What is?'

'The house,' she replied. 'I always knew it as Uncle Tom's Cabin …… I never called him Uncle Tom …… Just Tom …… but his house was always called Uncle Tom's Cabin.'

'Well it's been empty for two years now,' I stated. 'so it'll be cold and damp and no clean linen.'

She pointed. 'See the grey roof, the large one?' I followed the direction of her finger. 'There's a house behind it …… a tall one, with a double chimney …… three storey …… That's Uncle Tom's Cabin.'

'In that case,' I said. 'I'd better collect my bags and make my way down there and get out of these wet clothes. I hope I can get in …… I haven't even got a key to my own house. It's been good to meet you, perhaps we'll talk again sometime.'

'The back door's open,' she said wistfully, still looking down into the village. 'The back door's always open …… it always was open … … ever since I was a child it was open …… so I could go in and out when I pleased. There's clean linen in the cupboard on the landing. The bed's made up and there's some food in the pantry.'

I walked round in front of her and looked straight at her, not able to make sense of what was going on.

'Why?' I questioned intensely. 'You tend his grave ……you clean his house ……you leave food as if he's coming back ……you leave the door open so he can get in ……why? ….. I don't understand!'

She tilted her head to one side and looked beyond me, focussing on the clouds that were rolling effortlessly across the approaching night sky.

'Because he said you were coming,' she almost choked on the words. 'And I believed him …… despite all the lies to cover up for you …… I knew you'd come …… one day…… I knew you'd come.'

I had never been loved, never even been liked. I had lived a thoughtless, selfish life and trampled on anyone who got in my way. I had shouted, bullied, intimidated and terrorised and yet here was a beautiful woman who had patiently waited for years until I came.

Before I fully realised what I was doing, I reached out and pulled her to me; her cheeks were cold to my lips, but soft and tender. With a foolish display of animal arousal I enveloped her with my arms and smothered her with kisses. For one moment of ecstasy, she yielded, and then she was wrestling and shouting and pushing me away.

'No!' she shouted hysterically.

She broke into a run down the shingle path and I chased after her and caught her.

'No! I mustn't!' she screamed, pulling my hands away and pushing roughly against me. She ran off and I let her go.

'Wait!' I shouted after her. 'I don't even know your name!'

She had almost reached the gate now and her voice when she turned round was nearly lost in the sound of the wind and rain. 'Gwenlyn……Gwenlyn Bardell.' she shouted, and started running down the hill.

I walked slowly to the gate, soaked to the skin, and with a sickening feeling in my stomach.

Chapter 5

The house, when I reached it, was cold, dark and unwelcoming. I fumbled my way through the small, unkempt back garden and found that the back door was unlocked. A freshly lit candle sat burning in the kitchen which I presumed must have been placed there by Gwenlyn after she left me. I was grateful for that at least.

There were matches and a box of candles close by, so I lit a few more to enable me to see my way around. There was bread, dripping, vegetables and half a pail of thick, creamy milk on a cold slab of marble. A bucket of coal stood next to an old boiler which was ready for lighting with newspaper and sticks piled haphazardly inside. Out of interest, I noted that the date on the paper was September 5th 1948, three days after Thomas Bradbury had been buried and almost two years to the day before my arrival.

I threw in a lighted match and emptied in some coal. The kitchen filled with smoke but within half an hour a healthy blaze was helping to take the chill off the room. I ventured upstairs to escape the fumes, carrying a candle embedded in wax on a cracked saucer. Long shadows danced in the emptiness and my fingers touched layers of dust everywhere I moved. True to her promise, the bed in the largest room was made and as I smelt the sheets and bedclothes, I established that they were indeed clean and freshly aired.

I tried the water taps but nothing came out, but with a bit of exploring, I found the mains tap was turned off in the kitchen. Once turned on I heard the pipes coughing and the belch of water flowing into the sink upstairs. I rinsed my face then stripped out of my wet clothes and treated myself to a bath in icy cold water. There were no towels that I could find, but fortunately I had some in my bags. I returned briefly downstairs to blow out the candles before going back upstairs and curling my shivering body under the sheets and blankets. Even though I was hungry and cold, and even though the candles brought back some unpleasant childhood memories, I had one of my better night's sleep.

*****

I wasn't aware at first of what had awakened me. I could hear a noise; a rhythmical noise and not far away, but couldn't identify it. It was six o'clock. I got up, washed, and dressed and walked downstairs to the kitchen where I cut myself some bread and spread it with the thick dripping. It tasted strong and rich but quickly satisfied my appetite. I warmed some milk on top of the boiler which had miraculously stayed alight, and added some sugar to the creamy, white liquid. It was sickly but revitalising and it quenched my thirst.

The rhythmical noise continued outside, then ceased abruptly and I suddenly became aware of the silence inside the house. I felt a momentary sadness for the man who had lived here before, whom I had never seen, but who had paid all my expenses until my adoptive parents died. Even then, he had continued his support by leaving me his share in Latchley Aggregates and also the house itself. The house and its contents looked almost untouched since his death and lacked a woman's touch. Gwenlyn may have continually been in, but she had left it very much as a shrine to his memory.

I walked out through the back door and round the side and so to the front access which led directly on to a road which sloped very steeply down towards the little harbour. I wondered which of the nearby houses was Gwenlyn's, but the peculiar noise started up again from the direction of the harbour, so I followed my curiosity and went to find out what it was.

The harbour was roughly three and a half sides of a square, littered with the criss-cross plaiting of mooring lines, connected like umbilical cords to dozens of small fishing boats. The exception was a large vessel which totally occupied one side of the harbour and dwarfed the boats around it. It was this vessel which was producing the rhythmical noises.

It was a large craft sitting immobile while it exhaled a thick plume of smoke from its single funnel. A maze of pipes adorned the superstructure; a cacophony of whistling steam jets enveloped in a patchwork of grey paint and rust. A chain of dredging buckets slanted upwards like a row of hungry mouths waiting to be fed, while seagulls soared overhead with cries of complaint at the intrusion into their domain.

Amidst the well ordered bustle of the fishermen and the crew of the dredger, I was drawn to the sight of a man walking briskly along the harbour wall. He was dressed in a smart suit, completely out of place with the rough fishermen and he walked with ungainly steps too long for his body. He eventually disappeared though the door of a building at the far end of the harbour and I thought no more about him for the moment.

I wandered round the harbour itself, absorbing the atmosphere, the noise and the smells. It wasn't until I, too, reached the far end of the harbour that I noticed a small sign on the wall of the building into which the man had gone. It was a small, dulled, brass plaque which stated: 'Latchley Aggregates. Branch Office.' So I invited myself in.

There was a long corridor leading directly into a cramped, low-ceilinged office. The suited man I had observed earlier faced me from behind the desk.

'Good morning.' I ventured.

'Is it?' he replied, hoisting himself up to a more upright position. 'Can I help you?'

He was fresh faced, early twenties and kept pushing his glasses up his nose which wrinkled up every time he did so. He looked to be an intellectual rather than one to get his hands dirty; a combination of brains and naïve enthusiasm, but pleasant enough for all that.

'Yes, I suppose you can help me. I saw the plate outside and thought I'd come in and find out what you do.'

'What? At this time of the morning?' he began irritably. 'Most people should still be in bed, but not this lot! No way! Crack of dawn they're at it, seven days a week!'

'The fishermen, you mean?' I asked.

'No! The dredger! Out on the banks at eight. First barge there by ten ...... second by twelve ...... third by two ...... No time for lunch!'

I looked puzzled.

'You're new here aren't you?' he enquired.

I nodded.

'Well, they're dredging the shingle banks. What do you want to know for?'

'Just interest,' I said casually in reply. 'So why the noise so early in the morning?'

'Aha!' He exclaimed, pointing his pen at me. 'Because......it's simple really: the harbour is prone to silting up, has been for years. The dredger comes along, can't get into the harbour to moor because the harbour is prone to silting up... blaa ... blaa ... blaa ...So it dredges its own moorings. The fishermen are happy because the water is deeper for them; the dredging people are happy because they have somewhere to moor up at night, tides permitting......so everybody's happy! Symbiosis they call it ...... everybody helps everybody else!'

'So why dredge the shingle banks?' I questioned, somewhat bewildered.

'The Lord Mayor of Plymouth's bright idea, I believe.' he answered. 'Shore defences ...... of military significance ...... the war's over but the fighting goes on. They have to use up the budget somehow.'

'So they've got no shingle there?'

'No. They need a certain size; easily washable, to get rid of the salt. Not too small; not too big, in fact, just the size of the shingle off the coast at Windle Bridge......Nicholas Faversham, by the way.'

He extended a hand and I shook it firmly.

'Alexander Kinsey,' I said.

'Well, they dredge up the shingle, then when each barge is full they go off to .... Hey, aren't you ....?'

'Yes, I am,' I confirmed.

'I don't think I'm supposed to be talking to you.' He frowned, his manner changing.

'And why not?' I asked, as casually as possible.

'Mr Latchley said so! I mean, not directly. He said you were sort of …… nosey …… curious …… not to be trusted.'

I endeavoured to enlighten him. 'I only met him yesterday for the first time. He seems to judge people very quickly don't you think?'

'He's a mean sod! …… I shouldn't have said that should I?' he pushed his glasses up on his nose and looked like a naughty school boy.

'How long have you worked here, Nicholas?' He was a Nicholas, not a Nick or a Nicky.

'Oh! …… Stuff Jonathan Latchley! Three weeks and two days! Three weeks and two days of Hell! You been to Hell Mr Kinsey?'

I nodded. 'Oh yes …… I've been to Hell! ….. To Hell and back …… more than once!'

'Then you'll understand.'

I did …… but he didn't. He was too young for the war; he'd probably lived through it longing to be a spitfire pilot or a submarine captain. He'd not seen Hell …. he'd not seen anything even close!

'So what's your job?' I probed.

'I'm in charge of course!' he stated with pride. 'I co-ordinate the work with the tides: the barges, the shifts, the volume of shingle, the men …… God, I almost have to wipe their bottoms for them sometimes!'

I smiled at the thought of tough sailors being mothered by such a lad, but kept my mouth shut. He'd probably never had an office of his own before.

'So, tell me,' I said, 'I know nothing about dredging, nothing about shingle. How long have you been dredging here, how much has been dredged up and how long to go before they're finished?'

He picked up a piece of paper and a pencil and did some quick arithmetic while he talked. 'Each barge can carry about six hundred tons. We get …… if we can …… five loads, so say three thousand tons in one day. We've been going for about seven months, nearly everyday, so that's pretty close to six hundred and thirty thousand tons or so.'

I whistled, very impressed. 'That's a lot of shingle!'

'Ah yes!' he pushed his glasses up again. 'But there's a long way to go. One million is the target. The contract requires exactly one million tons; not a pebble more, not a pebble less!'

'Well I didn't know Latchley Aggregates was so heavily into dredging,' I commented. 'I thought they were mainly into quarrying. I didn't even know they owned a dredger.'

'Ah, you see, Latchley Aggregates doesn't actually own the dredger, that's sub-contracted in with a skipper first mate and engineer. The rest of the crew are local …… Half of them struggled to find jobs in fishing again after the war, but they all knew boats and the sea. They jumped at the chance of a reasonably steady job, and with the smell of sea air in their lungs again as well.'

'So what of the quarrying?' I asked.

'Oh ,…… I wouldn't know about that,' he shrugged. 'That's Mr Latchley's department. I look after the dredging, he looks after the quarries. Don't know the first thing about quarries myself, and he gets seasick walking across a puddle.'

'But you know where the quarries are, do you?'

I'd found out a bit about dredging, now it was time to find out about quarrying. If Jonathan Latchley was offering to buy me out for ten thousand pounds, I wanted to know if it was a good deal or not.

'You are nosey and curious aren't you?' he commented, but there was no animosity in his tone. 'There are a few maps in the desk; might be something marked on there I suppose.'

He delved into the bottom drawer of the desk and pulled out a pile of papers and maps and, true enough, there was one, old map marked with the quarrying interests of Latchley Aggregates. I asked to borrow a pencil and paper and noted down the sites accordingly. If the quarrying was on the same scale as the dredging, then my thirty percent share was worth a lot more than the already considerable sum of ten thousand pounds! I decided there and then to spend the rest of the week finding out.

I bade farewell to the helpful Nicholas Faversham, but it wasn't until I was nearly back to the house that I thought of one question I hadn't asked. I had omitted to find out why his predecessor had left. I vowed I would ask next time, if I had the chance. Meanwhile, I would sort out plans to tour half a dozen quarries; whether Jonathan Latchley approved or not.

*****

I had no car, so I had to use a mixture of local bus, train and hitch-hiking. It was slow and time consuming, especially as it took me all day just to get see the nearest two quarry sites. I was puzzled when I saw the site on the moors outside Buckfastleigh and equally puzzled when I saw the one at North Bovey. I presumed that there must be some sort of explanation, but thought that I would see the others before I came to any conclusions.

I arrived back that evening, weary of travelling and hungry after the day away. I did as I had often done in the Peaks when I had lived with Father John and Isobella and changed into shorts and vest and went for a run. There was a semblance of a coastal path over the cliffs to the north, so I followed it and ended up running along the flat road that separated the freshwater of Slapton Ley from the sea.

There were still rusting remains of military equipment lying around from the exercises there during the war and it reminded me too much of the beaches of Salerno. I decided to avoid the area in future, if possible. By the time I got back, I was hot and disturbed from the memories. The running hadn't helped my restfulness at all, and after a cold bath and some food and drink, I sat morosely in the dusty lounge following the dancing shadows from the candle.

I slept badly, tossing and turning as my mind revived the ugly scenes from Vietri. By five o'clock I was wide awake, so I dressed and wandered down to the harbour. A dozen boats had just come in and the quayside was a hive of activity in the early morning light. A tall, slim, fair haired man appeared to be orchestrating the events and he eventually came over when he saw me watching so intently.

'Will you be Mr Kinsey?' He enquired with a strong accent.

'Yes,' I replied. 'How did you know that?'

His speech was slow, and each word was pronounced with exaggerated carefulness. 'Nicholas … Nicholas Faversham … He tell me that you are here. I am Peers Lofgren. I am from Norway. I come here in the war and now I am living here. I am the master of the harbour.'

'Pleased to meet you,' I said extending my hand.

His grip was vice-like, his skin warm and abrasive against mine. He smiled in a non-committal way and withdrew a few steps. 'Perhaps you learn about crabs and fish?'

'Perhaps,' I concurred.

He walked away, taking long, shuffling steps in his waders. He spoke to one of the fisherman and I got up to go but the fisherman gestured to me to wait. They finished their conversation and the fisherman strolled over and presented me with two, good sized, fresh fish. 'Something for your breakfast,' he said.

'Most kind!' I said emphatically.

'Peers idea, mate.'

'Thank-you,' I said as he walked away and I waved at Peers Lofgren. He acknowledged with a nod of his head and I left the quay and walked back to a hearty breakfast at the house.

By eight I was on my way to Liskeard and to the quarry at Common Moor. Once again, I was puzzled and yet more so on seeing the site at Callington as well. I toyed with the idea of spending a night in Launceston and carrying on the next day but thought better of it and arrived back at Windle Bridge just as night was falling. I struck a match to light a candle, vowing that I must find a way to get the electricity supply to work, and found a note on the kitchen table. I hadn't bothered to lock the back door, it hadn't been locked for years, so why start now.

The note read:

'Would you care to join us for dinner on Saturday evening at 7-30 p.m.? One or two other guests will be present. I look forward to making your acquaintance.'

Yours sincerely,

James Bardell.

Some more milk had been placed on the marble slab and I wondered if Gwenlyn had put it there and left the message at the same time. The milk was too creamy for me to drink so I added some cold water and found it more to my taste. Tea was still in short supply so I had long ago got used to cold drinks.

I was off early again the next day and was lucky enough to get two quick lifts which took me nearly all the way to Holsworthy. I ran the remaining few miles to Hollacombe and by now was not at all surprised by what I found. Yarnscombe was the same and as I started the trip back, I had already begun to form a few searching questions for Jonathan Latchley to answer on the next, suitable occasion.

Hitching back wasn't so successful and I ended up sleeping in a hay loft on a farm somewhere in the middle of Dartmoor. I must have looked fairly dishevelled because it was the best part of an hour, come the following morning, before I got another lift and, even then, I had to pay half a crown for the privilege. It was midday by the time I arrived back.

I wrote a short, official sounding letter to Father John then went for a run, but south this time, to Start Point and back. It was refreshing and didn't trigger off any of memories, unlike my earlier run up Slapton Sands. My legs felt comfortably tired, allowing my brain to work better. I wondered whether Jonathan Latchley would be at the dinner party the next night. Maybe then I would get the chance to find out not only why the dredging side of the business was doing so well but also why all the quarries appeared to have been sold.

All of them had been sold at different times over the last few years, two of them within the last six months. It had cost me five pounds altogether to get anyone to talk, but workers from three of the quarries did eventually give me some clues. Jonathan Latchley had sold below the estimated market level because for some reason, he seemed in a desperate hurry to sell. No-one had been able to tell me why he should do so, as the quarries were a good business venture and showing a healthy profit. One perceptive foreman stated that it was possible that Latchley needed to get his hands on some ready cash very quickly and the only way to do that would be to sell up. Maybe tomorrow I would find out why.

I had to put up with the candles for one more night; the electrician couldn't come until the following morning. The house at least was warm, thanks to the boiler, and I now had the luxury of warm water.

I wandered down to the harbour after the sun had dropped below the horizon and decided to try one of the local pubs for a drink. There were only two in the village, both next to the harbour and hardly more than fifty yards between them. I now had a nodding acquaintance with some of the fishermen and also some of the crew of the dredger. Peers Lofgren said a hearty 'good evening' and I bought him a pint to thank him for the tasty breakfast he had sent in my direction.

It was good to mix with people who knew nothing of my past and who just accepted me. I felt comfortable for the first time in years and that night, I went to sleep with a faint glimmer of a smile on my face.

*****

Saturday dragged by.

By eleven in the morning, I had ironed my suit and shirt so I spent the rest of the day cleaning and dusting. By five o'clock I was sitting ready for my dinner engagement. With nothing better to do, I spent some time trying to think of a reason why Latchley would sell off the six quarries. I could come up with no logical solution, so gave up for the time being and dozed of for an hour or so in an armchair.

I had seen nothing at all of the Bardell family during the week, not even a glimpse of Gwenlyn. I wasn't absolutely sure which was their house, but I guessed correctly from the three closest to mine. I knocked firmly on the oak front door and it was opened by Peers Lofgren, looking uncomfortable in a jacket and tie.

'Good evening to you Mr Kinsey.' he said with his strong accent. 'You come into the lounge, I will be getting you a drink, yes?'

He showed me the way through the door into the lounge which was empty apart from a very formal looking Nicholas Faversham.

I greeted him cheerfully. 'Hello Nicholas, how's the shingle getting on? No trouble with the crew, I hope?'

'Getting along fine, thank-you, Mr Kinsey. They do as I tell them, so we've got no problems.'

Lofgren left the room and returned a few moments later followed by a fair haired young man who looked almost identical to himself, but twenty-five years younger. 'Mr Kinsey, Mr Faversham......this is my son, Peta.'

Faversham and I stood up and shook hands with Peta Lofgren. He was about the same age as Faversham, but taller, broader and altogether more physical. His top lip was turned up slightly on the left side of his face, giving the impression of a permanent sneer. There was no warmth in his smile and he merely greeted us with a grunt.

We all sat down and sipped at our drinks in an awkward silence. I heard voices from what I presumed was the kitchen, which grew louder as the door was opened.

A face appeared and smiled in our direction. 'They've all got drinks have they, Peers?' the man said, then withdrew. 'Is the soup ready yet, Gwenlyn?' I heard him shout in the corridor, and then he came into the room. He was short, slim and dignified and had the same finely boned face as his daughter. His skin looked too delicate to be that of a fisherman.

'Good evening, gentlemen.' He said politely. 'Peta, of course I know ...... You must be Nicholas Faversham.'

Faversham placed his glass on the small table next to him, stood up and nodded in acknowledgement.

He turned in my direction. 'And you? .... You must be Alexander Kinsey.' He spoke in a different, more inquisitive tone.

'Yes,' I replied, also rising from my chair.

He looked up at me, studying my face and shoulders. 'You've got your father's jaw anyway ..... and same colour hair.' He looked away. 'Peers, more drinks. I knew your father well,' he continued, addressing me again. 'A fine, upstanding man. You got my note, obviously. Welcome to Windle Bridge.'

I thanked him and sat down again and accepted another drink from Peers Lofgren.

James Bardell shouted something out into the kitchen and soon afterwards, Gwenlyn came in and was introduced to us all. Faversham only just stifled a gasp as she entered. Even with an apron on, she was stunningly beautiful. She, too, shook hands all round with no hint of recognition in my direction. Being the cook for the evening she soon left again for the kitchen, leaving Nicholas Faversham feverishly pushing his glasses up his nose.

We were soon invited into a spacious dining room where we took our places, however, there were still three seats vacant. I assumed one was for Gwenlyn and maybe another for Jonathan Latchley, but as for the third, I had no clue.

'Jonathan will be a little late,' James Bardell informed us. 'Held up with some business. He said for us to start if he wasn't here by eight.'

There was a noise behind James Bardell and the occupant of the third, remaining chair entered the room. This time, Faversham couldn't contain himself and a gasp escaped in the guise of a half formed whistle.

'This is Charlotte, my youngest daughter,' Bardell announced with obvious pride.

She smiled round the table at us all in turn, lingering slightly longer on Nicholas Faversham. Her dark hair was gathered with ribbons on top of her head, accentuating the neck and slender shoulders which led down to a low cut dress just half an inch below the level of decency. I could understand Faversham's reaction.

She sat next to Peta Lofgren and kissed him lightly on the cheek while all the time looking at Faversham. I had never seen such overt flirting in all my life, and Faversham, sitting opposite, couldn't take his eyes off her face and breasts. Peta Lofgren's scowling lips seemed to scowl even more, but Faversham didn't notice; in fact, I don't think he noticed anything else for the rest of the evening!

Gwenlyn served the soup and we were about to start when I heard a key in the lock. There was some shuffling outside in the hallway, then Jonathan Latchley marched in.

'Sorry I'm late, pressing business. I hope you started. Gwenlyn, be a dear and get me a drink would you?'

She dutifully got up and poured a drink from a decanter on the side board.

'Alexander, my dear fellow, so glad you could make it. Settling in alright? Been sampling the joys of Windle Bridge, have you?'

He was all sweetness and light compared to our initial conversation a few days before.

'Yes, thank-you. Nicholas here has been enlightening me on the ins and outs of dredging.'

I looked for any sign of discontent on Latchley's face, but could detect nothing.

'Good man is Nicholas.' Latchley agreed. 'Knows his way about by now, I'd say.'

Faversham only had eyes for Charlotte.

'I said 'you're beginning to get to know your way about,' Nicholas.' Latchley repeated more directly.

'What? ..... Oh! ..... er ...... yes, rather!' Faversham pushed his glasses up his nose, looked at Latchley and decided he preferred to look at Charlotte. 'All under control.'

'Good,' Latchley concluded, realising that Nicholas Faversham was absorbed for the night.

We finished our soup and started on the main course. Crab to me was a delicacy, but to these fishermen who caught them everyday, it had long since become a normal part of their diet.

Peta Lofgren was getting increasingly irritable as Charlotte cuddled up to him and yet cast continual furtive glances at Faversham across the table. The sweet, the small talk, and the cheese and biscuits followed afterwards and I was beginning to think that perhaps I'd been a bit harsh on Jonathan Latchley after all.

'So Alexander......or do people shorten it to Alex?' Latchley questioned.

'No......Alexander will do.'

'So then Alexander ...... tell us about yourself ...... Where you're from? What you do?

The rest of the guests looked slightly bored and sleepy after such a large meal, so I replied casually enough to fit the low key atmosphere. 'Army mainly ...... Officer training ...... Rank of Major, then the war finished. Moved about a bit, then discovered my roots at Windle Bridge ...... and here I am.'

Peers Lofgren, the drinks waiter for the evening, topped up our glasses and I saw him give a quick, chastening look at his son. Charlotte was still sitting directly opposite Faversham, who due to the effect of the alcohol, had begun to lose his inhibitions.

'I was never in the war ...... too young.' he admitted, with a slur in his speech. 'Tried to enlist when I was fifteen, but got flat feet ...... look, I've still got them.'

He bent forward and removed his shoes and showed to us, with a waggle of his toes, the nature of his flat feet.

'How extraordinary!' Charlotte commented emphatically. 'I've got flat feet as well!' She followed Faversham's example and leaned forward to kick off her shoes exposing a view down her dress which caused Faversham to gulp loudly. Peta Lofgren jerked her upright angrily, but she smiled provocatively and put a finger across his lips.

James Bardell acted as if nothing had happened and addressed Peers Lofgren. 'Peers served on Corvettes, didn't you Peers?'

Peers nodded.

'That's how you came to Windle Bridge,'

'Yes. This is why I am coming here. We sail from Norway, from the fjords. We come to England and we come to Plymouth. It is nice, so when the war is ended we come here ... my wife ... my son. Sometimes we go to Norway, but here is home now.'

'Is this your home now, Alexander?' Gwenlyn asked quietly. She had hardly spoken all night, and they were the first words she had spoken directly to me.

I sighed before I answered. 'That depends really......I've got no job ...... not as such, anyway. I suppose I could get some work around here.'

Latchley interrupted me. 'Ten thousand pounds, Alexander! Ten thousand pounds! The offer still stands, and that's in front of witnesses.'

I could sense an edge to his voice and suddenly the evening ceased to be just a theatre for Charlotte's flirtations.

'I don't think so, Jonathan. It's quite nice around here ...... nice people ...... nice scenery.'

'But you've got no job! ..... Oh, you'll get your share from Latchley's Aggregates, but will that be enough? To live on, I mean ... ... to live properly, as befits a Major?'

'Like I said, maybe I can get a job.'

Latchley got up, walked to the fireplace and looked around the room. 'What did you do in the war ...... in your army life that could be of use here? Did you have some sort of speciality .... some special training?'

I didn't see the trap coming.

'Okay, so I didn't learn a trade ...... but I can still learn.' I countered.

'Ten thousand ...... and another fifteen hundred for the house,' he said. 'Gwenlyn and I have to live somewhere when we marry. You can't say fairer than that can you? It's a good price, far more than the house is worth, and a generous settlement on your share of the company ...... What do you say?'

'No ...... No thanks. Not at the moment. I need to spend some time thinking about my future first.' I said.

He pulled himself to his full height and ran his left hand slowly through his greased hair. 'You didn't give eleven children too much time to think about their future, did you?'

Chapter 6

The room was instantly silent. Even Nicholas Faversham, in his semi-drunken state, paused in an attempt at doing up his shoe lace.

James Bardell slowly put his drink down on a table near him, and frowned. 'What are you getting at, Jonathan?' he asked sharply.

'Perhaps Major Kinsey would care to enlighten us. Or, there again, perhaps he wouldn't. It appears that our Major here does have a speciality. Murdering children seems to be what he does best.'

Gwenlyn went ashen, and when she slumped in her chair, I thought she was going to faint.

'It was ......' I coughed to clear my throat, my mouth suddenly dry. 'It was a mistake.'

'A mistake!' Latchley retorted. 'Your war record seems to be strewn with mistakes! If anyone got in your way, you destroyed them! I have my connections you know. I didn't like you when I first met you and I like you even less now! A friend of mine found out a few details about you: your reputation is still talked about even now. People don't forget, Major Kinsey; they don't forget at all!'

I searched round the room for some sort of help or inspiration but none was forthcoming. All eyes were on me; hostile eyes, judgemental, unsympathetic, hateful even.

Latchley stroked his greased hair again and addressed the room. 'I knew it!' he spat out. 'The minute I heard that Tom's bastard was coming here, I knew there would be trouble, but even I didn't expect to share the same table as the bloody murderer of innocent children!'

I leapt out of my chair, stretching out my hands to go straight for his throat but peers Lofgren had anticipated my move and stuck out his foot as I rushed past. It caught me just below the knee and I crashed forward, bashing my head hard on the coal scuttle by the fire. My arms darted out for support but all I found was Jonathan Latchley's leg. I crouched there, half stunned, trying to catch my breath whilst holding onto his leg in a desperate endeavour not to fall again.

I shook my head to try and regain my full senses and heard a woman's cry behind me. I tried to pull myself up but my arms felt weak and I only managed to get to my knees. I let go of Latchley's leg and looked up to meet his taunting gaze. He lifted a foot and with a speed I would not have expected for a man of his size, pushed me with the sole of his shoe and watched me sprawl backwards across the room.

I cannoned heavily into Charlotte who screamed in terror. 'Get off me! Don't touch me you......you......you beast!'

Latchley spoke in a slow, melodramatic monotone. 'Go away from here. Go away from this house ... from this village ... and don't come back! My offer still stands, I'll have my solicitor draw up the papers and then we can rid ourselves of you for good.'

I had never, ever been so humiliated, yet, worst of all, I could think of nothing I could say in my defence. I got up and walked, still dazed towards the door. I looked pleadingly at Gwenlyn, but she turned away. I pushed open the door and walked into the hall aware of the echo of my footsteps. The fresh air, when I felt it outside, was cold and numbing and I stood there feeling doomed to run away from my past forever. Still dazed from the blow to my head, I staggered back to my house feeling more dejection than I had experienced for as long as I could remember.

The boiler had gone out and a chill had crept into the building. I took laboured steps up the stairs to the bedroom and threw myself on the bed with a cry of total helplessness. The moon flickered in and out of the clouds, alternately illuminating and darkening the room. I saw a shaft of light that illuminated the villa at Vietri. I saw my own men lying, mown down, lifeless on the road, and I saw the sun rising over the body strewn beaches of Salerno.

I lay there for hours, my eyes wide open yet sore with tiredness and the more I waited the worse the visions became. I tried looking at different points of the room. But I couldn't distract my mind from my past. I began to shout; incomprehensible words that spilled out louder and louder until I was screaming at the top of my voice. I thrashed out at the atmosphere with arms and legs wanting to strike out at circumstances, but there was nothing there.

I reached the point where I couldn't stand it any longer, bounded from the bed and wrenched the bedside lamp away from its wired connection to the wall. The flex was eight or nine feet long and with trembling hands I tied a loop in one end. I stumbled out onto the landing and by reaching on tip-toe, I managed to tie the other end of the flex to the banister which lined the stairs up to the attic bedrooms. Still at full stretch I pulled the loop over my head and tightened it round my neck.

I gagged with the pressure on my throat and as I couldn't bend my head forwards to see what I was doing, I felt with my feet as I inched closer to the top of the stairs. I could also feel the banister sloping away from me as my toes balanced precariously on the top step. I took a short pace back, then launched myself into space. There was a horrifying tearing sound from my neck and a sickening crash as the flex snapped and sent me careering down the stairs.

I somersaulted at least twice and banged my legs with alarming force on the wall next to the stairs as I fell. I landed in a crumpled heap in the hall with the flex knotted round my neck stopping me from breathing. I tore frantically at the wire as I felt myself slowly choking into unconsciousness until one, final, frantic pull separated the wire leaving me gasping on the floor. It was a while before I could move, and I noticed a pool of blood from where the wire had dug into my flesh. I plunged my head and shoulders into a basin full of cold water in the kitchen and felt the liquid soothing the burning cuts in my skin. Large gulps of water helped to cool me down and as the water ran smoothly down my throat, I felt the tension dissipate as I slowly came back to my senses.

I sat in the kitchen for an hour, trembling with shock and released emotion. My shorts and vest lay on one of the chairs with some other of my clothes so I changed into them and, still shaking, I went through the back door.

It was dark, but I didn't care, I just needed to be away, anywhere, absolutely anywhere but in that house or that village. I headed up onto the southerly coastal path, running at a crazy speed. I reached the first incline and was already gasping for breath, but I wouldn't stop. There was the faintest glimmer of first light so I could just about make out where I was running.

I pumped my legs until they seized with cramp and as I started down a steep slope I could feel my feet slipping. The strength had gone and I vainly tried to stop myself but I had nothing left in my limbs. I twisted sideways so as to avoid hurting myself on the stones of the path and, in doing so, I fell into the straggly vegetation that grew on the slopes down to the sea. I stretched out my arms and legs to break my fall but I was already weak from the tumble down the stairs, so I could do nothing but let myself go.

I ended up face down on the beach, my landing broken by the soft sand above the level of high tide. I lay there breathing deeply, too exhausted to move. Perspiration ran down my forehead stinging my eyes with its saltiness, so I closed them against the pain and in doing so, a wave of fatigue enveloped me; and in that crumpled, prostrate position, I slept.

It was a blank sleep; a nothingness, only apparitions of solid walls and emptiness which made it all the more strange when I woke to the smell of cooking. I opened my eyes and spat out the taste of sand on my lips. My whole body seemed to throb with pain and stiffness and it was a huge effort to roll over onto my side and seek out the source of the smell.

I was only thirty yards from an old shack made from pieces of driftwood and corrugated iron. A boat lay on the sand midway between high and low water mark and a man was crouching by an open fire while the smoke wafted in my direction.

'You'll be needing some hot food.' came a voice over the sand.

I slowly pulled myself up and stretched, grimacing with the pains of the accumulated falls. I shuffled over and sat opposite the man, upwind of the drifting smoke.

'Fish stew. That's all we got round here.' he murmured.

He ladled a generous helping into an old tin plate and handed it to me. I accepted it without comment. It was hot, strong and tasty having been spiced with herbs and salt. I finished the plate and he gave me some more.

'Hungry? he asked.

I nodded.

'Coffee?'

I nodded again.

He poured some thick, black liquid from an army tin kettle into a metal mug and handed it to me.

His hands were broad, hairy and cracked along the lines on the palms. Sinewy arms led to rolled up sleeves which buried themselves into a multicoloured sou'wester, full of holes. A filthy woollen hat sat on his head and he talked through blackened teeth set into a mouth framed within a grey beard.

'I saw you fall. Then I heard you snoring, so I left you to sleep. I throws a blanket over you. Didn't look like you'd been breaking no bones.'

'Thanks,' I replied, noticing the old blanket which I'd left draped over the sand. 'And thanks for breakfast.'

'It been't no breakfast......breakfast were long ago. More like time for dinner!'

I checked my watch; it was gone midday, I had slept for nearly seven hours.

'More fish stew?' he offered, stirring what was left over the fire.

'No thanks.' I replied.

'Then let's have pudding.' he announced, getting up from his seat on the sand and marching back to the old hut. He reappeared soon afterwards with a large tin of sliced peaches and proceeded to lay it on its side and stab it with a large sheath knife. The tin burst open spilling juice into the sand. He lifted it up and by twisting the tin from side to

104

side he worked a big hole in it. He tipped half the contents into the same dish I had used for my fish stew and kept the other half for himself. He handed me a wooden spoon and as I was beyond caring, I ate the lot while he lifted the tin to his mouth and let the contents drop down his throat.

'Are you the soldier boy that moved to Windle Bridge?' he asked, while wiping his mouth on his forearm.

I put my dish down, surprised at the question. 'Yes, but how did you know that?'

'Ah! I've got eyes! I've got ears!' He pointed at them in turn. 'Things get round 'bout these parts.'

'What things?' I asked suspiciously.

'Oh, gossip and the like. Can't have a new face round Windle Bridge without the gossip starting. Not often we sees some 'un new here.'

'So you've heard I was in the army...what else?'

'That you're Tom's bastard.'

He said it as a statement of fact and without any sort of malice and I wasn't offended as I had been with Jonathan Latchley.

'I can see it in your face. Knew Tom well ...... for years I knew Tom.' He bowed his head reverently as he let his mind drift back into the memories of yesteryear. He must have been well into his sixties if not more. I found it difficult to tell with these fishermen; their faces showed age but their bodies were strong.

'What do I call you?' I enquired.

'Jabber's my name.' he answered.

'Well, Mr Jabber, thanks for the meal.'

'Just Jabber ...... No one's called me mister for years! Everyone knows Jabber 'round here.'

'That's rather an unusual name,' I commented. 'How come you get called that?'

'Tom ......' He laughed loudly. 'Tom, the old 'fitch!' When we was lads and first took up fishing, we went out one day and did what's known 'round these parts as 'Riding the Wind.' Tom, he stole my old man's boat and I sailed it ...... Tom said that when I concentrate hard I push my bottom lip up like this ...' He demonstrated by curling his bottom lip over his top one and making it protrude outwards. 'It makes my lip look like the jabber of a fish ... that's its bottom lip ... since then, everyone calls me 'Jabber.'

I laughed too, and we good naturedly passed off the next half hour while he related stories about my father and the mischief they had got up to together.

'But what's this 'Riding the Wind' all about?' I asked. 'Was it some sort of prank? It sounds a bit ...... well ...... sort of ...... unreal don't you think?'

He got up and walked down the beach to where the waves lapped up onto the sand. I got up and followed him, aware that he had gone quiet and an odd, faraway look had come over his face.

'It is sort of unreal lad,' he murmured wistfully. 'Nothing quite like it ...... Do you see out there?' He pointed his finger towards the far off dredger on the shingle banks. 'There's a current runs north the other side of the bank and another what runs south on this side. Now them shingle banks makes the water shallow and at low tide the water gets really shallow, right?'

I nodded, not fully understanding.

'Now, we get storms in this bay; easterly storms what drive the water into the bay. If you get's a storm when the tide is on the turn, the wind whips across the banks and what with the current and shallow water, you fair travel in a boat ...... It's a wild wind ...... uncontrollable ...... you just sits there and waits for the wind to take you ...... nothing you can do to stop it.'

He stopped and pointed back up the beach to his own boat. 'You don't see many boats like mine'ere' bouts anymore; heavy, small sail, oars. Used to all have 'em, but not no more. That's the boat to 'Ride the Wind'...... The sail's not too big, and the boat's heavy enough to cut though the waves.'

We strolled back up the beach and Jabber disappeared again into his hut. He came out excited and I wondered what it was that had made him so vibrant.

'Barometer's dropped!' He enthused. 'I thought I could smell it!'

I shrugged my shoulders. 'Smell what?'

'You can smell it in the air ...... Wind change ...... heaviness ... ... a storm; perhaps in two days, maybe less, maybe more, maybe not at all.'

He looked pensive and I watched while he curled his bottom lip over the top one, in deep concentration. When he spoke it was in a slow, measured tone. 'How'd you like to 'Ride the Wild Wind,' lad?'

I was taken aback at the mere thought of it. 'I ...... well ...... I don't know. I'm no sailor ... army, don't forget.'

'It may not happen,' he interjected. 'It has to be when the tide turns, otherwise the water's too deep over the shingle.'

'Mmm... I don't know,' I repeated hesitantly.

'Come on, lad!' he cajoled enthusiastically. 'It only happens a few times a year …… You'll never forget it!'

I capitulated. 'Oh! Alright. But I'm no sailor,' I warned.

'You don't need to be a sailor …… you just be needing to hold on tight. Come tomorrow night, sleep on the beach and we won't miss it!'

'I'd better go now,' I said, changing the subject. I thought to myself that I could always forget to come or find some excuse not to turn up.

'I'll be seeing you tomorrow?' he said, waiting for my agreement.

'Yes…O.K …… Tomorrow …… I'll come late.'

I started up the steep slope back to the coastal path, but was struck by a thought. So I retraced my steps.

'What else have you heard about me?' I asked.

He was just about to go back into his hut. 'Nothing.' He replied, puzzled.

'Then I'll tell you before anyone else does. Someone's bound to say something sometime ….. I was in the army, like I said, I was also a bully, and I also made a mistake. I killed eleven children and four nuns during an ambush on the wrong target.'

I waited quietly for his response. He looked guarded and a frown clouded his face.

'A mistake, you say?'

'A mistake …… Yes.' I echoed.

'We all make mistakes.' The frown moulded into a knowing expression. 'And you're Tom's lad …… I don't listen to no gossip … … If you says it was a mistake …. it was a mistake and you been man enough to admit it.'

I smiled a genuine smile of appreciation and began my walk home. Tomorrow, or the day after, I would join an old tramp in the ritual of 'Riding the Wind' simply because he was one of only a few people who had accepted me for what I was, without judgement ...... despite my past.

*****

By the following morning I needed to replenish my stock of food so I left the house and headed for the small collection of shops that graced Windle Bridge. I smiled at a woman I had seen a few times over the last couple of days but she didn't acknowledge me. I thought little of it; perhaps she hadn't seen me, but when another woman obviously crossed the road with her little boy on seeing me approach, I knew something was wrong.

I arrived at the shops, becoming suspicious of other furtive glances which I had received on the way. I entered the small green-grocers only to be greeted by cold stares from the proprietor and customers.

'I need some potatoes and some fresh vegetables,' I said, looking round at the counters. 'Some carrots perhaps, and swede, and some tomatoes.'

'I'm sorry, sir ...... we're closed,' came the stern words from the owner.

'Closed?' I questioned. 'But it's mid morning! It's Monday! Shops don't close mid morning on Mondays!'

'We're closed to you, sir ...... not to anyone else ...... just to you, sir.'

I didn't like the tone to his voice and made as if to object but then thought 'what's the use.' Word had obviously spread around, so I left with no further comment. Out of interest, I noticed that the other shops had hurriedly placed closed signs on their doors although there were still customers inside. I wondered what story they had been told; the truth was bad enough but I dare say it had been dressed up and exaggerated beyond recognition from one telling to another.

Sad, lonely and dejected, I walked up the hill, over the bridge, past the cemetery and onto the main road where I soon managed to hitch a lift into Dartmouth.

I thought of barging into Latchley's office but decided I was in enough trouble as it was, so I bought sufficient food for a week and a heavy duty bag in which to carry it all. On my return, I was fortunate to be picked up again by the same farmer in the jeep who had given me a lift on my first day in the area.

He dropped me off at the top of the hill leading into Windle Bridge and, ironically, when I walked past the cemetery, I saw Gwenlyn again at my father's grave. I stopped to watch her, hoping that she wouldn't see me, but as if touched by a sixth sense, she turned round and caught sight of me. We stood and looked at each other for what seemed like an age before she bent down to carry on with her job of replacing the flowers. I nearly walked on, but decided to at least try to talk to her alone without Latchley interrupting. I was careful not to get too close. She had been frightened on Saturday night and I didn't want to frighten her again.

'Nice flowers,' I commented, but she carried on with her arranging and tidying.

'I'm sorry about Saturday night. I would have told you ...... eventually. But I don't know you, at least, not well enough to explain ...... to tell you what really happened.'

She looked up at me. 'But it did happen, didn't it......those children......you really did do it?'

I struggled to know how to answer her question. 'Yes,' I went on. 'It happened ...... and I've suffered for it every moment of everyday and every moment of every night since.' I shuffled uneasily, sensing a hardness in her expression. 'I'm not proud of it, if that's what you think ...... I ...... I'd rather not talk about it .... not yet anyway. One day maybe.'

'Let's not talk about it, then,' she interjected, still sounding doubtful.

'Alright then, what shall we talk about? It's a lovely day, the sun's shining, the sky's blue, the birds are singing.'

'No it's not,' she said.

'Not what?' I questioned.

'A lovely day. It's lovely now, but there's cloud to the east, maybe a storm.'

I remembered Jabber's predictions about an impending storm and I, too, looked out to sea and, indeed, there was a thin layer of black cloud on the horizon.

'Tell me,' I asked, suddenly feeling bold. 'Are you happy ...... happy living here, I mean?'

She thought briefly before answering. 'I've always lived here...' She seemed reluctant to continue.

'That wasn't the question,' I pressed, 'Are you happy living here? ..... Here? ..... Now? Right now, waiting to get married? ..... looking forward to having children? ..... that sort of thing, you know what I mean.'

She pulled up an imaginary weed from the immaculately kept

grave and rose to her feet. A tight blouse and full skirt accentuated the slender lines of her body; graceful and smooth. I suppressed an almost irresistible urge to hold her again as I had done that first time we had met, but there was a barrier between us now.

'Am I happy? Who knows?' she sighed. 'What is happiness? We live. We sleep. Christmas. Easter. Decorations, presents, birthdays. We laugh, we cry. Is that happiness?'

'When do you and Jonathan plan to marry …. what date I mean?'

She put her head on one side and raised her eyebrows in a gesture of uncertainty. 'I don't know. Sometime, I suppose …… Sometime.'

'You've just got engaged then I presume?'

She shook her head.

'How long then?' I asked.

'Eight years …… nine years …… something like that.'

'What!' I exclaimed in disbelief. 'Nine years! He's been engaged to a beautiful woman for nine years …. and no plans to marry! The man's a fool! What do you do then …. do you go away for weekends, or holidays?'

'No!... We…..do....not!' she stated indignantly. 'I'm a virgin! And anyway, what's that got to do with you?'

She blushed, but it was anger and not embarrassment that caused the colour in her cheeks. 'And what right have you got to question me about my morals?' There's certain things a woman wants to keep to herself!'

'I'm sorry,' I said, backing off. 'Is he waiting for the business to improve or something?' I suddenly saw my chance to ask about the sale of the six quarries without arousing suspicion.

'No ...... the business is doing well.' She was still angry. 'As far as I know, anyway.'

'Well, the dredging is,' I assured her, looking out into the bay. 'I mean, they're at it now, but what about the quarrying? Aren't there some quarries as well? I know so little about that side of things; all I've seen is the dredging out there.'

'Jonathan says they're doing well, I'm not really interested ...... in quarries ...... or dredging. I've never been into money and buying things. I ask out of duty. He says the quarries are very productive ...... a good profit.'

'How many quarries are there?' I enquired.

'I don't really know. Six, I think, but I've never seen them. Like I said, I'm not really interested.'

She may not be interested, I thought, but I certainly was. Why did Latchley so emphatically want me out of the way and why did he tell lies about the profitability of the six quarries when he had already sold them? It was something I promised to find out.

'You still haven't told me why he's in no hurry to marry you?' I hesitated and framed the next sentence carefully in my mind. 'You can't spend the rest of your life tending graves ...... If I was him, I'd marry you tomorrow.'

She looked startled.

'Come on!' I insisted. 'There must be a reason ...... He's a man ...... He surely must want you! It's not natural if he doesn't ...... I would!'

I'd gone too far......again.

'It's none of your damn business!' she retorted sharply. 'Yes, he wants me, but he'll only get me when there's a ring on my finger! .....

113

I've told him that! He doesn't like it, but that's how it is: no gold ring ...... no me!'

'I admire you for that,' I said simply. 'He's still a fool ...... and you've still not told me why.'

She answered impatiently. 'Because I don't know why! Every time we talk about it, he says that the time will come when it's right......Meanwhile, I'll have to wait.'

'The man really is a fool!' I said, shaking my head. 'Anyway, I must be getting back. I had to go into Dartmouth today to do my shopping. The shops in Windle Bridge are closed to mass murderers, I'm afraid.'

She looked puzzled. 'What do you mean......closed?'

'Just what I said,' I emphasised. 'Closed.'

'But who told them ...... about you, I mean?'

I picked up my bags of shopping and started to walk towards the gate of the graveyard. 'Your guess is as good as mine. Perhaps that fiancé of yours, I don't know. He certainly didn't welcome me with open arms. The only person who's made a genuine offer of friendship is an old hermit down the coast.'

She pulled hard at my sleeve. 'Jabber......!' she asked sharply. 'You've met Jabber?'

'Yes ...... so what if I have?'

'And didn't I welcome you?' she protested angrily. 'Didn't I put food on your table ...... clean bedclothes ...... candles.'

I looked at her and gave a cynical laugh. 'Welcome me? ..... you didn't welcome me!.....you wanted a younger version of my father, and when it turns out he's made a few mistakes in his lifetime, you turn your back on him.'

114

'I did not!' she denied strongly.

I was indignant 'Oh yes you did! When Jonathan Latchley came up with his bit of dirt digging, did you bother to ask if there was another explanation?'

I waited for a reply, but it never came.

'Well! ..... Did you?' I attacked, raising my voice. 'No, you didn't. Yet I talked to that old hermit. I told him what I was accused of, and he accepted me. Perhaps it's because he and I are similar .... both outcasts ...... He gave me food and drink, and tomorrow, or even tonight, we're going out in his boat ..... the only one to accept me as I am.'

I noticed a change in her expression. The anger faded and a worried look appeared. Her eyes darted back and forth from the approaching black clouds to my face.

'You're not?......' she whispered.

'Not what?' I replied. 'We're going to ...... what did Jabber say? .....'Ride the Wind.'..... Ha! At least he showed some friendship.' She had gone pale. 'What's the matter, anyway?'

She looked at the clouds again, then at me. 'You can't!..... You mustn't!' she yelled, her voice rising.

She dropped her hands to her sides, her eyes intense. 'You don't know, do you?'

I was beginning to feel uneasy. 'Don't know what?'

'It's an expression ...... an expression they use around here.' she said quietly. 'If you're going to 'Ride the Wild Wind.'......It's a suicide pact.'

Chapter 7

'That's nonsense! A suicide pact!' I declared with the growing suspicion that Jabber hadn't told me the whole story. 'A bit of an adventure, yes, but that's all, surely?'

She shook her head emphatically, sensing my uncertainty.

'Alright then, Jabber might not have told me everything,' I admitted. 'So tell me …… go on, tell me ……what's so dangerous about it?'

She pointed out to the shingle banks. 'Out there.' She emphasised. 'Low tide, and easterly winds on the back of a storm causes ……'

'I know all that!' I said, butting in. 'Jabber told me all about it.'

There was fire in her eyes. 'For goodness sake, will you just listen! ….. For once, just listen!'

I was taken aback by the authority in her voice and raised my hands in a gesture of submission. 'O.K.' I apologised.

'Good!' she returned, but only slightly calmer. 'Jabber probably told you what happens …… what's supposed to happen …… but I don't suppose he told you that's it's forbidden, and has been since the turn of the century?'

I shook my head.

She shrugged. 'I didn't think he had,' she continued. 'There's been fishing here for centuries, right up this section of the coastline. The shingle banks have been there for just as long. Someone discovered … … I don't know who, or how or when …… but they discovered the peculiar currents that happen with the combination of an east wind and a storm on a low tide. It became an initiation …… before you became a fisherman, you had to 'Ride the Wind."

Most of them cheated! They delayed until the tide had got past turning and it was easier then …… not so dangerous. In the end, someone would go out and check …… make sure the timing was exact. Nearly everyone who tried after that was drowned.'

She noticed the shocked look on my face and attempted to frighten me even more. 'So they stopped it …… officially forbidden. For fifty years or more now it's been banned. Some have tried it ……'

'Jabber and my father,' I broke in.

'Yes. Tom and Jabber did it once. Others have tried it as well … … usually headstrong, young boys for a dare, and most of them didn't come back. You can't do it alone, you see. The traditional boats round here have to be manned by two people.'

'But ……' I said, interrupting again, 'Jabber's a hermit; lives on his own. Who goes fishing with him now if it needs two people?'

'It's different now,' she pointed out, 'you need two to handle the seine nets. One for the boat …… the other to string the nets out. It's mostly crabbing now or single line, which one person can do …… not easily, but it can be done. With seine nets though, which some of them still use, you need two.'

'So,' I said thoughtfully, 'people …… fishermen who went out to 'Ride the Wind' always went in pairs?'

She nodded.

118

'Hence this suicide pact thing.'

'Exactly. If the boat capsizes, it's impossible to swim in the water ...... at least not as far as land anyway. The current will pull you under, so every time anyone has attempted, and failed, then both have drowned. The expression 'To Ride the Wild Wind' has come to mean someone who commits suicide and doesn't care who else gets hurt in the process.'

'I see now,' I said breathing deeply.

'Thank goodness, you're not going to do it then.' She sounded relieved until she sensed my indecision. She stared at me searchingly, 'You're not! ..... Surely, you're not! ..... not after what I've just told you! ..... I don't believe it!'

My fingers unconsciously crept up to my neck and I felt the rawness of where the wire had cut into the flesh.

'What's that?' she observed, stepping forward. 'That on your neck ...... You've hurt yourself?'

'What? ..... Oh, it's nothing,' I responded. 'Just a scratch.'

She pulled my hand away and I felt her fingers delicately stroke against my skin. 'How?' she asked, unsuspectingly.

 I pulled her hand away sharply. 'How?' I answered bitterly. 'How?..... Alright, if you must know, I tried to hang myself! After dinner on Saturday night ...... the early hours of the morning. I tried, but the cable ...... electric cable from the bedside lamp ...... snapped. I fell down the stairs then nearly choked. I wanted a quick death not a slow death, choking ...... the friction of the cable cut my neck.'

She was visibly trembling. 'And now you want to try again!' she exclaimed. 'Drowning is just as slow as choking you know ...... Worse even ...... And Jabber as well? You're not a sailor ...... he needs a sailor, not a soldier!'

'So why does he want to do it?' I shouted back. 'What's he got to prove ...... he's ...... '

I suddenly realised that I was still holding her hand from when I had pulled it away from my neck. I released it slowly, feeling the embarrassment between us.

'I must go now,' I said, more gently. 'I may do it ...... I may not. I've got no widow, no children. Jabber seems determined. I've got no one to hurt. Maybe I will drown ...... but it won't affect anyone but me.'

I left her there and retraced my steps over the bridge and down the hill. I may do it ...... I may not. I knew inside that I would. The old compulsion of facing a challenge and always succeeding was still there. I knew I would do it ...... or die in the attempt.

*****

It was pitch dark when I scrambled carefully along the coastal path, feeling my way, sometimes on my hands and knees. It seemed a very long time before I saw the kerosene lamp that Jabber had placed outside his hut to guide me. The rain was beating down and I could feel the force of the wind on the side of my face. My heart was racing, but not with the exertion, rather with the apprehension of what was to come. Jabber was waiting for me, standing outside, soaked to the skin.

'You came, laddie!' he shouted above the noise of the wind and waves, and hustled me inside the hut. It was still noisy inside, but muffled. The heat of an open fire seemed to insulate us from the elements, but only temporarily.

'You knew I would come, didn't you?' I told him.

'You're your father's son, lad. Yes ...... I knew you'd be coming! I've got oil skins, boots ...... everything you'll be needing ...... but I can't give you courage.'

I saw the excited look on his face which took ten years off his appearance. I could easily imagine him as a young dare-devil with total disregard for any authority.

'No ...... you can't give me courage, but you can coax me into stupidity!' I declared accusingly.

He frowned and busied himself preparing some hot food and drink. 'What makes you say that?' he asked, avoiding my eyes.

'Gwenlyn ...... Gwenlyn Bardell. She told me. You and my father ...... years ago. It's banned now, isn't it, 'Riding the Wind'. Too many people drowned.'

He ladled some fish stew into the same tin bowl I had used before. 'But you're still here, aren't you, lad?' he said mischievously, trying to close the subject, and handed me a wooden spoon.

We sat in silence on creaky wooden chairs with our tin plates on an upturned tea chest, and finished the sparse meal with the obligatory tar-like coffee.

'What time?' I asked.

He smiled at me, exposing his black teeth. Coffee had dribbled down his bearded chin and I asked myself, not for the first time, why I was sharing the company, food and drink of such a character. I couldn't explain it, but there was something charismatic about him.

'What time.....?' he repeated. 'When the time's right. It'll be building a force eight or nine by early morning long before light. We'll be going out south towards the Point and moving round as the tide goes out. Then we sits tight until the tide turns, then we come in, in a blaze o' glory!' His eyes lit up at the prospect and his enthusiasm was infectious.

'I must be a fool,' I said, shaking my head.

'Why?' He replied simply.

'Doing this!' I drank the last mouthful of coffee and placed the empty mug on the table. 'I could be back in a comfy bed, warm and dry, but no! Instead, here I am, waiting for I don't know what!'

He got up from his chair and gestured at some old blankets and stuffed sacking which he had lain out especially for me. 'You'll need to get out of your wet things,' he instructed. 'Got to keep the body warm.'

I had had the foresight to bring some warm, dry clothes with me, so I changed into them and snuggled into the smelly bedding not expecting to get much sleep.

*****

I woke with a start, wondering where I was, the light of a candle shining on my watch showing it to be three o'clock in the morning. The noise outside was considerably louder than when I'd gone to sleep and as I came to full consciousness I found myself becoming more and more apprehensive about what I had got myself into.

Jabber was busying himself with oil skins and boots and also brewing coffee. He handed me a steaming mug full of the foul liquid, but I drank it nevertheless.

'No food, lad, I'm afraid; Just in case we goes swimming. Don't want no cramps in your belly.'

'The life jackets are in the boat, are they?' I asked nervously between sips of coffee.

'No ...... No life jackets! If you goes under, you stays under. A life jacket won't be helping you against the undertow. Too strong, so no point. Anyway, it's quicker round the boat with no life jacket.'

I felt the first twinges of fear. I had been a soldier and faced danger many times, but I'd never done battle against the elements like this before. We donned our sailing clothes while Jabber talked me through the way we would go about the trip. We would need to row, maybe for an hour depending on the wind, until we reached the far side of the shingle banks. The tide would help us so far. We would then wait, holding station with the oars, until the tide changed. Up would go the small sail which would then drive us in over the banks from about three or four miles out.

'It's a bad night,' Jabber said emphatically, and I thought I detected some concern in his voice.

'We don't have to go,' I remarked, giving him the opportunity to back out.

'It's my last chance,' he pointed out passionately, 'and with Tom's lad as well ...... just like old times!'

He opened the battered door of the hut and we were both nearly knocked off our feet by the force of the wind and spray. The noise was deafening and as we stepped out, a streak of lightning bisected the sky, illuminating the maelstrom of water that pounded onto the beach. Jabber shouted something to me but I couldn't catch a single word, so he came up close and shouted directly in my ear.

'Take a pair of oars!' he yelled. 'I'll go stern, you go for'ard!'

I nodded. It was a waste of breath shouting back.

We pulled the boat down the beach until we reached the water. It was tough work in the heavy oil skins and boots and within moments I was hot with perspiration. It poured down the inside of the waterproofs leaving me drenched and clammy. There was salt on my lips but I couldn't tell if it was spray from the sea or the taste of my own sweat. The boat seemed small and insignificant compared to the size of the waves, but in its favour, it was heavy and well built. I felt it rise under the buoyancy of the first wave and Jabber indicated that I should climb in. He pushed the boat further out himself, then leapt athletically into the stern. We both put our oars into the rowlocks and I followed Jabber's lead as we pulled against the incoming waves.

The boat rose up then crashed down on the bottom then lifted again and we pulled hard to save being battered to bits before we even got started. There was no let up in the ceaseless pounding of the waves and only the occasional crack of thunder managed to penetrate the wall of incessant sound.

My legs were good, but I wasn't so sure about my arms. They were soon tired and I longed to rest them, but I knew I couldn't. Once over the initial breakers we hit the long swell of the waves as they built up before hitting the beach. We turned south and rode the swell broadside on, tipping and tilting, ensuring that we weren't driven in with the waves. Fortunately, the out going tide was helping to pull against the waves. So we managed to steer a relatively straight course.

I chanced a look out to sea in the darkness and was rewarded by a flash of lightning which spotlighted the vast whirlpool of white water powering over the shingle banks. I dug in harder to fight against the rising fear within, but I was committed now; there was no going back.

I watched Jabber in the stern of the boat, probably twice my age, yet rowing with the grace and fluidity of movement borne from years

124

of practice, and amazingly deceptive in its power. I endeavoured to emulate his actions and found to my surprise, that my shoulders relaxed, and renewed strength came back into my arms.

The southerly current pulled us towards Start Point and then we had to turn eastwards to go round to the far side of the shingle banks. The boat tossed and dipped in the waves, but still we carried on with the relentless rowing. We turned north after about two miles, by which time I was close to exhaustion. We both instinctively stopped rowing at the same time and a chill ran through my spine.

The swell was enormous; as high as a house, lifting us and dropping us as if we were a toy. The continual up and down motion was tearing at my stomach, and the vomit, when it came was largely whisked away on the wind, leaving me with a throbbing head and a profound wish to be anywhere else but where I was. Water was pouring over into the boat, covering my legs to above the ankles, but still the sturdy vessel stayed afloat, stubbornly defying the elements against all odds. My hands throbbed as they gripped the oars as the effort to hold on got harder and harder and my legs cramped up in pain as I braced myself against the side of the boat. Yet the atmosphere had changed. There was an eerie whistle to the wind, low and penetrating

Jabber turned round and shouted to me, 'Do you feel it?'

'Yes!' I shouted back.

'We're too close …… too soon …… need to row out further … … then wait!'

It was a relief to get going again, to distract my mind from the horror that was being played out in my brain. I tried to suppress the notion of capsizing and those long minutes as water fills the lungs, with the limbs flailing to reach the surface and fresh air, only to succumb to the slow blackness of drowning. For another few minutes we rowed, riding up and down on the swell, a never ending nightmare as we were battered unremittingly from all sides.

He turned round again. 'Here ...... We wait here ...... I'll go first with the oars!'

He fought with the sea, pulling us first one way then the other, holding us in position head on to the coast a few miles away. He twisted round again nodding with his head towards a pile of rope barely visible on the bottom of the boat.

'Lift your legs and turn to face for'ard,' he ordered. Then tie yourself into the boat ...... round the waist, then row to keep us straight while I turn round and tie in.'

His voice was hoarse and he sounded out of breath. I noticed that his shoulders were drooping: he was tired too. I gingerly moved round, being careful not to lose my oars, and tied myself in, then began rowing while he turned round and used another piece of rope for the same purpose.

He had allowed enough leeway so that he could stretch forward to raise the small sail onto the stubby mast that grew out of the middle of the boat. He kept looking up at the night sky, waiting for the right moment, sensing the movement of the boat, listening with the whole of his body. I was glad to be rowing, to be doing something through the interminable waiting, and then I felt it.

It was as if someone was tugging at the boat, slowly pulling it, gathering momentum. I couldn't row against it and I knew the time had come.

'Ship your oars lad!' he yelled. 'It's coming ...... any moment now!'

I hastily pulled the oars in and stowed them in the boat and gripped on tight to the sides. There was a crescendo of sound like some inhuman monster rising from the depths. Jabber hoisted the sail in a flash and loosened the tiller from its lashings. As we had both had to change our seating positions, I had to look behind to see the sail filled, and I felt the boat lurch forward as the sound built to fever pitch.

'Let's ride, laddie!' I heard Jabber yell, and I felt the suction on the bottom of the boat as we were pulled right down leaving the sea towering twenty feet above us.

It was like being shot out of a cannon as we rocketed forwards and I gasped with the sheer force of it. I braced myself hard and slid down on the thwart so as to avoid being thrown backwards. We seemed to skim across the waves, leaping and dashing like the death throes of some demented, uncontrollable being. I screamed and yelled in a combination of terror and euphoria while my fingers clasped on for dear life to the sides of the boat.

We hit a spinning cauldron-like trough which hurled us down as if we were a matchstick. I had lost all sense of direction and was only aware of us gyrating round and round, plunging even deeper. I closed my eyes to shut out the sight of it but when I opened them, we were still there.

There was an enormous explosion of sound and we were suddenly thrust up to the surface, flying above the waves then landing hard onto the water again. Three times it happened. Three times we plummeted into the bottomless pit as if we were being thrust into the very jaws of hell itself, and three times we shot out until I thought we would be ripped apart.

I lay helpless in the bottom of the boat just looking upwards at the mighty waves while the lightning and thunder intensified into one continuous, deafening roar. I tried to clamp my hands over my ears to blot out the noise but it made no difference. A wave hit us broadside on and I crashed heavily into the side of the boat. I lifted my head to see how Jabber was at the tiller and to my horror, discovered that he wasn't there.

'Please God ...... No!' I screamed again and again as I tried to clamber over the obstacles in the boat to get to the tiller. I hadn't left enough slack in the rope I had used to tie myself down, so I was helpless to even attempt to steer the boat. I tore at the rope in a mad frenzy; ripping at the tangle with my finger nails until eventually the knots came free in my hands. I scrambled over the seats holding on perilously as the boat was smashed about with nothing to restrain its writhing.

I spotted a rope trailing over the end of the boat and hoped against hope that Jabber was still attached to the end of it. I gripped hard onto it and pulled with all my strength. The tiller whipped round and hit me a stunning blow on the head and I involuntarily let go of the rope. At the same time, the boat was lifted almost vertically and I found myself toppling over the stern. I made a last ditch attempt and grabbed onto the trailing rope as I was tossed overboard.

My arms were nearly torn from their sockets as my hands slid down the rope leaving me further and further from the boat. I was tempted to let go as I felt the undertow take its grip and leave me completely submerged. My foot hit something soft; once, twice, then again. It was Jabber, still tied to the end of the line, though how long he'd been out of the boat, I had no idea. I slid a few more feet down the rope until I could encircle my arms round his unconscious body and I inserted my hands and arms in the rope round his waist and prayed that it was secure enough to hold me.

There was no possibility of swimming, and no possibility of being

128

able to pull us back to the boat; we were at the mercy of the sea. I couldn't think of anything more I could do. I tried to breathe as best I could whenever the waves lifted us briefly to the surface and spat us out before they swallowed us up again. It seemed to go on forever: to be left suspended, tossed around and half drowned. I closed my eyes and waited for the inevitable but then we hit a deep trough and my feet touched the bottom.

I was so startled, I couldn't immediately think of what to do. There was another trough and again my feet touched firm sand, but this time, I was ready and pushed my legs straight and lifted us both upwards only to be knocked down by the next incoming wave. I repeated the manoeuvre every time there was a trough in the waves, praying that we were being swept onto the beach.

I saw the dark shape of the boat in front of us as it, too, scraped the bottom, but the waves took us first, and we crashed into it. I pulled my arms out from the rope to try to protect myself and found myself floating free. I began thrashing through the water trying to stay afloat against the weight of the oilskins, inhaling water, coughing and spluttering in a frantic effort to breathe.

I felt a body in front of me and thought I had found Jabber's inert form, but hands gripped me and pulled me up.

'Help me!' I sobbed, and the arms pulled harder, only to land us sprawling in the waves. We half swam, half stumbled until we could stand in the shallows.

'Where's Jabber?' came the voice.

'Tied behind the boat!' I screamed before I realised that it was the voice of a woman. 'Gwenlyn!' I shouted in amazement.

We waded to where the boat had pitched onto the beach, racing as quick as we could to the stern and to the rope that linked up to Jabber's bedraggled shape. Gwenlyn deftly untied the rope and we dragged the body onto the sand where I collapsed into a heap, retching up bitter tasting salt water. She wasted no time in sympathy on me seeing that I was at least alive, instead, she pulled away the clothes from Jabber's chest and rolled him onto his stomach and began beating his ribs with her fists.

It was crude, but effective and I heard the same sort of coughing and vomiting that I had just experienced myself.

'Thank God you came!' I found myself saying, with genuine feeling.

'You damn fool!' she snapped back. 'If he's hurt, I'll never forgive you!'

I was too exhausted to argue so I crawled over to check on his breathing. He was very weak from taking in so much water, but incredibly, the tough old man was still alive.

'We'll need to get him to the hut,' she ordered firmly.

'Which way?' I asked, realising that I wasn't having to shout quite so loud to make myself heard.

'That way!' she pointed behind me. About quarter of a mile. He'll need dry things and warmth …… and soon.'

'How on earth did you see us?' I asked, incredulous.

'The sail!' she responded. 'It stood out in the light once you came over the banks.'

I looked around me to see the dim, murky gloom of a new day. There was still torrential rain and dense cloud, but the faint sign of light was forcing its way through. There was something else I noticed as well, but my brain was numb and I couldn't place exactly what it was.

130

'Lift him up,' she instructed. 'We'll have to drag him back one way or another.'

Between us we managed to hoist him up with one of his arms around each of our shoulders. She was strong and never faltered as we pulled him along the beach and although I stumbled a number of times, she never paused in her efforts.

We reached the door to the hut and pulled him inside, collapsing in a crumpled heap and panting with exertion. Gwenlyn was the first to move as she quickly stripped him and rubbed warmth into his stiff, cold limbs.

'Get those blankets!' she commanded, nodding to the place where I had slept earlier on that night. 'Make sure he's well covered. Have you got any dry clothes?'

'Yes,' I replied, overcome with fatigue.

'Then you'd better change.'

I did as I was told. I had been hot from the exertion of carrying Jabber but my soaking clothes had quickly cooled me down and I felt myself shiver.

'What about you?' I asked.

She dismissed the thought. 'I'll be alright ...... You just get dry and wrap up warm.'

Again, I followed her orders and slumped down under the blankets any remaining energy slipping away with the relief of survival and within a few seconds, I was asleep, yet it was a disturbed sleep. I knew that something was wrong; very wrong, but I couldn't see what it was.

Eventually, my sub-conscious won and I suddenly sat bolt upright. 'The beach!' I shouted.

'Gwenlyn must have brought some dry clothes with her as well because she had also changed. The candles were out and daylight penetrated the hut. In the corner, Jabber snored deeply and regularly.

'What time is it?' I asked, looking at Gwenlyn.

She reached across to Jabber's pocket watch which lay on the upturned tea chest. 'Eight o'clock,' she informed me.

I had been asleep, I estimated, for maybe two hours but it had only felt like seconds. 'The beach!' I said again as I climbed out from under the blankets and headed towards the door.

The waves were still high and the wind was strong but the rain had stopped and the clouds were starting to break up. I looked up and down the beach wondering what had happened. A lot of the sand, shingle and shells which formed the beach had disappeared. Instead, the beach dipped sharply down to the sea. The old high water mark had vanished and though I was no sailor, I knew that it should be high tide again soon, yet, already, the water seemed to be much higher up the beach than usual.

I poked my head through the door and smelt the strong smell of coffee brewing. 'The beach,' I said slowly. 'Where's the beach gone …… most of it has disappeared! ..... that can't be right, can it?'

Gwenlyn poured me a mug full of black coffee and handed it to me. 'Must have got swept away in the storm,' she said, guessing. 'I heard a strange noise from the path when I was looking for you, but it was too dark to see anything.'

I was concerned. 'Has this happened before?'

'No, not in my lifetime. Is it …… I don't know …… Is it the undercurrent pulling the sand off the beach.

'Who knows?' I replied, mystified. 'How's Jabber?'

She leaned over him and pulled the blankets tighter up to his chin. 'Tired and old.' she said fondly.

'You seem to be attached to older men,' I observed, but she scowled back.

'Jabber and Tom were good friends ...... best friends.' she said defensively. 'I came down to make sure he was alright. Like you said, you've got no one who would miss you, but Jabber has. Maybe he is a bit eccentric ...... a bit strange, but there's people around here who would miss him.'

'And that includes you.' I stated.

'That includes me.' she replied firmly.

Jabber stirred as if the mention of his name had woken him up. He rolled on to his back and wheezed deeply as he opened his eyes and tried to speak. 'We ...... we did it, lad,' he managed to whisper before being seized by a fit of coughing

'If he's got pneumonia, I'll......' she rasped at me, leaving the sentence unfinished while she bent over to check on him.

'Gwenlyn ...... Gwenlyn, my child,' he murmured affectionately.

'You're a stupid, old fool!' she said, without remorse.

He struggled to find words. 'Yes ...... But we did it ...... didn't we, lad?' The effort was too much for him and he fell back onto the pillow, gasping for breath.

'We ought to get a doctor,' I suggested, looking worried.

She shook her head. 'He wouldn't have a doctor on the day of his funeral! He'd certainly not thank me for it anyway! If he goes unconscious, yes, we'll have to get someone, but until then, we'll wait.'

'Would you like something to eat?' I asked. 'I'm sure he wouldn't mind us helping ourselves.'

She shook her head again. 'No, but you have something. There's some eggs and a side of salted ham ...... and there's bread ...... in that tin over there.' She pointed to the back of the hut.

I lit the small stove and proceeded to cook a makeshift meal for myself.

'Won't your father be worried about you ...... if you're not at home, that is?' I enquired.

'No, not really. He's busy with the fishing. He forgets we're there half the time, or forgets I'm there.'

The emphasis on the words was unusual and I felt a tension in the air so I had a couple of mouthfuls before I dared pursue the conversation. 'So...... Charlotte then ?' I probed tentatively. 'It's different for her, is it? He doesn't notice you, but notices her?'

She frowned. 'My mother died soon after Charlotte was born, so I've been the mother figure ...... she's been the daughter.'

I detected no jealousy as such, just a tinge of regret. 'You're both very beautiful......I've not seen a pair of sisters so attractive before.'

'Thank-you,' she said with true modesty. She was the one who accepted her beauty as a normal thing, while Charlotte was the one to flaunt it.

'Am I right in saying ...... now don't take this the wrong way ... ... but am I right that, in your father's eyes, Charlotte can do no wrong?'

She waited a bit too long before answering, as if weighing up how much she should say. 'She's ...... she's a whore.' She said it flatly, as a statement, but this time I sensed some deeply rooted, personal hurt, and I made as if to change the subject.

'You sure you won't have something to eat?' I tried.

She wouldn't let it go. 'You find it difficult to accept don't you? That in a quiet little Devonshire village there's a girl of easy virtue.'

'For money! ..... Surely not!' I argued.

Her face was a picture of sadness. 'No, not for money ...... for favours. You saw her with Peta Lofgren. He buys her things; spends nearly all his wages on her, then she sees this new boy who works for Jonathan .... Nicholas ...... Nicholas Faversham. She had her claws in him straight away. He's young, easily led, you saw him after he'd had too much to drink ...... she could have got anything she wanted from him.'

'And your father?' I commented carefully. 'Won't he do something?'

She gave a half-hearted laugh and shook her head. 'The sun shines from her eyes! He would never admit to anything going on at all. She's careful mind you ...... never at home ...... never openly, except for flirting of course. Most people know, but no-one talks about it.'

I spoke quietly. 'I'm sorry ...... for you, I mean. If you've sort of mothered her that is, and then this happens.'

'One day,' she sighed, 'one day she'll learn......I hope. But it's the people she hurts, and she'll get hurt herself, it's inevitable.'

Jabber gave a groan in the corner, and Gwenlyn quickly turned her attention to him to see if he was alright. He shuffled under his blankets and began snoring again.

'Was there much food?' she asked.

'Not a lot. He obviously catches a lot of fish, but he won't be doing that for a day or two.'

'Could you ...... would you go into Windle Bridge and get some food for him?' she requested. 'Just basics, he doesn't have anything fancy; bread, eggs …… even some fish, things like that.'

I smiled cynically. 'You forget one thing! I'm not exactly Windle Bridge's favourite citizen at the moment.'

She looked embarrassed and her face flushed red. 'I'd forgotten. With everything that's happened, it slipped my mind.'

I got up to leave, gathering up the wet clothes that she had thoughtfully put out to dry. 'No problem. I've enough food in the house. I did some shopping in Dartmouth yesterday. There'll be enough there. I'll come back later. Are you staying all day?

She nodded.

'Can I get you anything?' I continued. 'Anything you need?'

'No, I'll be fine. A hot water bottle …… for Jabber, not me …… it'll help to keep him warm. It should be in one of the cupboards somewhere, if it's not rotten by now.'

I left them both and set off on the coastal path back to Windle Bridge. Some of my strength had returned and I felt sprightly in the crisp, morning air. I broke into a run so as to loosen the muscles that had got fatigued while in the boat and in the water. I kept looking down at the beach and the small inlets that poked into the rocks, and all the way along, vast amounts of sand had gone.

I wasn't unduly worried. I didn't know the coastline, so maybe it was normal after all, despite what Gwenlyn had said. I reached the part of the path which overlooked the village and stopped in my tracks realising that it was anything but normal!

Half of the harbour had vanished!

Chapter 8

I walked rapidly along the final section of the coastal path into the village. A small group had congregated at the edge of where the harbour wall had collapsed into the sea. It was the most vital area of wall in that there was now nothing to stop the full force of the sea coming into the harbour itself. Around half a dozen boats had already succumbed and were lying half submerged; others bobbed around like corks, straining on their moorings. Only the much larger dredger seemed able to cope with the rise and fall of the unchecked waves.

'What happened?' I enquired of no-one in particular.

James Bardell was there, as was Peers Lofgren and Peta and a number of fishermen I recognised. Others, who obviously worked on the dredger, were also in a huddle away from the scene of the accident.

'Anyone hurt?' I tried, but met no response. 'What happened?' I repeated, but only received a chill stare from James Bardell. 'Damn you! Will someone please tell me what's going on.'

Peers Lofgren looked at Bardell, waiting for his authority to speak. Bardell eventually gave a nod of assent and Lofgren began his explanation. 'The harbour wall has collapsed, Mr Kinsey,' he informed me in his slow, over pronounced way.

'I can see that!' I remarked impatiently. 'But why? Was it really such a bad storm ...... the expected sort of damage?'

Lofgren shook his head. 'No ...... The storm was bad but we see worse. The harbour has been here many years, yet now it chooses to fall down.'

'And damage?' I asked in return. 'To boats I mean ...... and the dredger? ...... No-one hurt I hope?'

James Bardell joined in the conversation, holding his chin thoughtfully between thumb and forefinger. 'No-one hurt. Four boats sunk, others damaged.' He turned in the direction of the dredger crew who had been listening to our conversation. 'The dredger alright?'

One of them nodded his head and said that apart from scratched paintwork, the larger vessel was unscathed.

One or two scrambled down onto the edge of the rocks that still stood above water level to survey the damage. They were joined by a few from the dredger who wandered over from their separate meeting.

'It's that bloody dredger what done it!' I heard one of the fishermen say, and I had a feeling that he had verbalised the suspicions of some of the others.

'We don't know that, Dan,' Bardell said defensively. 'When they inspected last year they said it wouldn't affect the fishing.'

'I'm not talking about fishing ...... But we can't fish with no harbour,' the fisherman said in return. 'They didn't say nothin' 'bout our harbour fallin' down did they?'

One of the dredger crew stepped forward who had the same gaunt features and ruffled black hair as the fisherman. I guessed they were related, possibly brothers, and that there was no love lost between them either!

'You be shuttin' your mouth Dan Bredan. You don't complain

when yon dredger comes along and makes your channel deeper!'

Bredan jumped back onto the sound harbour wall and stood staring angrily into the face of the other. 'So ...... what you goin' to do about it, big brother? Couldn't get a job on a fishing boat if you tried, could you? It's you and your other mates what's done this ...... takin' our livin' like!'

He spat on his brothers boots and there would have been a fight if Peers Lofgren hadn't stepped in between them.

'Look, this is help to no-one.' Lofgren emphasised. 'Go home, all of you. We will sort it out.'

The circle broke up and the men slowly drifted away leaving Bardell, Lofgren and myself standing by the harbour wall.

I complimented Lofgren. 'You handled that well.' But he wouldn't be flattered.

'You misunderstand me, Mr Kinsey,' he said flatly. 'If it is the fault of the dredging, I will take the side of the fishermen. Those two brothers are always fighting, but it will not be just them, everyone wants to look after their interests: I, the fishermen ......you, the dredging.'

'I'm not interested in the dredging!' I asserted. 'I'm no more interested in it than ...... than just about anything you could think of!'

Lofgren was not convinced, neither was Bardell.

'What about you?' I said, addressing Bardell. 'You're a fisherman with a daughter engaged to the majority holder of the dredging company! If it comes to sides; whose side are you on?'

I thought he might at least stop and think; weigh up the arguments. I had taken him for an intelligent man, but there was no hesitation in his answer.

'I am a fisherman ......! A fisherman first and last! There's no question in my mind about loyalties!'

I looked down at the mass of collapsed stonework with the waves now pounding over the once formidable structure: a salutary lesson on the vulnerability of man when pitted against nature.

'Does Latchley know about this?' I asked. 'It's probably nothing at all to do with the dredging ...... What about Nicholas Faversham? Is he at the office yet?'

They both shook their heads.

'Faversham lives in Dartmouth,' Bardell answered. 'I've not seen him today. He would have been out by now if he was here. We can't telephone Jonathan because the lines are down, so he won't know.'

I didn't fancy having to notify Jonathan Latchley, but it looked as if it was going to be my responsibility whether I liked it or not. 'O.K.' I said finally. 'I'd better get into Dartmouth and let him know. Like I said, there's probably no connection at all, but I had ...... We had better get him here to see for himself.'

Bardell and Lofgren walked off, deep in conversation, leaving me with the necessity of hitching into Dartmouth. Gwenlyn and Jabber would have to wait for food until I got back, whenever that would be.

The road was quiet and I had to wait for twenty minutes for anyone to give me a lift, but a rambling old truck was better than nothing as I was impatient to get to Latchley's office. I appreciated that the local community were quite volatile people and the quicker Latchley could calm them down, the better.

I got dropped off in town and ran to the office only to see Latchley climb into his car and drive off before I could get close to him. I glanced round for inspiration just as the farmer with the jeep drove past and stopped a few yards away.

I made a quick decision. 'Hello ...... Remember me?' I said cheerfully.

He looked me up and down while chewing on the inevitable pipe. 'Right I do.' he said between chews.

'Look ...... It's a bit of an emergency ...... I need to notify someone about something very important and he's just driven off ... ... Could I borrow your jeep?'

He looked me up and down slowly again as I got even more impatient. I didn't know how far Latchley was going or whether I would be able to catch him up anyway. I quickly fished in my pocket and withdrew a note.

'Ten shillings?' I suggested.

He nodded and as quickly as I could, I was in the jeep and driving in the same direction Latchley had gone. With all the steps in Dartmouth most people tended to walk, even if they had transport, unless they were going some distance. I drove up the steep hill west out of the town going as fast as the road permitted.

I caught a glimpse of a car in front and saw it turn left onto the main road down to Kingsbridge. I hoped it was Latchley because I could see no other vehicles. Tough though the jeep was, it was not meant for speed and, no matter how hard I tried, I couldn't make up much ground on the car in front.

I drove into Kingsbridge looking from right to left and saw Latchley leave his car parked next to where the inlet from the sea poked into the middle of the town. I flashed the headlights but he was looking the other way, so I parked behind his car and jumped out to follow him.

He had arrived at the front door of a house and I was about to open the gate and follow him when the front door opened and I stopped immediately. Latchley's back was towards me, and I didn't think anyone else had seen me, so I rapidly moved away down the road with my mind full of questions. The harbour wall didn't seem quite so important anymore.

I turned back and crossed the road, being careful to face away from the house. I moved the jeep a hundred yards back along the road and sat and waited. He was in there for half an hour, after which he came out, turned the car round, and drove off in the direction he had come.

I ducked down in the jeep so he wouldn't see me and after waiting for fifteen minutes or so, to make sure he was not about to return, I ventured out of the jeep and along the road to the house.

It was opulent, large and with meticulous gardens. I knocked on the door smartly and fabricated a smile. The door was opened and I launched into my roughly prepared speech. 'Good morning, I'm looking for some short term accommodation in Kingsbridge and am told that there may be some available here?'

I saw a movement down the hall and I strained to look without being too obvious, but it was enough to confirm what I had originally thought.

'Not here, I'm afraid,' came the reply. 'Two doors down. I think they do accommodation there.'

'Thank-you,' I said graciously. 'I must have been given the wrong house number.'

I kept up the smile and walked down the garden to the gate and out onto the road and back to the jeep. I didn't know quite what I had stumbled onto, but I suspected I had found a possible reason for the sale of six quarries. I would need to do some investigations, but I now had something to go on.

I drove back to Dartmouth and because my mind was so busy going over the implications of what I had discovered, it wasn't until I drove into the town itself that I recalled the original purpose of my visit. I had been longer than I had thought, and it cost me another half a crown to placate the owner of the jeep.

I walked into the office only to disturb Latchley's secretary at the typewriter. 'Is he in?' I asked as I marched towards his door.

'Yes ...... No! ..... No! ..... He's not available at the......'

'Thank-you,' I said briskly, and opened the door into his office.

He was momentarily startled but recovered quickly. 'Ah! ..... the ... er .... Papers,' he stuttered. 'They'll be .... um .... ready tomorrow. I've seen my solicitor this morning.'

His smile was triumphant, and if I hadn't experienced the humiliation of that Saturday night, I would have said, openly friendly.

'There's no time for that now,' I said sharply. 'There's some .....'

'Oh, there's plenty of time, Major.' He interrupted. 'Twenty four hours will be time enough.'

I dismissed his comments with a wave of my hand. 'There's some problems in the village. Part ...... a large part of the harbour wall has collapsed.'

He was immediately concerned. 'The dredger? The dredger's not damaged is it?'

'No.'

He looked relieved. 'Good. We've got nothing to worry about then, have we?'

'Oh, yes we have!' I insisted. 'Some of the fishing boats have sunk …… No one hurt, but there's the ……'

'The fishing boats are not my responsibility!' he interjected loudly. 'The dredger doesn't get in the way of their boats, in fact, it dredges a channel for them!'

'If you'll let me finish,' I said quietly. 'Then you might learn something.' I waited for another comment, but he stayed silent, so I knew I had his attention.

'Thank-you,' I said politely. 'As I was saying: a few boats …… no one hurt, but you have a problem … No! ….We have a problem!… Some of the fishermen are blaming all the dredging that's been done for the collapse.'

He shot forward in his chair, the arrogance suddenly gone. His tough self confidence seemed to evaporate in a split second and all at once he looked very worried indeed. 'No! ….. That's ridiculous! ….. the idea …… the methods! …… the whole project was checked.'

He gave the impression that he was speaking more to himself than to me. I shrugged my shoulders, surprised at his reaction, but then again, perhaps I shouldn't have been. With no income from the quarries, then that left the dredging as the only source of revenue, and if that was to be stopped; where would that leave him …… and me?

'It may be ridiculous,' I declared. 'On the other hand, it may not be; but there are certainly some down there who have put two and two together.'

'I'll go and see,' he concluded quietly to himself, standing up and lifting his jacket from the back of the chair.

'Could you give me a lift?' I asked, but his thoughts were elsewhere. I followed him out through the door and into the outer office where he ignored his secretary's questions and walked into the street and to his car. He made no comment as I climbed into the front seat beside him, and we drove the first few miles in silence.

'Is there a big investment in dredging?' I chanced.

At first, I thought he hadn't heard, but he eventually spoke. 'What?'

'The dredging,' I said again. 'Is there a heavy investment in the dredging?'

He bit his bottom lip before answering. 'Mmm ...... you could say so.'

'What's that supposed to mean?' I queried.

'None of your damn business!' he snapped.

I was mildly amused to see him in such a state, so I decided to do some probing while his guard was down. 'It's a good job the quarries are flourishing. At least you've got another source of income. Or should I say, we've got another source of income.'

He wouldn't be drawn, and we continued in silence.

'What's the contract for?' I tried after a few minutes. 'The dredging, I mean ...... the money side of things ...... the volume of shingle?'

I already knew the answers from Nicholas Faversham but wanted to hear Latchley say it for himself.

'One million tons.'

'And the finance?' I asked.

'A set amount per ton.'

'Payment on delivery?' I added.

'Payment on delivery.' he concurred.

'So .....' I summarised, 'no dredging ...... no shingle ...... no shingle ...... no pounds, shillings and pence.'

He nodded his head and pushed his foot hard on the accelerator in anger. I was tempted to ask direct questions about the defunct quarries, but since witnessing the morning's episode in Kingsbridge, I decided I needed to do some homework before I could tackle him.

We drove down the hill into Windle Bridge and he parked the car round the corner from the office.

'Where's Faversham?' he asked sharply.

'He wasn't here when I left ...... he may be here now I suppose?' I speculated.

Latchley glanced over at the dredger, still at its moorings. He hardly seemed to notice the collapsed harbour wall. When we walked into the office, Nicholas Faversham was in deep discussion with the captain of the dredger.

'What's going on?' Latchley demanded brusquely.

'The harbour wall's collapsed,' Faversham replied meekly.

'I can see that!' Latchley replied. 'But the sea's dropped, why isn't the dredger out there?'

The dredger captain whom I'd seen once or twice, was a mild, silver-haired man with a precisely shaped beard and no moustache. He was nearing retirement and I think, until now, had enjoyed the relative ease of the dredger work.

'The sea was too high to take her out, Mr Latchley,' the captain explained. 'Then there was some dissent from the fishermen so we thought it best to stay moored up today.'

I thought Latchley was going to explode. His eyes squinted narrowly and his lips squeezed bloodlessly together. He began hitting the table with his pointed finger while he thought up the right words to use.

'If you think that that ship is going to sit around here doing nothing while I'm paying for it, you've got another thing coming!'

The captain moved towards the door, probably not worried about himself, but worried if he was to have to tell his crew that bonuses were to be removed.

'If you say so,' the captain said calmly.

'I do say so!' he barked in return and waited, still fuming, for the captain to leave the office before turning on Faversham. 'And what about you ...... ? You're supposed to keep this contract going ...... at all costs! We don't stop just because a bunch of fishermen are a bit upset!'

To give Faversham his due, he did try to speak up for himself.

'But Mr Latchley, the weather wasn't good and I thought it best to stay here until things got sorted out.'

'Oh! You did, did you! And under whose authority?'

'Mine.' Faversham said succinctly.

Latchley continued his tirade. 'Well listen here, young man, I make the decisions, so get that lump of scrap out of here and get the lot of them to do some work!'

Latchley whirled round and stormed out of the office leaving Faversham to reach for the telephone, presumably to reorganise the barges to come and collect the dredged up shingle now that the dredger was about to start work again. I wondered how successful he would be? If the lines were down between Windle Bridge and Dartmouth, I didn't give much hope for any contact with Plymouth. I followed closely behind Latchley and espied Peers Lofgren and James Bardell walking across the harbour.

Latchley's mood changed instantly and he was transformed into a picture of care and concern. 'James ...... Peers ......' he began, frowning. 'I came straight away. A tragedy for Windle Bridge. I was stunned when I heard. It must be desperate for all the fishing folk of the village. Obviously some fluke that this should happen, but I'll get an inspector down immediately. As you know, we went through things thoroughly before we started, so it won't have anything to do with the dredging. After all, the banks are a long way out, so there could be no connection between the two.'

Peers Lofgren spoke first.

'Very well, Jonathan. We will give you time to see what has gone wrong. This is a fishing village and we do not like it when things go badly wrong.'

Latchley looked relieved, and James Bardell seemed placated. I was anything but reassured, but kept my thoughts to myself.

'We'll leave it to you, Jonathan,' Bardell said. 'Let us know the outcome as soon as you can, won't you?'

They shook hands all round leaving me out of it and Bardell and Lofgren walked off together. Latchley started back to the office and I walked alongside him for a few paces.

'The telephone lines are probably down,' I informed him. 'If you want any dredging done today you'll have to notify them from your office. I doubt if Faversham's got through.'

He made no comment. Try to be helpful, I thought sarcastically, and decided to leave him and collect some food to take along to Gwenlyn and Jabber. I looked at my watch, they would be lucky to get one barge load of shingle done by the evening as it was already late afternoon.

I packed a bag of appropriate foodstuffs and set off along the coastal path to Jabber's hut. I looked back to see the dredger moving slowly away from its moorings, setting off for the shingle banks. I felt like running, having spent too much of the day inactive and having experienced surprisingly little reaction from the excesses of sailing with Jabber early that morning, but the bag was heavy and I had to be content with a brisk walk.

I reached the hut and on entering, I found Jabber sitting up and sounding remarkably well after the ordeal he had been through.

'You're looking better,' I said cheerfully to the old man.

'Where've you been?' Gwenlyn rebuked before Jabber had time to reply.

'One thing at a time ….. How is he?' I said, addressing Gwenlyn.

'Stubborn …… aching all over, but not coughing so much now …… some stomach cramps from too much salt water, but otherwise, he'll be alright …… but what about you? Why so long?'

'Do you know about the sand?' I said to Jabber. 'The beach …… a lot of the sand has disappeared.'

'Aye, the lass told me,' he replied. 'Things was different this time when we was riding. Them whirlpools …… not been there before … … reckon them was holes the dredger dug and the water drilling down into them.'

I looked pensive. 'And could …… is it possible then …… that the sand was being sucked off the beach to fill the holes left from the dredging? There's been hundreds of thousands of tons dredged up.'

He breathed deeply and I heard the rasping of his lungs. 'Possible,' he said thoughtfully, with his bottom lip over the top one. 'Possible.'

'There's worse happened back at the village.'

I informed them about the harbour wall and that having to go to find Latchley had caused me to be late in returning.

'I'm sorry,' Gwenlyn said genuinely. 'I shouldn't have jumped to conclusions. There again, Peers and my father shouldn't have jumped to conclusions either. Fishermen are so protective of themselves and their boats.'

A thought suddenly struck me. 'Jabber's boat! We left it down the beach, will it be alright?'

Gwenlyn got up to rummage about in the bag I had brought, pulling out the contents with a nod of approval. 'I moored it fast,' she said. 'And pulled it further up the beach at high tide. It'll be alright there until Jabber's better and he can sail it again himself.'

She cooked a meal while Jabber and I talked over the adventure of 'Riding the Wind.' We both agreed that having done it; him twice, me once, we could rest content with the memory of so narrowly escaping death. I fingered the marks on my neck, thinking to myself that I had in fact, had two narrow escapes and not just one.

We ate heartily in a relaxed atmosphere enjoying each other's company. I would have been happy to have stayed there forever, but the night was drawing in and it was dangerous to walk the coastal path in the dark, as I well knew.

'I must go,' I said. 'It'll be dark soon.'

Gwenlyn stood up and spoke to Jabber. 'And so must I. You'll be alright. I'll see you tomorrow. You need to sleep and get some good rest.'

She kissed him lightly on the cheek, oblivious to his old clothes and general tramp-like demeanour.

'You're a good lass, Gwenlyn Bardell. Walk safely and, yes, I'll rest …… and goodnight lad …… We did it! ..... We did it didn't we lad! I done it with father and son ….. but I'll not be doing it with grandson …… I'll be long gone by then.'

We left him to reflect on happy memories: some old, some more recent, and walked along the cliff path. We talked easily, avoiding controversial topics and when I could, I looked at her, admiring her beauty and the graceful, unpretentious way she moved.

The walk ended all too soon as we reached the high point above the village. We could just make out the harbour, or what was left of it, and it dampened our spirits. We decided that it would be prudent if we weren't seen together; there was enough trouble as it was, so she went down into the village ahead of me. I followed ten minutes later and had a last look at the collapsed harbour wall before I headed back to the house.

I stood between the two pubs, listening to the night air, but somehow the sounds were different. I was perplexed at first, until I realised that there was no-one else around but me. The whole village was deserted, not a soul to be seen anywhere. I walked past the one pub and heard raised voices inside, then I walked past the other and heard similar sounds.

I was ill at ease, but knew that I couldn't go into either place because of the gossip that had been spread about me. It was impossible to pick up what they were saying so there was no way to satisfy my curiosity, instead I resigned myself to continuing back to the empty house none the wiser to the situation.

I busied myself with household chores, exploring some of the rooms that I had barely entered previously, absorbing some of the personality of Tom Bradbury. It was uncanny, trying to discover the history of someone so closely related, yet about whom I knew almost nothing. I found some faded photographs, mostly of the village and its people, even one of Jabber who looked equally eccentric even in younger years. His facial features looked different and vaguely familiar, however, I passed it off as I noticed a picture of Gwenlyn. She was young, seven or eight perhaps, and sitting on my father's lap. She already had the delicate shape to her face and the alluring features which she had continued to develop to the present day.

I found some more pictures of her and became totally engrossed as I followed the course of her transition from child to woman. In fact, I was so preoccupied that it was a while before the noise from outside registered in my ears. I replaced the photographs in the drawer where I had found them and walked over to the window.

I turned off the light and opened the curtains, but could see nothing, hearing only shouts from the direction of the harbour. The sounds increased and seemed to be coming closer and eventually, I saw shadows in the dim light at the bottom of the hill. I went downstairs with the purpose of investigating and was greeted with a continuous pounding on the front door.

I was in the habit of using the back way, so the door was stiff, but I managed to pull it open to be met by the panic stricken shape of Nicholas Faversham. His clothes were dirty and torn, and blood flowed from a gash above his right eye which was already closing. His face and arms were grazed and cut and he stumbled and fell as he pushed past me.

'Help!' he screamed as he lay shaking on the floor. 'They're going to kill me!'

Chapter 9

Faversham had barely got through the door when a group of angry fishermen arrived at the front gate. The leading ones were short of breath from sprinting up the hill, others followed behind, more slowly. There were at least twenty of them; some brandishing thick pieces of driftwood ready to be used as makeshift weapons should the opportunity arrive. I could smell the ominous tang of alcohol wafting towards me in the night air.

Dan Bredan was the spokesman, while Peta Lofgren stood off to one side. I noticed that in general, it was the younger fishermen who were present, with only a few of the older brigade tagging along at the rear.

'Where is he?' Bredan demanded.

'Come on, calm down ...... Now what's going on?' I asked in reply as mildly as I could.

'Let us have him!' Bredan demanded again, encouraged by a chorus of agreement from behind him.

'That's enough!' I warned sharply. 'What's got into you anyway? Haven't you done enough harm already?'

'We'll have his balls!' came a call from the back, and as if orchestrated by a conductor, they all surged as one towards the front door.

'Are you all mad!' I shouted in amazement. 'You can't just go round dispensing your own barbaric form of justice! This is a civilised world we live in! What's he supposed to have done to deserve this ... ... this sort of insanity?'

'You be new here mate. You wouldn't understand,' Bredan said, with at least a semblance of reason.

'Try me,' I snapped back in reply.

Bredan looked around for support and was cheered on with repetitive shouts of, 'Tell him, Dan!.....Tell him, Dan!'

'O.K. I'll tell you! Yon lad's been going with Peta's girl, now Peta don't like that ..... fact is; none of us likes it!'

I thought for a moment of when Charlotte had appeared for dinner and how she had toyed with Faversham's emotions for the whole evening. I also remembered the obvious jealousy shown by Peta Lofgren. I looked down to where Faversham had fallen, but he'd gone, crawling away down the hall and probably out of the back door, and escape.

'So, what if he has seen Charlotte,' I said decisively. 'She has the right to choose whoever she wants.'

Peta Lofgren shook his head violently, but still didn't speak, preferring Bredan to do his dirty work for him.

'Not round here you don't!' Bredan muttered under his breath. 'Peta's girl is Peta's girl.'

'Come on ......'I said bluntly. 'The girl was born here ...... lived here all her life ...... you know her, you've grown up with her ...... you know what she's like, she probably led him on, it's just as much her fault as his.'

A hush descended on the crowd and I began to relax a little, thinking that they were beginning to come to their senses. I soon realised that it wasn't my powers of oratory at all that had done it when I saw a new member arrive at the back and push his way through.

'What's going on?' James Bardell said with evident authority, and I heaved a sigh of relief at the command he had over them. I was just about to speak when a drunken voice sang out in the silence.

'He called your daughter a slut, Mr Bardell!'

I tried to shout above the resulting noise, but no-one could hear me. Bardell raised his arm and silence fell again. His face suddenly flushed with rage and I remembered Gwenlyn relating that in his eyes Charlotte could do no wrong.

'And he's with the dredger as well!' came the same drunken voice again.

'Silence!' rapped Bardell and looked me up and down disparagingly. I could see that it was hopeless, so I started to shuffle slowly back so as to be able to slam the door if needs be. One of the men spotted my intention and wedged his block of timber by the hinge. He gave a sly grin and a wink of his eye.

'And did you, Mr Kinsey?' Bardell began. 'Did you call my daughter ...... a ...... a ...... a slut?' The words were spat out, and I could tell that he had already made up his mind.

I assured him. 'Of course I didn't. All I implied was that she's an attractive girl who readily accepts the compliments of the young men in the village ...... Look, this is ridiculous! ..... People are not allowed to go around beating up other people ...... Have you seen Nicholas Faversham?'

He shook his head, but didn't seem interested,

I continued. 'Well, you should see him! ..... See what this lot ...

... this irresponsible mob has done to him! ..... He's black and blue! ..... kicked and beaten by the look of it! You're supposed to be the one in charge in this village! ..... you're the one who's supposed to keep control!'

'You called my daughter a slut.' he repeated quietly.

I threw my hands in the air in utter despair. 'No! ..... No! ..... No!'... I protested. 'I did no such thing! ..... can't you see......or are you blinded by your own prejudice?'

'Then you implied it,' he concluded.

'And he's a dredger man!' sounded the voice yet again.

'I asked you into my house......' Bardell began again. 'I welcomed you, only to find that you're a murderer.' A murmur ran through the group of fishermen. 'And a murderer of helpless children as well ......' The murmur was louder this time as was his voice. '... ...and now I find that you're a liar as well ......!'

His next sentence was interrupted by Dan Bredan casually picking up a stone and tossing it through my front window.

'Hey, you can't do that!' I shouted, and made the mistake of stepping out of the doorway.

Others followed Bredan's example and began smashing the rest of the windows either with stones or with their wooden clubs. Two powerfully built men tried to bar my way, but I was annoyed ......very annoyed! I had made my mistakes in the past, but I was no coward when it came to facing up to adversity. I lifted my right leg and kicked one of the two sharply between the legs causing him to instantly double up with pain. The other's attention was distracted so I smashed my fist just below his heart and heard him cry out in agony.

Two more came at me! They were fishermen and they were strong but they were not fighters! I had years of fighting in me, learnt the hard way! Fighting clean, or fighting dirty! They would get me in the end, but not before I had taken a few down with me.

They tried to rush but it was a confined space and I was faster than they were. One lifted his piece of timber exposing his throat which I stabbed forcefully with my straight fingers and immediately lashed out with my left foot to catch the other on the shin. He dropped his guard and I brought my knee up to connect with his face.

They were all pushing and shoving now, and I let them force me into the hall where no more than two at a time could get at me. All the old craft came back as if it had been yesterday; the words of my old instructor echoing in my ears. 'Make them come on your terms ...... narrow down the options......there are no rules, use whatever you've got ...... strike vulnerable areas ...... speed of reaction ...... attack, reassess and attack again.'

I took two more of them out at the foot of the stairs, hitting one over the head with a clock from the wall forcing him to collide with the one next to him, who stumbled over and crashed through the banisters.

It was too narrow a space in which to use their wooden weapons so some dropped them causing others behind to trip over the extra obstacles in their path. As two fell, I knocked their heads together and watched them crumple senseless at my feet.

I'm convinced I could have taken them all, but James Bardell was next in line, pushed forward by the throng behind who couldn't see what was happening. He could fight with words, but not with fists and the look on his face was one of absolute dread.

I smiled crookedly at him, wordlessly accusing him of inciting the violence and I raised my fist ...... but I couldn't hit him ...... I was in love with one of his daughters!

The realisation hit me so abruptly that I hesitated a fraction too long. A blow landed on my left cheek at the same time as one caught me in the stomach; not painful in themselves, but sufficient to throw me off balance. The sheer impact of the rest of them made me lose my footing, while their momentum propelled them forwards until they were trampling all over me. I lifted my arms in a final, forlorn effort to protect myself against the worst of the spiteful blows that rained down on me incessantly. The sickening reality of the situation was drilled into me with every cry of pain that was uttered from between my lips. Inevitably, I reached the point where I couldn't resist any longer, and I blacked out.

I wondered in and out of consciousness, feeling the pain, but aware that the stamping and beating had ceased. The house was empty and dark and I was unable to move. I tried an arm and then a leg, but nothing would do my bidding. I started to panic but deliberately slowed my breathing and I felt myself gradually relax.

Any perception of time was lost to me, one minute, it was dark and the next, there was brilliant sunlight and soon afterwards dark again. I felt a pounding in my head and the floor and walls seemed to spin around me in my delirious state. I was cold and shivering but my limbs would do little else.

I closed my eyes again but woke when I felt something touch me. A man stood over me, someone I'd not seen before, who felt around my head and neck and then all over my body. There was nothing I could do to stop him, but sensed from his gentleness that he meant no harm. Occasionally it hurt when he touched me and I let out a low groan. Finally, I felt something in my arm and I drifted off into sleep.

When I awoke, the hall light was on and I heard voices in the front room. Blankets had been placed over me and, somehow, under me as well. I tried to speak but only managed to produce a whisper, but it was enough and I heard rapid footsteps coming into the hall.

'He's conscious!' I heard a voice say, so I made an effort to move.

'Shhh ...... Quiet ...... Don't strain.' came the words, and I peered up to see Gwenlyn's troubled face. I tried a smile but failed in the attempt. A man appeared by her side who went through the same routine of feeling all over my body.

The man spoke. 'He'll be very stiff. There's probably some ribs gone, but he's strong. Bruising and lacerations mainly. It's a good job he curled up and covered his face ...... I'll leave something for you to give him.'

I endeavoured to move again and got some reaction from my arms and legs. I clasped my teeth together to fight against the burning sensation in my chest and screwed up my eyes as I forced my joints through the pain barrier. I stretched my fingers up and down and then my ankles and succeeded in making myself more comfortable on the floor.

The doctor and Gwenlyn went into whispered conversation before he left through the back door. Gwenlyn knelt down by my side and replaced the pillow that had been supporting my head.

'What day is it?' I sighed.

'Thursday.' She replied.

I raised my eyebrows, which was about the only movement possible without pain. 'Nicholas ...... Nicholas Faversham ...... Where is he? ..... Is he okay?'

'No-one's seen him......He's not been to the office. Charlotte won't say anything.'

'And Latchley?'

'I've not seen him either.'

'The others?' I queried. 'The ones who were here?'

For the first time, a slight smile broke the serious lines of her face and her head did its characteristic tilt to one side. 'What did you do to them?' she said with more than a hint of humour in her voice. 'It was like a battlefield yesterday...... bandages ...... stitches ...... plaster. They all agreed that you had a small army hidden away in here, and that they'd all been heroes. Dan Bredan's got the worst headache of his life, and the Doctor's said no alcohol for a month ...... As for the rest of them! ..... No fishing at the very least.'

'No-one badly hurt?' I enquired in all seriousness.

'None as bad as you! But it's about time some of them were taught a lesson ...... It'll teach them a bit of respect.'

I wriggled around again, pushing myself onto my back. I lay there for a minute while the pain eased, then moved again.

'I need to go to the bathroom.' I stated.

'But you can't walk.'

'Well, I'll have to. Can you give me a hand up. I must stink as well, lying there for two days. And I could do with a drink.'

With the use of a chair as leverage, and with Gwenlyn's help, I managed to stand up. The hall seemed to spin round and I was nearly sick, but fought it and held my balance.

It took half an hour to negotiate the stairs, and I was exhausted by the time I got there, but I made it. It was painful to pass water, but there was no blood, so I assumed no internal damage had been done. I cleaned my teeth with difficulty as my hands felt clumsy and swollen, and I was conscious that I needed a bath.

I tried to turn on the bath taps but they were more stiff than those on the wash hand basin, and I couldn't grip them. There was a knock on the bathroom door and Gwenlyn enquiring if I was all right. She finally had to come in and turn the taps on for me.

She undressed me slowly and carefully, whispering quietly as I cringed with pain. My back in particular was severely bruised and my legs were badly grazed with the worst area being by the ankles. She helped me into the hot water, neither of us embarrassed by my nakedness. The water stung at first, but when I got used to it my aching body responded by feeling refreshed and relaxed. I tried to make small talk but my brain was going sluggish and it took an almighty effort to get out of the bath, towelled dry, and into bed. Jabber had the one and only hot water bottle, but I was content enough with a soft mattress and the bedclothes after being on a hard floor for so long.

Gwenlyn gave me one of the doctor's tablets to kill the pain and I was soon fast asleep and didn't wake for the next twelve hours, after which I felt much stronger, but still unbelievably stiff and sore.

She brought me breakfast at nine which I devoured hungrily and I hardly noticed that she had said very little since she came in. She appeared to be distant and some of her friendliness had evaporated.

'What's the matter?' I asked quietly. 'You seem ...... quiet ...... remote all of a sudden.'

She lifted up the heavy tray and headed for the door. 'Nothing.' She claimed.

'Come on,' I pressed. 'What's happened? ..... What's changed? ..... Has someone said something to you? Or are you just a moody sort of person and I didn't realise before?'

'No,' she replied in a faint voice. 'No-one said anything.'

I let it drop and she took the dishes out and I heard her washing up in the kitchen sink downstairs. She returned with a hot drink and sat at the opposite end of the room while I drank it, looking at me in a vaguely fearful way.

I was mystified. 'I don't bite you know. What is it? Someone must have said something …… I've not seen you like this before.'

She hesitated as if to speak, then shook her head. 'I must go,' and made for the door, but I wouldn't let her go without an answer.

I tried another approach as she stepped onto the landing, looking impatient to leave. 'What's your job?' I persisted. 'What do you do all day? ….. Do you have a job at all?'

She continued shuffling away, but at least she spoke. 'Some sail making …… repairs …… I look after the house of course …… cooking, washing, that sort of thing.'

'So you have to dash off now to do sail-making all day do you?'

She shuffled a bit more, looking frightened and embarrassed. 'You ……you talk in your sleep.'

'How did you know?' I asked slowly in return.

'I stayed …… I stayed most of last night. I was frightened; the things you said. I thought you were delirious, a blow on the head or something. I tried to calm you …… quieten you down …… talk to you, but you wouldn't …… couldn't hear me. You grabbed me by the wrists.' She rolled up her sleeves to show the red, swollen forearms. 'You shouted and screamed, and I couldn't get away. I didn't want to hurt you, but I had to kick you on the ankle where I knew you'd been injured, and then you let go. I nearly didn't come back this morning. You ……you had your eyes open …… I thought you could see me, and …… I thought …… I thought you were mad.'

I rested back on the pillow, not knowing what to say; feeling sad that, once again, I'd hurt one of the few people who had begun to get close to me.

'What did I talk about? I was asleep, I don't remember anything. I have nightmares nearly every night, but I don't know what I say.'

She was uneasy and kept looking onto the landing and wanting to go, then, as if she'd made a firm decision, she took a purposeful step back into the room.

She breathed deeply. 'Killing ...... all you seemed to do was to order people to be killed ...... murdered! It was horrible! All the time, names, things, places. I was frightened. Then when you got hold of me, you kept saying you were going to kill me. Is it ...... is it to do with what Jonathan was saying when you came round to dinner?'

I sighed. My past had caught up with me again. 'Will you listen to me?' I requested. 'If I tell you what happened. The truth, all of it ... ... good and bad. Will you listen and not ask questions ...... not until I've finished?'

She nodded her assent.

'Come and sit on the bed?' I invited, but she didn't move. 'Please?' I continued persuasively. 'I'm awake now. I won't hurt you. I didn't mean to hurt you in the night. You're the last person on earth I'd ever want to do that to ...... and you've been so kind.'

She sat awkwardly on the end of the bed, not close, but more intimate than when she was standing at the door. I saw her again as on the day I'd first met her in the cemetery by my father's grave, so beautiful, so assured, so loyal, so protective, so caring. Now I had to trust her with my past ...... so I told her everything.

For two hours, as the late autumn sun came through the windows, I told her of the Italian beaches and prior to that, to my childhood, my feelings, emotions, my hates, my fears. All the time she stared directly into my eyes; unflinching when I told her of the things I'd done. I left nothing out, nothing at all, even trying to explain my logic, my reasoning and my thoughts up until I first met her.

When I had finished, we sat in silence.

The retelling had awakened a host of disturbing memories, and instead of feeling comfort, I sensed a gulf between us. I wasn't particularly looking for forgiveness from her; on the other hand, I did not want judgement. All I really desired was a measure of sympathy for the way in which I'd suffered.

'The people ...... the parents of the children, how do they feel now? ..... how did they feel then?' she asked in hushed tones.

I looked at the sunlight filtering through the closed curtains, trying to understand why she should be more concerned with their feelings than mine.

'Sad ...... I suppose,' I said after a pause. 'But people get over these things, they rebuild. But me; I've had to suffer everyday, every night since. You saw the torment last night ...... Saw me! ..... Heard me! ..... Everywhere I go I feel it, can't get away from it. Like after last Saturday night when I tried to hang myself. One day, I'll succeed ... ... finish it all off, be done with it. I can't stand this guilt much longer.'

She gave a stifled sob and pulled out a handkerchief to wipe her eyes. I couldn't make out the expression on her face but she moved along the bed and I felt the touch of her fingertips on my hand. They crept up my palm and then intertwined with my fingers. Her other hand touched me as well, caressing the back of my hand, fondling, squeezing, firm then gentle, her eyes never leaving mine.

'What do you feel?' she asked gently.

I lay still, confused at what she was doing. I said nervously, 'The touch of a woman.'

'What sort of touch?'

'A ...... a gentle touch ...... soft ...... sensuous I suppose.' I could feel the colour rise in my cheeks, I'd not experienced anything like this before.

'I understand your friend, Father John,' she said, withdrawing her hand. 'He couldn't help you because ...... you won't be helped ...... you've never loved have you? ..... I've asked you that before.'

I slowly shook my head.

'A pet? ..... a dog? .... a cat?'

I shook my head again.

'You've never even loved yourself, have you? Never even thought of yourself as anything worthwhile?'

I waited silently for her to continue, but she got up and drew the curtains letting in a bright shaft of light that framed her in a dark silhouette so I couldn't see her properly, only feel the emotion in her voice.

'The parents, brothers, sisters, aunts, uncles, grandparents of those children ..... there will always be an emptiness in their memories. The wives ...... lovers of your men ...... always an emptiness in their memories too. They'll remarry ...... some of them ...... but still an emptiness, a hole that can never be completely filled.'

She walked over and sat on the bed and touched my hand again. 'The touch of a woman,' she repeated my words. 'Gentle .... soft .... sensuous. That's all on the surface. You can't get rid of your guilt because it's not guilt that you feel. It's self pity. You've never loved ... ... never had anyone love you. You don't know what it's like to lose

someone, and until you love, and then lose the one that you love ......
you won't understand.'

'I love you,' I stammered.

She shook her head. 'No....the touch of a woman .... gentle ....
soft .... sensuous .... but not love ...... not love for me ......' She
stopped and waited. 'I'll go now. You'll be tired.'

She rose from the bed and walked to the door: a vision of
loveliness that I couldn't reach; physically, yes, but not in the way I
longed for. She closed the door without looking back, leaving me alone
with my thoughts.

I slept again and woke in the afternoon thinking it all a dream.

*****

By the following Monday I was up and about, still in pain, but
moving. Gwenlyn came in each day, keeping me up to date with the
news. The inspector had been and confirmed that the collapse of the
harbour wall was a fluke and was nothing to do with the dredging.
There was an uneasiness in the village with families divided, especially
those where some were fishermen and others worked on the dredger.

The two pubs had become the two opposing centres, one for the
fishermen, the other for the dredger crew. I'd thought of calling in the
police over the fight at my house, but Gwenlyn said that they would
close ranks and deny everything. In any case, no-one would admit that
it was only me who had inflicted so much injury.

I was at a loose end so I asked Gwenlyn if there was any way I
could get hold of a car. I didn't tell her that I intended to follow up one
or two things about Jonathan Latchley. As it turned out, she used her

father's car for shopping in Dartmouth and there would be no problem if she drove, and as long as he didn't know that I would be with her.

I lay in the back seat so that no-one could see me, and switched to the front seat when we reached the main road. Conversation was reserved for non controversial subjects. Jabber was fine now. Some more sand had slipped from the beach at high tide the previous day, but nothing significant. Nicholas Faversham was now working out of Plymouth and the local office was temporarily closed while he ran the dredging programme from a safe distance.

I persuaded her to drive to Kingsbridge, telling her that I hoped to meet an old friend, but that it wouldn't be appropriate if she was there as well. She asked no difficult questions and sat by the water's edge for an hour while I made my way, rather slowly, back to the house I had seen Jonathan Latchley enter when I had followed him.

The visit confirmed my worst suspicions and after dropping in to the post office to make a half a dozen telephone calls, I had the information I needed. I then returned, somewhat achingly, to where I had left Gwenlyn.

'You look awful!' were her welcoming words. 'You look pale, and you're shaking. Is everything all right?'

I grimaced. 'My ribs. A bit sore. Done a bit too much on the first day out of the house. Too much walking I think. Look, we'd better get back, your father might suspect.'

She got up and started walking to the car but had to slow down as I was lagging behind.

'Your father,' I said, catching my breath. 'Does he know that you've been round to see me; that you've been looking after me?'

She opened the door and helped me in before going round to her

167

side. My ankles were aching as well, and I was developing a bad headache.

'I think he does,' she said, starting the engine. 'He knows he did wrong, but he's a proud man. He knows he shouldn't have allowed them to give you such a beating, but he's still adamant that you insulted Charlotte. He won't admit that there's the remotest possibility of her being anything other than the perfect daughter.'

'Does he ask about me?' I questioned.

She shook her head, 'No ….. no comment at all, not by mouth anyway. He's more quiet, looks troubled, probably just as much worried about the harbour wall and the lack of protection for the boats in an easterly wind. They've started pulling the boats on to the beach above the high tide mark when an easterly is expected, but one broke free last night when a strip of sand shifted.'

I moved my position, trying to get comfortable in the car. She glanced at me, sensing my distress.

'You do look bad you know. You're looking worse. You've done far too much haven't you?'

I felt my forehead. I was hot and feverish and my whole body seemed to be throbbing. She stopped the car, suggesting that it might be better for me to lie down in the back seat and travel the rest of the way in that position rather than fighting to stay upright. I did as she instructed, but was still very weak by the time we arrived back.

She checked that no-one was looking and helped me upstairs and into bed. I was hot and shivering so she gave me two more of the doctor's tablets saying that she would get him to come to see me in the morning if I was no better. She said she would call in later but that she had to get dinner for her father and sister and that if she wasn't careful, they might get suspicious.

She gave me a worried look and left me curled up and shivering, trying to rest my aching head.

I must have slept for a while because when I woke, it was pitch dark. I crept along to the bathroom and sponged off some of the sweat from the fever, then decided on a soak in a warm bath before returning to bed. I felt better but still weak and I left the landing light on for comfort. My watch said nine o'clock and I was ready for a long night.

I dozed for a while then woke up again when I heard a noise on the stairs and a moment later, Gwenlyn appeared. She switched on the bedroom light and came over and sat on the bed, placing her hand on my forehead.

'How's the patient?' she asked cheerfully.

'All the better for seeing the nurse.' I replied.

She laughed. 'Well you seem a bit better anyway.'

'Hmmm …. not shivering so much.' I said, 'I'll have to get my hot water bottle back from Jabber; I need it more than he does right now.'

'I'll get it tomorrow,' she promised. 'No long walks for you for a while though. Food? Do you want anything?'

I shook my head.

'Anything to drink?'

'No thanks. I got a drink from the bathroom not long ago. I'll live! What do you think, nurse?'

'I think you'll live too.'

There was a sudden stillness in the room, a change of mood, a change of atmosphere, so I hesitantly asked, 'Have you been to my father's grave again?'

'No, not recently,' she said softly.

'Why?' I asked, even quieter.

'Why? ..... Because ...... because his son's alive.'

I felt her hand touch my cheek, and I reached out and touched hers. I felt her lean towards me; slowly but deliberately, and my hand fondled gently through her hair. She sighed deeply and I pulled her to me, kissing her lightly on her forehead, her cheeks and then on her lips. She encircled my head with her hands pulling my lips towards her, longingly, searchingly.

It was a fleeting moment of ecstasy, as with my eyes closed, I sensed rather than saw another presence in the room. My eyes shot open and I pushed her away rapidly at the same time. She was startled and instantly frightened at the sudden movement, but not half as frightened as when she looked across and saw Jonathan Latchley standing in the doorway.

Chapter 10

Gwenlyn leapt off the bed in alarm, with one, despairing look around telling her that there was no means of escape. Latchley took three strides and grabbed her by the hair. He pulled her head back and struck her a fierce blow with the back of his hand, followed immediately by a savage strike with his open palm.

I managed to get out of bed, but there was so little strength in my body and my movements were far too slow and cumbersome.

'Stop it!' I yelled, but he just hit her again letting her slump to the floor, unconscious. 'You maniac!' I bellowed at him. 'You touch her again and I'll tear you apart!'

He rounded on me then, stepping over her prostrate form and tearing at me like a mad bull. Under normal circumstances, I would have taken him easily, but in my weakened state I knew that just one blow and I would have nothing with which to counter him. He threw a punch at my face, but I ducked and fell across the bed and rolled over onto the other side.

I had forgotten that despite his size, he was very nimble on his feet and in no time had quickly worked his way round the bed. He kept his eyes on me all the time, ready to move if I tried to get away across the bed again. My ribs were screaming in pain from the effort and I was finding it increasingly difficult to breathe.

'Come on, soldier boy! He sneered, trying to intimidate me by beckoning me to come to him. 'Or is it different facing a man instead of a child?'

He'd forgotten about Gwenlyn's body on the floor and tripped over it, momentarily loosing his balance. I took my chance and advanced a step and kicked out, catching him on the side of his head, but there was no power in the attack and I was bare-footed. I jumped onto the bed again and wriggled across but he recovered rapidly and came round the other side again. I launched a pillow at him to distract him but he deflected it easily. It gave me enough time to jump off the end of the bed, but then I realised that I had nowhere else to go.

'Come on, soldier boy.' He taunted. 'Come and get me ...... if you can?'

I looked helplessly to right and left, but there was nothing to assist me, so the only way was forward. I bent over and thrust myself at him, catching him a stunning blow in the stomach. He pulled me on top of him and encircled my waist, pinning down both my arms. I could hear him panting from the pain I had caused him, but now of course, he had time to recover as he squeezed the very breath out of me.

I used the only weapon I had left and bit hard into his right ear. He released me with a yelp and as I fell, I rolled over onto my back. He was less hurt than I was however, and was on his feet first. My reactions were slow and as I pulled myself up, my legs buckled under me and I grabbed for the bed post to restore my balance. I winced as a searing pain rammed through my chest and I could see the glint of victory in his eyes as he saw that I was helpless.

In a flash it came to me: all I needed was a few seconds in which to speak. I briefly overcame the agony. 'You can't hurt me, Latchley,'

I boasted, with more confidence than I felt. 'I know too much!'

For the first time, he halted in his advance, 'Who says so, soldier boy?'

He, too, was having difficulty speaking and we were both grateful for the respite.

'I know it all ......' I gasped, and then coughed hard. 'I've been to Kingsbridge!'

There was a stirring from Gwenlyn on the floor.

'She's coming round, Latchley ..... Shall I wait until she's conscious?' I paused to take some deep breaths. 'Three letters......I've sent three letters. To be opened on my death: Solicitor, Bank and friend ...... It's all there.'

'You bastard!' he murmured.

'No more than you.' I replied. 'You dig dirt on me ...... I do the same with you.'

He straightened up, taking his time while dusting down his suit, unsure if I was bluffing or not. 'I'll get you!' he promised bluntly. 'One day, I'll get you.'

'Perhaps,' I said, also straightening up. 'But not today ...... and I'll have that ten thousand if you don't mind ...... or can't you pay? Six quarries sold! Where's all the money gone? Or have you used it all as a pay-off?'

He turned on his heels and stormed out leaving me hugely relieved that he'd fallen for the deception. I hadn't written any letters, let alone sent any.

I bent down to Gwenlyn; I wasn't sure if one of his blows had knocked her out or whether she had fainted, but I helped her onto the bed and gave her a sip of water. Both sides of her face were swollen and she was a dazed and confused, but otherwise in one piece.

'What happened?' she said vaguely.

'Our friend, Mr Latchley ……' I began.

'Did you…… talk?' she stuttered.

'Talk!' I exclaimed. 'Look at the mess of the bedroom!' She looked. 'Yes, we talked! We certainly talked! ….. And other things besides! Let's just say that he'll have a stomach ache and a very painful right ear……or was it left? ….. No ……right …… and my lungs haven't been quite so compressed in a long while!'

'You mean, you had a fight! In here! With me on the floor! But you …… you're not well!'

'The exercise did me good.' I insisted, but the pallor of my face told her otherwise.

She sat up and grimaced as she massaged the swollen areas of her face. 'But he's gone! How come? ….. Just like that.'

'Never mind,' I sighed wearily 'he's gone, that's all you need to know.'

She wanted to press things further, but I wouldn't let her. Instead I suggested a hot drink in the kitchen. I also insisted that she should have the back door key and that, from now on, I would keep all the doors locked. I also needed to get the downstairs windows repaired as they were still broken from the near riot. The doors into the rooms had been kept closed, and when we opened them to investigate, the rooms felt cold and damp with the smashed panes only acting now as partial barriers against the wind and rain.

'You need something cold on your face,' I suggested while looking at the swelling. She went to the kitchen sink and using a sponge and cold water proceeded to apply the prescribed treatment.

'Do it again before you go to bed ...... and it's probably best if your father and sister don't see you tonight, or certainly not close up. They'll only ask questions.'

She kissed me goodnight and withdrew back into her world, leaving me in a turbulent mood wondering what I should do next. Shock set in and I sat there until the early hours shaking while I turned things over and over in my mind, only to conclude that at the moment I could do nothing anyway. I wearily climbed the stairs to bed and dreamt of 'Riding the Wind,' Gwenlyn, the harbour wall, Jonathan Latchley, broken windows......and dead children.

*****

Within a few days I had recovered considerably. I hadn't ventured outside the house, except very late at night when there was no-one around, meanwhile Gwenlyn had kindly provided me with any food that wouldn't keep for long. I ran up and down the stairs repeatedly to restore my legs to some state of fitness again, and did other exercises for the rest of my body as well. My ribs were still painful if I overstretched but generally, I was well pleased with my recovery.

Against Gwenlyn's advice I wandered down into the village one morning. I told her that I had to face people at some point, so it may as well be sooner rather than later.

Apparently, so Gwenlyn had told me, feelings were running high between fishermen and those who worked on the dredger. Much of the blame had been placed on my shoulders, so it came as no surprise when I was largely ignored on my arrival at the harbour. Rejection was something I had faced all my life, so it didn't bother me unduly.

I sat on an upturned wooden box and made a careful inspection of my surroundings. Most of the fishing boats were out at sea, but some were moored up on the opposite side to the dredger. A line of crab pots, boxes and entangled nets blocked access to the dredger, and half a dozen fishermen sat astride the obstacle. I watched, fascinated, because I knew that it was getting very close to the time when the dredger normally got under way.

Sure enough, five minutes before the usual time, individual dredger men appeared from their homes and congregated across the road from the harbour. There were ten of them this time, and when all assembled they marched across the road towards the fishermen and their makeshift barrier.

I looked up and saw windows open and faces peer out. Others poked their heads around half-open doors and braver ones ventured into the street. I tensed with anticipation and saw the fishermen do the same. It was as if the whole village had come to a halt so as to witness the spectacle. I even noticed one of the shops quickly put up a closed sign and the shopkeeper appear at an upstairs window. Apart form one shout of 'Traitors' from somewhere behind me, it was a quiet condemnation of the dredger crew.

The ten reached the barrier and began to clamber over, much to the consternation of those blocking the way. I don't know who pushed whom first, but within seconds there was a violent scuffle in progress and the whole situation looked to be turning very nasty. I contemplated trying to intervene but then thought better of it. I was in no fit state to take on anyone at the moment, especially in an open space. Then one of the dredger crew fell backwards and I heard the crack of his head hitting the solid stone surface. I jumped to my feet, but felt a hand on my shoulder firmly pushing me down again.

'Stay out of this! You have caused enough damage already!' commanded Peers Lofgren as he paced over to the confrontation. I followed him across the road, keeping well behind wanting to hear the conversation but with no desire to be part of it.

Their fighting ceased abruptly at the sight of the harbour master who bent down to check on the fallen man. I heard them all shouting at once, with Lofgren shaking his fist, trying to get them to be quiet. I took an inquisitive step closer in an attempt to pick up some of what they were saying, but one of the dredger men spotted me and pointed an accusing finger.

'It's his fault!' he shouted above the rest, while another echoed in agreement. At least they were united in something.

I took a few more paces but Lofgren stopped me from going closer.

'I told you to be staying out of this, Mr Kinsey. It is bad enough without you interfering!' he ordered.

'I wasn't interfering!' I argued. 'But I do have a right to know why, all of a sudden, I get the blame for everything that goes wrong in this place.'

Peers Lofgren looked unsure of himself as he endeavoured to think of a good reason why I shouldn't ask questions, but one of the others beat him to it.

'You be knowing quite well why it's your fault,' said the voice of one of the dredger men whom I'd not seen previously.

I challenged him, 'You seem well informed. I don't think we've met, so how come you know so much.'

'Me name's Rudd.'

'All right, Mr Rudd.' I continued. 'If you're so well informed,

177

perhaps you could inform me.'

'You knows bloody well why! ..... Mr Latchley wants to stop dredging, but he says you wants your money, your share, so he has to keep dredging to get the money for to pay you ...... We doesn't want to fight; these lot used to be our mates, but we has a job to do. We don't get paid 'til Mr Latchley has enough money to pay you, so the quicker we gets going the quicker we gets our pay again!'

He spat in my direction and without more ado pushed the fishermen out of the way, and continued his walk to the dredger.

I shouted after him. 'You believe that! You honestly believe that!' I was totally dumbfounded that Jonathan Latchely had managed to twist so comprehensively what I had said to him.

'Fine,' I said to myself, turning away. Beaten up by the fishermen, rejected by everyone else in the village and now accused by the workers on the dredger, who I had thought until now were partial allies. If it hadn't been for Gwenlyn, I would have packed my things and left there and then. I glanced over my shoulder at the fishermen skulking away from their blockade and didn't look where I was going and collided with Jonathan Latchley.

'Ah ...... Major Kinsey!' he chimed, with a broad, beaming smile on his face. 'Having some trouble there were we?'

I smiled back. 'No! ..... No trouble at all.'

'It looked to me as if you were, but never mind; such good men, it's a shame they've got to work so hard ...... and it's all your fault of course. But they were understanding, so considerate ..... It's a pity you are as you are ...... and with such a past as well!'

I pushed round him, doing my best to ignore his jibes.

'Yes, Major, we all have a past, but some of us are better able to

...... how should I say? .... dispose of our past ...... Now take, for instance, a house in Kingsbridge. It's empty, I'm told. See what I mean. People can disappear, but alas, gravestones are memorials ...... never forgotten ...... never disposed of.'

I believed him. I believed the house in Kingsbridge was empty; he was too confident for it not to be. I was cursing myself for telling him that I knew all about it, but at the time I had had no other option. I gave him a mocking smile, which he mimicked and he gave me a gentlemanly bow into the bargain.

'Perhaps you could now be persuaded to leave Windle Bridge, Major. You're not exactly very popular, are you? And at some point, you are going to have to get some sort of job. There's only fishing and dredging here, Major, and you're not on very good terms with either camp at present! Why don't you do yourself a favour and leave us alone; let us get on with our lives and you can get on with yours. What do you say?'

I didn't say anything. I simply walked away, with his smug laughter ringing in my ears.

The house seemed unfriendly and unwelcoming after the incident at the harbour. I entertained the thought of leaving, but where could I go? Similar events were bound to dog me wherever I went.

I thought of Latchley: I didn't know that much about him, only the little I had learnt by direct contact and from the visit to the house in Kingsbridge. Maybe there was something else I could use to make him back off, but there was no-one I could ask; certainly not Gwenlyn! Jabber sprang to mind: he had known my father well, so possibly he knew something of Latchley, even though Jabber himself spent little or no time in the village.

I half walked, half ran to Jabber's hut. The fitness was returning but I didn't want to overtax myself. When I arrived, Jabber was nowhere to be seen, so I sat on the sand and waited until I spotted his boat coming in from fishing. I helped him beach it and then we both entered the hut where he hummed tunelessly while he brewed the usual tar-like coffee. I wondered how come he had such a plentiful supply but never got round to asking. It was an acquired taste but one to which you could easily get addicted.

'Tell me about Jonathan Latchley?' I asked after the small talk had passed.

He mused, 'Jonathan Latchley? ..... Now there's a question! Gwenlyn tells me you saw off some of them young fishing lads. They had it coming right enough! Now Jonathan Latchley ...... how far's you wanting to go back, laddie?'

'The beginning,' I said resolutely.

'The beginning! ..... Well, lad, the beginning ...... No brothers, no sisters, doting parents, too much freedom, then one day his mother dies and his daddy has to bring him up and brings him up real spoilt, like.'

I interrupted, 'His mother: what did she die of?'

'Weak heart, lad. Can't be in fishing and have a weak heart. I used to live in the village, fish with some of the old 'uns: all gone now. And the women folk can't have a weak heart. The women lift and carry, and sort and weigh ...... and fish as well. Those seine nets are heavy. She had a weak heart and dies when young Latchley would be four or five.'

I drained the dregs of coffee from the tin cup. 'Let me get this straight, his father brought him up, so how come the dredging and quarrying and not fishing?'

'You want some more of that?' he pointed as I put the cup down.

I waved my hand, 'No thanks.'

180

He got to his feet and made for the door. 'Come with me, lad and I'll explain something to you.'

I followed him out onto the beach, or what was left of it, and he showed me the boat we had used to 'Ride the Wind'.

'Look you here at this boat; weather beaten, exposed; but tough, hardworking. Young Latchley was fair skinned; didn't have the roughness of the other lads, so his father got ambitious, gave up the fishing and moved into quarrying. Not doing it himself, mind, getting other men in to do the work, just being manager himself. It was 'Latchley and Bradbury' in them days: well known hereabouts ...... slate, granite ...... and sand. Your father and Bill Latchley got together, started off and did well they did.'

I examined the boat; the faded paintwork, the battered and worn woodwork, the cold, grimy water slopping in the bottom, the deeply impregnated smell of fish and thought of the gnarled and roughened hands that would be needed to sail such a craft. I agreed that I couldn't imagine Jonathan Latchley as any sort of fisherman whatsoever.

'So how come?' I said, inquisitively. 'my father only ends up with thirty percent? Presumably they must have started fifty-fifty?'

Jabber looked sad, and I wondered if I had opened up some old wounds when I talked about the past and my father.

'Greed!' he said firmly. 'Bill Latchley's fault ..... Not him necessarily that was greedy like, but young Latchley. Now he was ambitious! Nought wrong with ambition, but he starts steppin' on people's toes. Bill and Tom let him in with nearly a third share, then he comes up with these fancy ideas for cutting corners. I used to know young Latchley well; a good brain, but wasted. Spoilt he was, and it ruined him ...... ruined Tom as well. Tom wouldn't have nothin' doin' with ought dishonest, but Bill got carried away, supported his son

through everything. Tom wouldn't sell up, so Bill sides with Jonathan
...... majority between them, changed the name to 'Latchley's' and
Tom's out on his ear.'

I summarised out loud. 'So Latchley's a spoilt child, gets a bit
power mad, and now here he is insisting that his dredging continues,
despite the strong possibility that it's the very dredging itself that's
undermined the harbour ...... and may well have undermined the
whole coastline for all we know, now that so much of the beach has
gone. His father's dead, I suppose and left everything to his only
offspring.'

Jabber played with the lines that lay piled in the stern of the boat.
'No, Bill Latchley's still alive! Saw the error of his ways, but too late
like ...... shame on the family name ...... Lost the friendship of Tom
Bradbury as well, so he moves away and won't have ought else to do
with his son anymore.'

'Which leaves Jonathan Latchley doing whatever he pleases, and
no-one to stop him!' I concluded.

Jabber nodded his head in agreement and shifted his gaze out to
sea. 'Yes, you got it about right, lad. Bill Latchley runs away, leaving
young Latchley a law unto himself ...... You want some grub, laddie?
Gwenlyn brought me a pie yesterday, wouldn't want to eat it all by
myself.'

'Fish pie?' I asked.

'Fish pie,' he confirmed.

It had to be fish pie of course, everything round here had fish in
it, but very tasty just the same. I was growing rapidly accustomed to
the staple diet of a fisherman.

'The beach?' I asked after we had eaten. 'The beach and the harbour

...... do you think it's due to the dredging? The inspector says not.'

Jabber laughed in reply. 'Ha! And who do you think pays the inspector? His majesty's government or Mr Jonathan Latchley? It's always been like that. Young Latchley would always buy himself out of trouble.'

Jabber did the business with the tin of peaches and we devoured the contents between us. I was thinking about my suspicions regarding the way Jonathan Latchley handled his financial affairs and on the spur of the moment, asked Jabber about some of them.

'What I don't understand.' I explained, as the last peach slithered down my throat, 'Is why he insists on the dredging? The villagers are up in arms, he can't be short of cash, or is he?'

Jabber tapped his spoon against the now empty tin. 'Greed! Like I said: Greed! ..... He wants more!'

'But the quarries,' I pressed, 'why's he sold the quarries?'

He looked genuinely surprised, 'Sold the quarries ...... I'd not be knowing he'd done that!'

I was tempted to tell him my reasons for thinking why Latchley had sold them, but there was a knock on the door of the hut and the sound of Gwenlyn's voice. Her eyes lit up when she saw me, and for a split second I felt certain she hadn't even noticed that Jabber was there.

'Hello,' she said, smiling. 'You must be better to walk this far.'

'Half ran,' I replied proudly. 'Could have run all the way, but thought I'd best be careful.'

She turned her attention to Jabber who had tactfully moved over to the stove to put some more water into the kettle for another hot drink.

'One of these days you'll drink too much of that stuff,' she chided him.

'One of these day,' he mocked. 'One of these days …… all sorts of things may happen …… very tasty pie though …… and …… we've …… er …. just been talking about Jonathan Latchley's father.

Her cheerful demeanour changed immediately. 'Oh …… and what have you been saying?'

'Nothing much,' I said hurriedly, trying to direct the conversation away from anything to do with Jonathan Latchley. 'I had some of your fish-pie. I shall have to ask you to make one for me sometime …..'

I was aware of something going on between them; subtle, two way glances as if looking for confirmation from each other.

Jabber finally spoke. 'It's no good, laddie.' he said with resignation, as he lined up three mugs. 'She knows all about it.'

I was embarrassed and didn't want to place Gwenlyn in an awkward situation. I tried a reassuring smile, but she wouldn't be fooled.

'What did he say?' she persisted.

'Like I said, nothing much. Some of Jonathan Latchley's background; why he is as he is. Jabber was just saying that it was his father's fault …… spoiling him …… you know how it is, only child …… no-one else to shower their attention on, then Bill Latchley disappears into the sunset, leaving Jonathan to cause havoc wherever he goes. I agree with Jabber …… I blame Latchley's father as much as Latchley himself.'

Her eyes narrowed. 'Oh, you do. Do you?' she murmured.

'Yes …… Why not? Someone's got to be responsible somewhere along the line. We were discussing the sand and the harbour and how Jonathan insists on carrying on despite pressure from the fishermen.'

She fell silent, giving Jabber time to hand us each a mug of the black coffee. 'And he's doing an extra load as from today,' she said casually.

I wasn't sure I had heard her right. 'Pardon. Did you just say what I think you said?'

'He's doing an extra load ..... everyday ...... as from today,' she confirmed.

'What! After all that's happened! ..... But he knows the dredging must have something to do with the harbour collapsing ...... and yet he's still insisting on carrying on! He must be mad!'

She took a sip from the side of the mug. 'He's told the fishermen that within two months he'll be finished. He actually gave them the day he would finish. He's told them that given the winter storms and tides, any holes in the shingle banks will be made good by sand being brought down by the northerly currents. Within a couple of years at most, the shingle banks will be the same as they were before. He's also said that no more dredging will ever be done after the next two months, so most of them are a bit happier. He hasn't told them officially about the extra load each day, he's letting them find that out by word of mouth.'

'And what do you think?' I asked.

She shrugged. 'I don't know......The inspector says the shingle and the harbour aren't connected.'

'I didn't ask for the inspector's opinion, I asked for yours!' I said, agitated, then retracted the question. 'I'm sorry ...... I didn't mean to snap at you.' I softened my voice a little. 'It just seems that whatever Jonathan Latchley wants , he gets.'

'And you're jealous, is that it?' she fired back.

'No! ..... I'm not jealous ...... Not of his influence. Jealous that he's engaged to you maybe ...... if he still is ...... is he?'

185

She looked at the ring on her left hand, not knowing what to say.

'I can't understand you Gwenlyn Bardell,' I declared. 'He hit you good and hard the other night, and yet here you are not being able to make up your own mind. I would have thought it's obvious.'

'It's not as easy as that.'

'Why not?'

'Stop bossing me about as if I'm one of your soldiers! It's not easy because it's been a long time …… you can't drop someone just like that.'

I could tell she was confused, but I still argued back. 'That's not logical! Engagement …… marriage …… it's all about trust and love …… and, I admit it, things I don't know much about. As for bossing you about, what about the way he treats you? What about the way he treats the rest of the villagers? For all we know, every dredger full of shingle, every barge that sails for Plymouth could be a nail in the coffin for this village. It might be the whole of the harbour next time! It might be half the main street, houses, people …… children …… and you don't need to be reminded that I know what it's like to be responsible for children …… and you say it's not as easy as that! I know what I feel about you …… I might not understand fully, but my motives are honest if nothing else! ….' I broke off my rhetoric. 'I'm sorry, Jabber,' I said, turning to the old man. 'We shouldn't be conducting a scene like this in your house …… it's not fair on you.'

I looked at Gwenlyn again. 'And I'm sorry …… I didn't mean to shout, but someone's got to do something! There may be a major disaster here for all we know, and all the villagers are doing is arguing and bickering! As Jabber says, Latchley's father is just as much to blame for letting his son loose like this. I'd ring his neck if I could get hold of him!'

Jabber moved uneasily, coughing nervously as he did so. 'You don't have to look far, laddie. If you're looking for young Latchley's father, then you've found him ...... cos' I am.'

Chapter 11

'You are!' I cried out, dumbfounded.

For a moment I was speechless while my mind juggled with the consequences of his revelation.

I was suddenly very angry. 'So …… So you let him …… this son of yours …….. You let him take over!' I was incredulous. 'You let him do whatever he wants …… and without lifting a finger!' Realisation dawned. 'Ah! ….. Come to think of it, I can see the likeness now. I saw some old photographs at the house; there was one of you! I couldn't place it, but now …… Yes! I see the likeness! ….. And you've just let him get away with it!'

He busied himself doing nothing in particular, trying to avoid any sort of confrontation with me.

'So you walked out and left,' I reproached him. 'You do understand what you've done don't you? ….. I could have been killed that night when the fishermen came round, yet you kept quiet …… not a murmur …… not a whisper! All the trouble Latchley's caused …… and you stand around and watch!'

'Tom saw it first,' he said meekly. 'I doesn't see it, not at first. Then I opts out …… I couldn't be no part of it, so I left him to it.'

No matter how much I liked the old fellow, I couldn't believe that he had allowed his own flesh and blood to walk over him like he had. I was soon on my feet waving an accusing fist at him while I blamed him for nearly everything that had befallen me since my arrival at Windle Bridge.

'Leave him alone!' Gwenlyn butted in, laying a protective arm on his shoulder. 'He's an old man ...... what do you expect him to do?'

I snapped back. 'What do I expect him to do? He wasn't an old man when all this started to happen!' I looked at Jabber. 'No, you weren't old then, were you? And does Latchley get his greedy ideas from you? ..... Like father, like son? You seemed eager enough to start with, when he began working with you ...... and did you listen to Thomas Bradbury? We'll forget that he's my father for a moment. Did you listen to your business partner ...... Did you listen?' He shook his head. 'Well, you should have done ...if you had, this village wouldn't be in such a mess. You stupid old fool: it's all your bloody fault!'

Gwenlyn leapt to her feet and slapped me hard across the left cheek.

'You leave him alone ...... you! .... you! .... hypocrite! What right have you got to accuse him of anything ..... or shall we talk about you? What about the effect you've had on others? Shall I spell it out ..... shall I?'

Her eyes were blazing with anger and she stabbed the air with her finger to hammer home the point. Behind her, Jabber slowly got up and sloped out of the door, his shoulders hunched, looking every bit his age. She waited until he had gone then rounded on me again.

'How dare you!' she fumed, continuing her outburst. 'How dare you even think that you can come here and start behaving as if you know all the answers! Jabber's the one person to offer friendship, and what do you do? Throw it back in his face! You've been doing this all

190

your life, haven't you? You're nothing but an arrogant ...... self centred
...... self righteous hypocrite; and it's about time someone told you!'

It was my turn to slap her face then, and I was sorry the moment
I did it. She didn't flinch, staring me straight in the eye all the time.

'Feel better now?' She said bitterly. 'You accuse Jonathan of
bullying me; now you've done exactly the same thing ...... his level
...... do you feel satisfied now? It's all you've ever done isn't it, just
push people around ...... push people out of the way! Well I've got
news for you, it doesn't work with me! I've waited years for Uncle
Tom's son to come here ...... but he's not come yet ...... not the son I
was led to believe existed!'

She stormed out slamming the door leaving me feeling nothing
but shame and humiliation.

I waited for ten minutes while I wrestled with my thoughts. I had
spent the whole of my life justifying my own actions and it was a
difficult habit to break. In due course I wandered outside to find Jabber
tidying up the lines and pots in his boat. Gwenlyn was nowhere to be
seen. I joined him, and in silence we sorted out the tools of his trade.

'Gwenlyn gone?' I ventured.

'Aye, lad,' he replied, not looking up.

We lapsed into silence again, but the animosity had subsided.

'She's a fine lass,' he said after a while.

'Yes ...... most definitely, Yes,' I agreed. 'Look ...... I'm ......
I'm sorry, very sorry. It was rude, uncalled for, ungrateful and
inexcusable. I had no right to yell at you like that; not after the friend
you've been, especially when I've had no others.'

'No lad, you were right. I'm an old man, been running away from
things too long.'

'You've run away?' I emphasised. 'Are you kidding? That's nothing compared to me! She gave me a right telling off in there! I've had all sorts of people have a go at me before now, and all I did was ignore them. But not Gwenlyn!' I shook my head vigorously. 'Oh, no… ..not Gwenlyn! She put me well and truly in my place.'

'Perhaps we both had it coming?' Jabber surmised, smiling. 'And let's not be forgetting it either.'

'So what now?' I asked.

'Not sure. You got any ideas, lad?'

'None …… None as yet.'

'I've got one.'

'You have? That's a start anyway. What is it?'

'Well …… 'he continued, running his fingers through his beard and pushing his bottom lip over the top one. 'Young Latchley's hell bent on doing this dredging for to get his shingle and he be filling them all with lies 'long the way. I thinks the best thing to do would be to have a public meeting, like ….. in the fish hall just back of the harbour. It's the only place what's big enough. Then we can explain, you know …… say what we're worried about …… or I can; you'd best be staying out of it. We can say we're worried about the rest of the harbour if more dredging goes on and sees what they say.'

I agreed. 'O.K. …… Problem is, how do we go about it? I can't ask anyone.'

'Leave it to me , laddie. I'll go in and see Peers Lofgren about it this afternoon. We'll be arranging it for tomorrow. Most of the village …… those what's working …… is usually in the fish hall come six o'clock. If he tells them today, they can spread the word and get everyone there come tomorrow.'

192

'Good,' I said enthusiastically. 'And possibly they'll listen.'

'Possibly, lad …… Possibly. Them's nice folk, but mighty stubborn!'

*****

I'd not been into the fish hall; in fact I'd not even noticed it was there. It was across the road from the harbour and looked like the frontage of two large houses but with one set of big double doors. The fish and crabs were brought in through the doors and after sorting, filleting and packing, were taken out through the back to be delivered to varying destinations further afield.

By six o'clock the day after the talk with Jabber, most of the village had congregated in the hall. The smell of fish was overwhelming but I seemed to be the only one aware of it. There were few chairs, and villagers who weren't standing were perched on the stone slabs that were normally used for a surface on which to gut the fish. The day's work was over and the mess had been cleared into large, metal bins that were yet to be disposed of. It was these that gave off the pungent odour.

There was a raised stone area at the far end which was used to lift the packing cases to the level of the delivery lorries, and it was this that was used as a platform for the proceedings. Peers Lofgren had produced a small table and also a single chair which remained unoccupied behind him. I positioned myself at the back, watching carefully, noticing that Jabber and Latchley stood at opposite sides of the stone platform and didn't acknowledge each other at all.

'I know you have all been having a full day,' Lofgren began, his accent getting stronger as he raised his voice to reach everyone in the hall. 'And maybe we are tired, but people have been worried about the collapse of the harbour wall. I, as harbour master, have been concerned as well, but I am thinking that the inspector has put my mind at rest. But this is not sufficient for some of you, so Mr Jonathan Latchley will explain what he plans for the future.'

Latchley stepped forward to mild applause from the dredger crew who had collected together at one side of the hall. He placed a file on the table, opened it and thoughtfully contemplated it's contents. 'Mr Chairman,' he said in confident tone, first addressing Lofgren and then the assembly, 'Ladies and gentlemen of our village of Windle Bridge.' He paused for effect as he surveyed the motley collection of villagers who constituted his audience. 'It gives me great pleasure to speak to you this evening so as to put your minds completely at rest. As you know, we were approached some time ago as a source of shingle for the new harbour defences at Plymouth. We have now grown accustomed to seeing the dredger moored in our harbour here, and it is thanks largely to its crew that we are now ahead of schedule.'

There were muffled cheers from the crew members.

'Thank you,' Latchley continued. 'This has supplied work for many of you who were not able to procure regular employment in the aftermath of the war. There has been a good working relationship with the dredger resulting in the digging of a deep water channel thus enabling the larger fishing vessels to use the harbour even at low tide.'

Shouts of 'Here, here' echoed from various parts of the hall.

'Thank you again.' he said modestly. 'However, we have had the unfortunate incident of the harbour wall collapsing.'

His voice took on a new seriousness and the occupants of the hall were hushed as he wallowed in sincerity. 'My immediate response was to contact His Majesty's Inspector, who had originally surveyed the shingle banks, and to discuss the possible repercussions on our community of dredging there. I have the findings in front of me.' He leaned forward and lifted up the contents of the file he had placed on the table. 'Mr Chairman, ladies and gentleman of Windle Bridge, His Majesty's Inspector states that the collapse of the harbour ...... and, I might add ...... the loss of some sand from neighbouring beaches ... ... appears to be one of those accidents of nature and has nothing whatsoever to do with the dredging.'

There were some subdued objections from one or two fishermen whom I had seen manning the barricade by the dredger, but otherwise the audience was eating out of Latchley's hand.

'Now legally, Latchley's Aggregates can continue to dredge for evermore, but that would be unfair, so this is what I intend to do. His Majesty's Inspector also states that the south flowing current will easily pull sand in from the north to replace the shingle loss. So with this in mind, we will cease dredging in two months ...... two months at the most ...... but before that, I intend to do something about the harbour.

We need a harbour wall, but until that can be done, I suggest that when the dredging is over, we do one last trip and deposit a few thousand tons of shingle as a temporary breakwater!'

There was louder applause this time, and Latchley was getting progressively more confident.

'My initial idea was to cease dredging immediately but by now you will know that a partner in the firm of Latchley Aggregates has appeared on the scene. I am attempting to buy up the rest of the shares so as to maintain the standards expected from this reputable company. Unfortunately, this new partner insists on receiving his share now, so the dredging has had to continue to meet these expenses. As you can see, the decision has therefore been taken out of my hands. Despite wanting to stop dredging, even though no connection has been established, it is with great reluctance that Latchley Aggregates had been forced to carry on.'

Heads turned and accusing eyes peered in my direction. Latchley obviously hadn't expected me to be there because he seemed to lose his composure somewhat when he saw the reason for the stirring in the audience. I knew it was pointless for me to jump up in protest at the string of lies, because by now, their minds had been cleverly and systematically poisoned against me anyway.

'Yes ...... er ...... in conclusion, Mr Chairman, ladies and gentlemen. You can rest assured that the harbour and village are safe, and that nothing will be done to make it otherwise.'

He was rewarded with restrained applause and much nodding of heads. I stood on tip-toe and spotted Gwenlyn with her father and Charlotte near the front. Charlotte was forever angling her head from left to right, flashing smiles at any young suitor who strayed within her line of vision.

'Thanks you Mr Latchley,' Peers Lofgren said getting to his feet. 'I am sure that we can all rely on your goodwill in this matter.

Now ...... most ...... or all of you will know Jabber. One of the senior members of our community. We know he lives his own life down the coast a little way, but he is still one of us.'

Jabber moved along to the table looking nervous. He had smartened up a little, but was still the unmistakeable hermit-cum-tramp who lived in a hut by the sea.

He looked up and mumbled something which provoked a response from the back of the hall. 'Speak up .... Can't hear you!'

So Jabber spoke up. 'Half me bloody beach has gone!' he shouted, and gained everyone's attention immediately. 'Now it strikes me that only thing round here what's changed is yon dredger! There's people lived here for hundreds of years or thereabouts; they didn't lose no beach ...... They didn't have no dredger!'

There were murmurs of approval from around the hall interrupted by a shout from one of the dredger crew who I recognised as Dan Bredan's brother.

'You've got no proof, old man!'

Jabber looked a bit confused, but quickly recovered. 'Maybe no proof, but what proof has this inspector person got? God is he? To tell what the tide does ...... where it goes ...... where the wind blows!'

His eyes suddenly opened wide with a flash of inspiration. 'I have got some proof!' He claimed. 'That storm we had recent like ...... Force eight or nine ......' The room fell silent; they were men of the sea and well used to the vagaries of storm and gale that besets any coastline, but they weren't expecting Jabber's next words. He spoke slowly and precisely, 'I 'Rode the Wild Wind!'

The place was in uproar in an instant; people shouting and waving their hands, clamouring to be heard. I couldn't see their faces, so in the confusion I slid round to the side of the hall so that I could at least view them from side on.

James Bardell was on his feet, and despite Gwenlyn trying to pull him back, was soon standing face to face with Jabber. 'That is expressly forbidden!' Bardell shouted above the mayhem. 'How could you! ..... How could you even contemplate doing such an insane thing?'

I looked at the faces of some of the young fishermen; too young to be wise, too young to know fear. I saw the sudden respect they now had for the old man who at times had probably been their subject of ridicule. A smile came over Jabber's face at the reaction he had caused and he launched into the next part of his speech.

'Rightly or wrongly, I 'Rode the Wind!' I done it before, I knew what it was like, but it were different this time. The wind's supposed to bring you straight across the banks, but not this time! The holes dug by yon dredger's made whirlpools that pulls your boat down! Three times I went down ...... Three times I popped up like a cork. The currents not bringing sand, it's letting them whirlpools pull the sand off the beach ...... I seen it meself ...... I didn't want to tell you all this because I doesn't want to see young lads doin' it. I knew I was wrong ...... but it's proved me point!'

For the first time in the proceedings Latchley looked worried. Lofgren was on his feet waving his arms to gain some semblance of order, but they paid scant attention to him. It was Jabber himself who managed to silence the noisy crowd. There was a hush as he began to speak again.

'There be no guarantee that the next storm won't sweep the rest of the harbour away: where would your living be then? No harbour! No fishing ...... I says we should stop the dredging now ..... before it's too late!'

There was loud applause this time, except for the dredger crew who I noticed were directly in front of me. In the commotion, to my surprise, I hadn't realised how far round the hall I had strayed.

Latchley moved up to the table again, looking angry, but controlling himself. 'How do we know this old man 'Rode the Wind?' he derided. 'Did anyone see him? ..... He's probably telling lies ...... there's no way he can prove anything.' It was Latchley's turn to have some inspiration as he paused to look at his father. 'Your boat's a two man boat ...... Yes, you can sail in calm water by yourself .... but you can't 'Ride the Wind' alone, it needs two, so you must be lying!'

James Bardell was looking round the gathered crowd when his eyes alighted on me and I saw his mouth drop open as he simply put two and two together.

As quickly as I could and without drawing attention to myself, I moved towards the door.

'So you can see, people of Windle Bridge that .....'

James Bardell broke in, 'Just a minute Jonathan.' he said firmly, not taking his eyes off me as I moved. 'Jabber, were you alone in that boat?'

Jabber didn't get time to speak.

'You weren't alone, were you? ..... Was a certain Major Kinsey with you?.....Did he set you up to do all this?'

'I ......I' stuttered Jabber.

'So I'm right!' Bardell snapped. 'This man comes to our village, a known murderer and disrupts our lives, then he tries this pattern of deceit ...... even influencing a helpless old man!'

I gave up trying to be cautious and barged my way the short distance to the door. The fishermen were still disorientated but the dredger crew knew what to do and promptly gave chase. I caught a glance from Gwenlyn out of the corner of my eye. She was pushing her way through the crowd but with being at the far end, she was a long way away.

I was first out of the door, knowing it was a waste of time reasoning with them. Jabber had said they were stubborn, but they were also headstrong. I wasn't fit enough for a long chase and they knew the streets better than I did. It was pointless running to the house because they would easily break in so I was left with no other options.

I sprinted across the road and without hesitation, dived headlong into the icy cold water and struck out for the middle of the harbour. They spilled quickly out of the fish hall but only two were brave enough to follow. I kept ahead of them by a few strokes until we were almost in the middle then to keep the initiative, I ducked under and circled back beneath the surface. With the loss of sand, even at low tide, the water was deep. I reached up with my arm and found a leg trailing through the water. I pulled down sharply and twisted round, and as I dragged him under, I jerked my head into his face. It was a dirty trick and I knew it, but it guaranteed that any aggressor would think twice before attempting another assault.

My other assailant had realised by now that I had come up behind them and disposed of his companion, but his movements were cumbersome, hampered by his heavy clothing. I took advantage of his handicap and kicked hard with my legs which lifted me out of the water a few, extra inches, enough to bring my fist round to catch him on the point of his nose. He took a sharp intake of breath and as he did so, I pushed him under. I held him there for ten seconds then let him come, coughing and spluttering, to the surface.

I let him alone to join his friend while I swam in the direction of the nearest boat moored in the harbour. My breathing was heavy with the exertion and my ribs hurt again. A number had produced torches and were shining them over the dark water and I could hear my two attackers being pulled out of the water while questions were fired at them as to my whereabouts.

I hid on the seaward side of one of the boats, but one brave individual had ventured onto the top of the collapsed part of the harbour wall and seen my head bobbing in the water.

'Over here!' he shouted.

I was about to move my position again when I heard something land in the water next to me. I looked across, horrified to see in the light of the torches, that he was throwing rocks at me. I dived under the boat, only to come up the other side in full view of the harbour wall and the dredger.

I thought of aiming for the open sea, but the man on the collapsed part of the wall was already being joined by others who showed no fear of wading into the water on top of the newly submerged rocks and cement. They hurled rocks at me, large and small, effectively blocking my way out.

I dived under again and swam to my right, only to be greeted with another shower of stones when I surfaced. I tried to the left next time, attempting to stay under for longer to confuse them. I bumped into a mooring line, which I held on to firmly and allowed myself to gently rise up where I slowly let out my breath. My mouth and nose were barely out of the water and I thought I had given them the slip.

I had failed to notice a few others who had moved around in anticipation of my movements and I let out an involuntary yell as a stone hit me on the back of the head, rapidly followed by others aimed in my direction. I had just enough time to get my bearings and observe that the harbour wall adjacent to the road was the part most in shadow. It was all of thirty yards, and right under their noses, but it might, just work. I dipped under the surface again and yanked off my shoes, then deliberately showed my whole head pointing in the direction of the open sea. A hail of rocks and stones hit the water but I ignored it and breathed deeply.

I took a stroke forwards to mislead them, then dived and twisted round to head back in the direction which, I hoped, would lead me into the shadows. I relaxed my body as much as I could to make the most of every stroke, but the wet clothes, while assisting in keeping me under the water, also slowed me down. Very soon, I could feel the blood pounding in my head but I still hadn't touched the wall that could spell safety.

I counted the strokes and vowed that I would do ten more, but each stroke was progressively shorter and less powerful than the last until I knew that I would have to go to the surface to breathe. I tried to let myself up slowly, but desperation for air denied any caution and I shot up hitting my head on an outcrop of rock. For a moment I inhaled seawater because I couldn't find the surface and I panicked until I tilted my head back and breathed in life giving, fresh air.

I seemed to be in some sort of air pocket, presumably actually underneath the harbour wall itself. It was several yards from front to back and extended at least as far as my arms and legs would stretch from side to side. There was about three inches of air between the surface of the water and what I assumed to be the foundations of the road and buildings above, but sufficient to keep me alive. The salt water was irritating my eyes and nose but I had to be content to stay where I was for as long as I possibly could.

It was, of course, pitch black and I had no way of knowing how long I had been there, or how long I could stay. I did know, however, that the water was extremely cold and that I wouldn't be able to stay too long without losing all my body heat. No sound penetrated through to my prison so I didn't know what was happening around the harbour. I hoped that they would all calm down and disperse, but I had no way of knowing if, or when they would. I kept moving my arms and legs rhythmically to keep the blood flowing, but after a short time it became too much of an effort and my thinking began to go sluggish.

I came to the hasty conclusion that I couldn't actually afford to wait any longer as my body was slowing down so much that it wouldn't do my bidding. I took a deep breath and ducked under the overhang which I presumed would reconnect me with the rest of the harbour. I had to go down three or four feet before I managed to get underneath, and was amazed that I had succeeded in swimming so deep and for so long to escape from the rock throwers.

I emerged in the shadow of the harbour wall next to the road, and although I couldn't see if there was anyone directly above me, the other two sides of the harbour were empty. I pushed myself along the side of the wall making as little noise as possible. The dredger sat silent in the darkness and I thought that the best way out would be to use one of the access ladders that were scattered round the harbour, two of which were hidden behind the dredger.

By this time I could see that the whole harbour was deserted, though there was considerable noise from the two pubs. I kicked one of the iron ladders with my foot, and even though I could hardly see where I was going, I laboriously began to pull myself out. It was almost impossible to grip with my hands as they were so cold, and my legs were slow and heavy, but I got clear of the water and paused to rest.

It was only then that I realised the consequences of what I had discovered when I had accidently found my hiding place. By the look of it, the sea had done massive damage way beyond what I or Jabber had dreamt of. Not only had much of the harbour itself been washed away, but the harbour wall next to the road, and possibly all the sea defences themselves, had been undermined. Not only that, but even in my sluggish state I remembered that every time the dredger came into the harbour it had dug a channel to cope with its draught. This was supposedly to help the bigger fishing boats as well, but it was likely that all it was doing was further reducing the stability of the foundations of the harbour, and even perhaps, the whole village. The implications were catastrophic; the road itself would be a veritable death trap and it was anyone's guess as to what might have already happened to the foundations of other roads and buildings in the village. Windle Bridge was like so many other places around the coast which relied heavily upon good access to the sea, being long and narrow, with steep streets reaching precariously back up the hillside.

Realisation spurred me on and I pulled myself up the remainder of the ladder, but it wasn't until I got to the top and poked my head up over the level of the harbour that I discovered that I wasn't alone.

'I thought I'd find you here,' came the quiet voice. 'If I waited long enough I knew you'd come up somewhere secretly ...... You army types are all the same. Mind you, you had me worried there ... ... I thought you might have got away.'

I thought about jumping back into the water, but my body was cold and weak and all my movements were pitifully slow. Instead I was forced to let Jonathan Latchley drag me numbingly and painfully up the final steps and onto the harbour wall.

Chapter 12

'Onto the dredger, now!' Latchley ordered, grabbing me by the arm and steering me up the walkway and onto the deck. I was too cold, too stiff and too despondent to offer any resistance. He kept a careful watch over the houses along the waterfront to check if anyone had noticed us, but the village had receded into its usual late evening inactivity.

The dredger was larger than I had at first thought, and I briefly entertained the idea of making a break for it, but my legs were hardly able to hold me up, never mind allow me to run. My feet seemed to catch every protrusion on the dark deck of the boat, but they were so numb that even though I was wearing no shoes, I felt no pain. He pulled open a door which moved noiselessly on well-oiled hinges and, on entering, directed me to the left along a short passageway. We turned a corner which led into a blind alley with four doors, one of which was marked 'Captain.' He ignored that and opened the door next to it which gave access into a small, but well fitted cabin with bunk beds, a table, two chairs and a small wardrobe. He ordered me to sit down on one of the chairs, then sat himself down opposite me.

We looked at each other, the winner and the loser, and not surprisingly, he smiled. 'I would never have thought it!' he said emphatically. 'It said on your military report that you were stubborn

..... Stubborn!.....That's not the word for it! I respect you, Major Kinsey ...... and I regret that I've had to employ such demeaning tactics. I think I should have been more gentle that first day when you came into my office. We could have worked hand in hand ...... But you see ... ... I'm stubborn too! Nevertheless, I would like to shake your hand as the only person who ever came up against me without giving in ...... Well, not quite the only person ...... There was the situation at Kingsbridge of course, but this is slightly different, don't you think?'

I didn't offer my hand, but he reached across anyway, giving it a firm shake.

'My good man! But you're freezing!'

He got up and went over to the wardrobe, stopped, went to the door and locked it and placed the key in his pocket and went back to the wardrobe again. 'Can't be too careful can we?' he said, keeping one eye on me while he reached inside and produced a blanket which he gave me. I would have removed my clothes but my fingers could hardly move by now, but I managed to get the blanket round my shoulders and started the long process of warming up.

'Better?' he enquired.

I nodded.

'Good!'

He produced a large bottle of brandy from inside the wardrobe and responded to my unspoken questions.

'Not to worry, Major ...... My own, personal cabin ...... not that I use it much, but I keep it here for emergencies ...... such as now! We have a lot to discuss, and a lot on which to agree, so a drop of the hard stuff should help us on our way. The brain is probably as cold and numb as feet and fingers......Yes?'

I nodded again.

'In that case ......' he put down two glasses. 'Let's get down to some serious business.'

The first glass was like nectar after tasting nothing but salt water over the last hour. The second glass warmed my stomach and reminded me how little alcohol I had taken since my theology student days in London. He watched me drink, topped up my glass, then had one himself.

'You're an interesting man, Kinsey; stubborn, like I said, but interesting. We could have worked well together you know, but so be it, this is how we are. The question is ...... the future? So, what about it?'

I started to speak, but my face and lips were so numb that the words came out in an unintelligible jumble. I stretched my mouth wide, pushing my tongue against my cheeks and pulling my lips in and out then took another mouthful of brandy, I swilled it round my mouth and swallowed it with a gulp.

'Open ...... Open to suggestions,' I stammered eventually.

'Good, that's good,' he replied, refilling my glass. 'Slight problem though, I offered you ten thousand, but, alas, you discovered a certain hindrance in Kingsbridge. Now it's cost me a pound or two to sort that little one out. Unfortunately, that means I can't find any money to buy you out ...... Another drink?'

I sipped at the glassful, shivering intermittently. I was beginning to feel very drowsy and yearned for a nice, warm bed. He took a sip from his glass and topped up mine again.

'So what now?' I said sleepily.

'What now?' he frowned. 'Now that's a good question. Easily answered as well. Basically, I need to finish the dredging, otherwise

I'm out of pocket. You discovered the quarries have been sold, a necessity when you're trying to keep someone quiet. Rather an embarrassing situation, having to race over to Kingsbridge every week, especially when greed sets in. Hence …… the dredging, a final payment …… all the paperwork done …… then, damn it, you come along.'

'What difference do I make?' I asked even more wearily.

'My……my, we are slow aren't we. Obvious, I would have thought! Invest everything in the dredging, one million tons of shingle at a good price …… at a very good price, and everything is sorted! Then along comes our Major Kinsey and does his best to stop me, and him a partner in the firm as well! And that's the problem you see, no dredging; no payment on delivery. No payment on delivery; no pay-off for Kingsbridge …… no money in the bank …… no money to reinvest to buy back into quarrying, no Latchley Aggregates and no Jonathan Latchley. Simple enough for a military mind to work out I would have thought.'

'You forget,' I murmured. 'That swimming around in a cold sea rather numbs the brain …… I don't suppose Jabber owns any of your seventy percent does he?'

He leaned back in his chair and let out a jocular laugh which echoed round the small cabin. 'Jabber! Damn silly fool. No, signed it over to me. Never could face up to reality, too much of a dreamer. Mind you, I'm impressed with you, Kinsey, 'Riding the Wild Wind!' That's the ambition of every young man in the village! They lie in bed at night you know, just dreaming of the homage they would get …… if they survived that is! Then along comes an outsider, and an army man at that; not even a sailor, and does it! I'm impressed! ....really impressed! A toast! To Kinsey and Jabber, sailors on the high seas …… against the elements ...... the victors!'

We touched glasses and I swigged down another glassful and screwed my eyes up with the sting of the taste. I had nothing left to lose I thought, no ten thousand now, but at least I could drink a good bottle of his spirits. He leaned across the table, excitement in his eyes.

'Tell me; what was it like? When we were kids, we heard all about it. Jabber told me about it when he did it with Tom, but I never really believed what it was like.'

'I ...... It was ...' I belched loudly and felt nauseous. 'It was hell ...... Sheer Hell! An adventure, and I ...... we ...... should have known better. I was the damn, silly fool not him ...... or not just him ......like you say, I'm army not navy; fools go in where angels fear, and all that. I had no idea what it was going to be like!

As for those whirlpools! If you want to be in a small boat with twenty foot of water above you, twisting you round and tossing you about like a bit of matchwood ...... if you enjoy that sort of thing, fine, you do it! If I'd known, I wouldn't have gone anywhere near ...... and if Gwenlyn hadn't ......'

'Gwenlyn!' he shouted. 'What was she doing there?'

'She fished us out.' I said, wishing I'd kept her well out of it, aware, too late, that my brain was functioning very slowly.

'She wasn't in the boat with you? She didn't ride with you?' he asked, alarmed.

'No,' I said, and he looked relieved. 'She was waiting. She knew we were going to do it, so she waited and when we came in, Jabber was half drowned and I wasn't much better. She pulled us onto the beach. Never again! Sheer hell! ...... and it means a lot for an army man to say that! Give me dry land any day!'

He lifted the bottle to pour me another drink but saw that I hadn't finished the last glassful, so I obliged and he filled it up again.

'You're trying …… You're trying to get me …… get me drunk,' I said woozily, my eyes closing.

'There's no denying it,' he replied. 'I'd rather deal with you weak, wet and drunk than stone, cold sober any day! Those two gentlemen who went for a swim with you just now, won't be at work for ages, so, yes, I'm trying to get you drunk.

'Ha!.....Then tell me why?' I said, slumping onto the table.

'Why?' he asked. 'Well, you're not a very reasonable man when you're sober, so, we'll see if you're reasonable when you're not. I want you to go away …… and stay away. Don't come back in other words.'

'And …… and why should I?' I slurred. 'Why should I indeed?' I could feel my eyes closing with sleep but succeeded in grabbing the glass and knocking back its contents. 'Why should I …… indeed?'

Latchley leaned forwards to where my head was resting on my arms and whispered into my ear. 'Because if you don't …… Then I'll hurt Gwenlyn!'

It took a while for the words to sink in, but when they did, I sat bolt upright, feeling my head spin round and my eyes go in and out of focus. I squeezed my eyes tightly shut and opened them again, but Latchley was just a blur in my vision.

'Did you hear me?' he said, louder this time. 'If you don't leave, I'll hurt Gwenlyn!'

I coughed and tried to speak, but my mouth had gone dry, so I took a swig straight from the bottle and as an afterthought, tried to use it as a weapon. I swung it round aiming for Latchley's head. Either he was quick, or I was slow, but in any case, I missed completely, slipped off the chair and fell onto the floor.

He bent over me and removed the bottle from my grasp before lifting me up and dumping me on one of the bunks. 'You heard me! You leave, or Gwenlyn gets hurt!'

'H ….. H ….. How' I stuttered, 'if you're …… you're supposed …. supposed to get married. Why, on earth, would you want to hurt her?'

He replaced the top on the bottle and put it, and the remains of its contents back in the wardrobe. 'Because, my dear fellow, she doesn't want me, she wants you! But if you're out of the way she might want me again. But if you stay I'll make sure she's not worth having ….. !'

He stopped and looked knowingly at me, 'But I don't think you'll go away, will you?'

'Eh?' I replied, on the border of consciousness.

'You won't go away,' he said, more to himself. 'Not even if I persuaded you. You're stubborn, like me. You'd come back eventually, unless I could make you go away for good.' His eyes lit up. 'Now there's a thought!'

He looked very pensive, mumbling away to himself. Finally, to signify the making of a decision, he stretched up to his full height and pointed a finger at me. 'I have it, Major!' he exclaimed. 'I shall return soon!'

He left me in drunken slumber on the bunk, but appeared again soon afterwards. I was half awake, half asleep, but even so, he approached with great caution. He had some thin, but strong rope with him and used it to tie my wrists to one end of the bunk and my ankles to the other. He supplemented the rope with some fishing line which he pulled tight so that it dug into my flesh. To finish off, he tied a noose around my neck connected to a cord which stretched to both ends of

211

the bed. To demonstrate, he rolled my body a few inches and I felt the noose tighten.

'You're probably wondering how I learnt to do that aren't you?' he said. I wasn't, but I knew he'd tell me anyway. 'Up on the moors, when we were children,' he continued, straightening up to admire his handiwork. 'we used to snare rabbits and foxes ...... learnt lots of rope tricks there. You will notice that if you try to struggle, you will only do yourself an injury ...... so my advice to you is to stay exactly where you are ...... I'll come back early tomorrow morning, before the crew arrives of course, and then I'll carry on!'

As a parting gesture he threw the blanket over me, presumably so that I wouldn't shiver myself into a choking position. I certainly didn't think it was for the good of my health. He switched the lights out and locked the door, leaving me in complete blackness and unwilling to move. I tried a gentle tug on the leg but felt the rope tightening round my neck. The same applied when I pulled my arms so I had to be content to lie there and speculate on what tomorrow would bring. I tried moving my body as slowly as I could so as to get some degree of comfort, but it was impossible. Every time I moved, I felt the pull on my neck; ironic that so recently, I had been trying to do the same thing to myself, but now, for once, I had something ...... someone to live for.

The hours passed by in slow torture with my arms and legs going into cramp but knowing I could do nothing about it. I tried screaming at one point, partly as a tension relief, and partly because I thought it might attract someone's attention, but being deep in the bowels of the ship, I suspected that I was well and truly isolated.

As the effects of the brandy wore off, I found myself thinking more clearly, but it only left me wishing that I could get my hands on the bottle again to blot out reality. I longed for Latchley's return so that

I could be freed and more or less agree to anything he said. The thought of Gwenlyn being hurt in any way was unbearable, but I didn't know whether I had it in me just to walk away.

I heard a key turn in the lock, but hopes of it being anyone else were dashed when Latchley, very tentatively, leaned through the door and turned on the light.

'Caution's the word,' he said as he stepped into the room. He carried a small pistol in his hand which he held clumsily, unused to its feel.

'Where did you get that?' I demanded.

'Ah! The Major has sobered up! If you must know, I found it on Slapton Sands. I went over there before they did the final clearance after practicing the Normandy landings. Never knew I might need it. It works. I tried it once …… just one bullet. Definitely works, though I'm not used to using this sort of thing …… unlike you of course …… second nature to you, I suppose?'

I twisted my head round to see him better, but felt the rope tighten round my neck. He looked as if he hadn't slept either. 'All right. What are you going to do now?' I didn't expect him to use the gun, that was more of an insurance measure than anything else. I'd thought overnight that he would come with an ultimatum to force me to leave the village, together with various threats to ensure I didn't return. His answer, when it came, sent shivers down my spine.

'I've been thinking. The idea came last night. You dived into the sea …… right? You were pelted with stones and then disappeared. Now, as far as everyone else is concerned, you either got away …… or you drowned. No one has found your body …… yet! But they will! Quite convenient you climbing up that ladder out of the water last night!'

In a mixture of fear and panic, I impulsively kicked my legs hard and pulled my arms rolling over at the same time ...... It was a spur of the moment bluff ...... and to some extent it worked, though he was slow in coming over and I could already feel myself blacking out.

'Bloody fool!' he shouted as he pulled the rope away from my neck. 'There mustn't be any marks!'

It was bliss just being able to turn a little and move my cramped legs and numb body. 'What now?' I tried. 'You've had your little game, now let me go ...... you can't expect to get away with this, it's murder! That's not your style.'

He looked down at me, keeping a respectable distance just in case I had any further tricks to play. 'Not my style!' he replied. 'My style is to get things sorted out! To get answers ! This is exactly my style! With you out of the way, there's no-one to stir things up is there? Jabber would never do it by himself, you would never go away, not even if I asked politely ...... so all I need is to arrange an accident. As far as the village is concerned you're already dead ...... drowned ..... so it makes things easier for me.'

I could feel a cold sweat breaking out all over my body. 'All right, I'll go away ...... wherever you want. My honour as a soldier never to come back!'

He smiled. 'Say that again, Major.....I love to see you grovel.'

I stayed quiet.

'Say it again, Major!' he shouted. 'I want to see you grovelling!'

'I said I'd go away ...... Now let me go. We can forget this ever happened. I'll give you my share ...... I don't want anything.'

He shook his head slowly and came a step closer. 'No deal, Kinsey...... my way, I can guarantee you'll never come back.'

214

He raised his gun and checked the safety catch. I felt certain he wouldn't shoot me, that would be anything but an accident, then I realised that he'd put the catch in the on position. He leaned over the bunk and took a swipe at my head using the gun as a club, but I saw him coming and tilted my head backwards quickly. It caught me on the cheek causing excruciating pain and while I recovered, he grabbed my hair and while holding my head immobile he lifted his arm, hardly giving me time to yell before the butt came down and knocked me out cold.

*****

When I came to, I could hear noise all around me. I seemed to be in some sort of cage. My head was pounding and I felt acute pain when I tried to move my neck. I could see daylight but couldn't see where it was coming from, and then the cage started to move. There was thick, iron mesh over my head which appeared to be fixed in position while the cage moved underneath it. I was in some sort of metal container about six feet across and four or five feet wide and the same distance high. I looked around, waiting for the movement to stop so that I could get my bearings and, hopefully, regain full consciousness. I sat back on the cold surface and massaged the back of my neck. The ropes and fishing line were gone and I was free to move, but there was no way out of the cage.

There was a sudden jolt and the cage twisted over to a slightly different angle and I was able to catch a glimpse of a murky grey sky through the mesh. The noise grew louder and I looked around for clues as to where I was. The cage jolted again and I got a sensation of falling while the mesh moved more quickly over my head.

Another small impact propelled me backwards, thrusting my already bruised and aching body against the cold, hard steel. The shock was enough to alert my senses to the sickening realisation that I was imprisoned in one of the huge buckets that went under the surface and dredged up shingle from the bottom of the sea.

In an instant I was tearing frantically at the wire mesh, shouting and yelling at the top of my voice. I span round, frantically searching for a way out, but I was sealed tightly into my tomb. The mechanism was slow and laborious and I knew that the time would soon come when the bucket I was in would be plunged under the surface and dragged along the bottom of the sea, compressing me under a couple of tons of suffocating shingle.

I felt a change in the angle of the bucket so I braced myself and waited for the inevitable. I had to face it, this time, there was no way out! It wasn't as if I could sit down at my leisure and come up with some carefully constructed plan, as there was only seconds to go. There was simply a grim resignation that this was the end. The only glimmer of hope I had was that occasionally; very occasionally, people had been buried alive and lived to tell the tale. With that faintest of hope in mind, I shielded my face with my hands but left my eyes open so as to be able to breathe until the very last moment.

The bucket tipped and the sound of the engine powering the drive chain crescendoed to a deafening roar. I was plunged into total blackness and before I knew it, water was pouring into the bucket and I was submerged. I kept my legs and feet well away from the sharp edge, but I could feel the vibrations as the bucket dug into the shingle. It was like being hit in the chest with a battering ram. A vice like force clamped my arms and legs, crushing my body and moulding me into a contorted, dying figurine. As the dredger dug deeper I could feel what little air I had in my lungs being squeezed out of me. It seemed like an eternity and I knew that my lungs wouldn't hold out for much longer. I began counting, knowing that I could perhaps hold my breath for a minute and a half, maybe two, but certainly no longer before I would be forced to succumb.

I felt a sudden jarring and the bucket stopped! ..... I couldn't believe it! I was buried under the water and the machinery had come to a halt! I had counted to sixty by now and could feel myself weakening. The machinery started up again, but I was almost beyond caring. Visions passed before my brain, from childhood, to army days, memories of running through the heather in the Peak District, the freedom and the fears, the nightmares and the rare moments of happiness, all doomed to end as a murder victim off the coast of a Devonshire village.

The bucket began to shake more and more and I felt the whole thing tipping forward, there was a noise like a thunderclap and then I was falling. I was semi-conscious and I couldn't figure out what was happening, but the shock was such that I inhaled a mixture of sand, air and water. There was no opportunity to do anything else before I landed flat on my back with all the wind knocked out of me.

I waved my arms around wildly, managing to scramble onto my side, then something hit me, like a sledgehammer in my back. I opened my eyes and just caught sight of movement above me. I had travelled under the boat, and the bucket in which Latchley had dumped me had eventually tipped over and emptied into the hold of the boat. I had then fallen twenty feet or so onto the pile of shingle that was building up ready to be transferred to the barges.

A further sledgehammer blow hit and stunned me as yet another bucketful of shingle was piled on top. I knew that unless I moved

217

quickly, having escaped drowning, I would be entombed under hundreds of tons of shingle. I pushed with my legs, trying to pivot round but it was like being in quicksand, so I resorted temporarily to pulling some of the shingle away from my face to try and get a view of what was happening, but it was of little use.

I did discover, however, that by pulling my knees up and rapidly straightening them, I could at least move, so I pushed with my legs and pulled down with my arms, almost like swimming, but the more I tried, the more the shingle was piling up on top of me. It was getting progressively more difficult to breathe and I knew that as my strength failed, the weight above would only seem greater and greater.

I decided on one, last, almighty effort, a do or die attempt! I forced the legs down, then up again, like pistons against the resistance of the shingle, each time stretching my arms up above me. Finally, I pushed my hand into fresh air and with a superhuman extension of my legs, my head reached above the surface of the shingle, only to be smothered again by the next load. I pushed again, succeeded in freeing my arms, then wriggled like an eel to free the rest of my body.

Looking up, I saw the never ending conveyor belt of buckets continuing to steadily dump their loads on top of me, so in anticipation of the next one coming, I swivelled rapidly out of the way only to crash violently against the side of the hold.

The big question then was where to go next? I couldn't keep digging myself out, and a quick look around showed that there was no-one about to help me. The only way out therefore, was up, so I stretched with my arms and grasped onto the top edge of the hold and despite being showered with shingle, I levered myself up and over.

There was only a thin edge between the top of the hold and the side of the dredger and my tired arms hadn't got enough strength left to hold me. I had no alternative but to fall overboard and into the water below, where I landed awkwardly and yet again, had the wind knocked out of me.

When I surfaced I could touch the dredger on my left but could also see the moving bulk of another boat very close by. One of the barges that was being used to transfer the shingle to Plymouth was drawing alongside to accept its first load, but in the process was going to crush me against the side. I knew it to be empty, and therefore of shallow draught, so took a chance and dived down underneath it before I was squashed.

I plunged as deep as possible, feeling the movement of the water above me as the barge sailed over my head as I feverishly swam forward to get to the other side. I kept going until my breath was nearly out then took three strokes to reach the surface and was relieved when I gulped in fresh air. The barge towered above me just a few feet away, where it had come to rest next to the dredger.

It took a minute or two before I regained my breath and had the energy to swim along the side of the barge and look for help. It was a valuable few minutes as the relief of survival passed into the reality of weighing up what to do next. It was too far to swim for shore, especially in my battered state, but neither did I want anyone, in particular Jonathan Latchley, to know that I was still alive. If he ever did find out that I had survived he would quite possibly harm Gwenlyn, but as long as I was supposedly dead, she was safe, and so was I.

The decision was taken from me as a face appeared looking over the side of the barge. I was too conspicuous not to be seen, but fortunately he was so taken aback that he didn't immediately shout out. He was smartly dressed, and obviously not a sailor and I blinked a few times to clear my eyes of salt water before I saw that it was Nicholas

Faversham. We recognised each other at about the same time and he was about to call out when I raised a finger to my lips. I swam as close as I could, then trod water while I spoke to him.

'Don't tell anyone I'm here,' I ordered as loud as I dared. He looked even more puzzled. 'Can you get me on board without anyone seeing?'

He nodded and gestured for me to swim towards the stern of the barge while he casually walked back himself, occasionally glancing over the side to check my progress. I got dangerously close to the idling propellers before I saw a rope being dropped over the side of the barge. I clasped it between my fingers then began the painful process of climbing up using arms and legs that had very little power left in them.

I got to the top but didn't show my head. I could see Faversham's back and hear him talking to someone across the other side of the deck. The weight of my body was nearly pulling my arms out of their sockets, but I had to hold on. Faversham put an arm behind his back and waved me up so I threw myself over the top and landed on a convenient tarpaulin. He reached down, tossed a corner of it over my prostrate body and whispered the command that I should stay still and not move at any cost, so I did exactly as he said.

It seemed a long time before anything happened but I felt an increase in engine revs and eventually the rise and fall of the swell of the open sea and a few minutes later, Faversham's voice.

'I don't know what's going on,' he said mystified. 'Are you in some sort of trouble?' His voice sounded muffled and a long way off from my position concealed under the tarpaulin.

'Trouble ….. !' I replied. 'That's not the half of it! I need to get off secretly at Plymouth …… no one to see me, is it ……'

He gave me a hard kick which immediately shut me up, and then sat down heavily on top of me. I heard the sound of approaching footsteps which seemed to stop right next to me. I wondered why Faversham was on the barge in the first place and thought that I would ask him later, meanwhile I wished the member of the crew, whoever they were, would go away and let me get comfortable.

'Morning,' I heard Faversham say. The reply was a long time coming and when it did, my heart skipped a beat.

'Nicholas, my dear fellow,' Jonathan Latchley said evenly. 'Do you always talk to yourself like that, or is this some new habit of yours?'

Chapter 13

I held my breath, not daring to move, while Faversham and Latchley continued their conversation. I felt my legs seizing up from all my exertions, plus my arms were pinned down with Faversham's weight. The talking ceased, but it was some time before Faversham was able to change position and give me the all clear to stretch my limbs.

'Okay, you can move, but slowly and don't show yourself. Be ready to jump over the side when I give the word. Use the rope again. We stop at a wharf for unloading, but there's a low jetty over your side. Do you know where the Plymouth office is?'

'No,' I replied.

'Citadel Road. The other side of the Hoe, but don't meet me there. Mr Latchley will probably go back with the barge on its return trip, but I'll make sure first. Stay hidden until you see me walk into the office, it's about half way along …… There's someone coming …… I'll give you a kick when it's time to jump.

'Thanks a bunch!' I thought to myself. Everybody seemed to be wanting to kick me, but I stayed still anyway, and waited for my cue.

The kick, when it came, wasn't too hard, so I poked my head out from under the tarpaulin and had the briefest of looks before I snatched the rope and launched myself over the side. True to his word, there was a small jetty with light commercial craft moored on the other side. I guessed that this was the biggest craft that the wharf would normally accommodate, as there was only just enough room for the barge to fit in.

I landed safely and let my eyes adjust to the morning sunlight, then walked briskly away from the barge without looking back. Once on the Hoe itself, I asked someone the time and was surprised to find that it was still morning. I had forgotten that Latchley had said that they were going to fit in another trip each day, so they were obviously starting earlier in the mornings.

I waited out of sight, close to the office, and Faversham appeared half an hour later. He went into the office and I crossed the road to join him but he was out again in barely a minute and hustled me down the road.

'Mr Latchley is going back straightaway. He doesn't travel on the barge very often because he sometimes gets a bit seasick, but he likes to keep a check on the crew occasionally. He may call briefly at the office, so we won't take any chances ...... You look awful, Mr Kinsey.'

He looked me up and down, taking in my bedraggled clothing and unshaven face.

'Thanks for the compliment,' I said, 'I don't always look this good early in the morning!' I assured him.

'Early!' he exclaimed. 'I've done half a days work by now!'

'An extra trip a day ...... Is that right?' I asked.

'Yes. For two months ...... only small bonuses ...... but for the crews, not for me! Part of my job I'm told, but it has its advantages.'

'But I thought you were the office type.' I stated. 'Not one of the seafaring boys.'

224

He looked around as if to make sure no-one on the street was eavesdropping. 'It's Charlotte really. Sometimes I get to see her. I take my binoculars. I check on the lads on the dredger, that's my first priority, but sometimes I get to see her: from a long way off, of course ...... Shall we have coffee somewhere? ...... I'll treat'

I raised my eyebrows at the boy's innocence.

'We've met in Dartmouth.' he continued. 'And she's been over to Plymouth ...... One of the dredger lads passes messages.'

I smiled at him. Innocence was probably the wrong word. 'What about Peta ...... Peta Lofgren?' I ventured.

'Here ...... I've tried this place before, we can sit by the window ...... Peta?' A frown came over his face. 'Yes ...... Peta ...... I don't know, she won't say. She's had a bit of a sheltered life really ...... of course she knows all the local lads; grew up with them, I mean, you have to in a small place like that. I thinks she likes to get away ...... mix with someone who's seen the world a bit ...... been around ...... I know that sounds awfully arrogant, but I think she prefers a bit of sophistication.'

I bit my tongue, smiled, and rapidly changed the subject. 'You escaped all right from my house that night, did you?' I asked with a touch of sarcasm in my voice.

He blushed. 'Ah ......Yes ......Two coffees please.' he said, thankful for the waiter's brief intervention. 'I, er ...... I suppose I should thank you for that ...... but I heard that you sorted them out! You weren't hurt yourself were you? ..... Not too bad anyhow ..... you look all right; I mean, I know I said you looked awful, but I meant that you seem to be all right ..... but you look ...... well you just look as if you need a bath and a shave.'

I rescued him from his embarrassment. 'Don't worry ...... You've made up for it by saving my neck on the barge.'

He seemed relieved but then looked me up and down again, as did the waiter when he brought the two coffees to our table. 'I must admit that I'm a bit confused. Why the morning swim? Why all the secrecy? I only get things second hand and I don't go on the barge everyday, so I don't know everything that goes on.'

I sipped the coffee, which tasted much better than Jabber's evil brew and would probably cost Nicholas Faversham an arm and a leg. 'You'd never believe me,' I said.

'Try me and see.'

'Mr Jonathan Latchley tried to kill me!'

He paused with the small cup halfway from table to mouth, 'You're right! I don't believe you!'

'There you are!' I continued. 'If you don't believe me the police certainly won't! I was supposed to have drowned yesterday, so how could Latchley kill me if I'm already dead. And of course, there's no witnesses ...... no evidence ...... his word against mine. He wants me out of the way because I've suggested that the dredging is causing the harbour and the village to be undermined.'

He was pensive. 'Yes ..... I saw the harbour wall ...... but that was just a fluke of nature, that's what the inspector said. Or that's what Mr Latchley told me the inspector said anyway.'

'True enough.' I commented. 'But what is said to be happening and what is really happening are two different things! But I swam under the harbour ...... you know: the main wall by the road.' He gave me a strange look. 'I know ...... It's a long story. Suffice to say that I was using the water as an escape route and thought I was swimming back

226

underwater to the harbour wall ...... and found myself underneath it! The foundations have been sucked away ...... or fallen away ...... whatever, it doesn't matter, but there's little there supporting the harbour ...... or the road ...... or the edge of the village for that matter! Another bad storm ...... and remember there's no seaward breakwater with that part of the harbour gone ...... In other words, it's one, simple recipe for disaster!'

He finished off his coffee and his boyish face did its best to look wise and mature. 'What about approaching Peers Lofgren?' he suggested, then screwed up his nose. 'Perhaps not! Neither of us are doing very well with that family are we? ..... Mr Bardell? ..... No! Same applies ..... the inspector?'

I shook my head.

'But maybe worth a try though?' he hinted half-heartedly.

'Don't think so,' I said doubtfully. 'I believe our inspector enjoys a little financial help from Mr Latchley.'

'Coast Guard perhaps?' he tried hopefully.

I shook my head again slowly. 'Doubt it ...... doubt it very much ...... and even then it would be a long wait. It was low tide when I found it ...... they'd need divers. No-one in their right mind would go down there of their own accord.'

He rested his head on his hands and stared out of the window. The waiter came with bill and I had to nudge him out of his contemplative frame of mind for him to pay up.

'I suppose we could ...... no, that wouldn't work.'

'What wouldn't?' I asked.

'It depends what you ...... we ...... are trying to do. I might find myself out of a job here. Are you ...... are we ...... just trying to stop the dredging? If so; then no barges; no dredging ...... no, that wouldn't work either ...... maybe for a day, but no longer than that. No dredger perhaps ...... but that's more difficult than no barges! You say you've got no-one in the village, no-one with influence?'

'Afraid not,' I concurred. 'No influence now anyway ...... Jabber? Do you know Jabber?'

He nodded hid head. 'Not actually know him; heard of him ...... hermit ...... tramp, something like that. But what's he got to do with it?'

'Jonathan Latchley's father,' I stated.

Faversham looked surprised and lifted his head off his hands. 'Father? .....' he looked around him. 'We'd better move ..... someone wants this table.'

We walked outside into the sunlight but turned in the opposite direction to the office.

'Father!' he declared. 'You do surprise me, Mr Kinsey. Not what I would have expected ...... But no influence now you say?'

'Not now.' I added sadly. 'We tried ...... he tried ...... but Latchley's got them pretty well conditioned. They more or less believe everything he says ...... even the fishermen, and it's their livelihood that's being messed up.'

We walked in silence for a while, trying to think of a way out of the dead-end.

'There is one idea,' he said thoughtfully, slowing down. 'If there was a way to discredit him ...... publicly ...... but there again?' He speeded up, but he'd set my brain going and it was my turn to slow down. He turned round to see where I'd got to and I gestured towards a seat that we'd walked past earlier.

'Mmm ...... that is an idea, you know,' I mumbled.

228

'But only an idea,' he replied. 'To discredit him ...... you have to have something with which to discredit him.'

'But there is!' I said excitedly, and told him about Kingsbridge.

His face lit up with surprise then dipped into a frown.

'I don't believe you,' he said flatly.

'What do you mean you don't believe me? I've just told you what I saw!'

'What I'm saying is, that I do believe you, but what will they think?' A child murderer who's caused no end of trouble! ..... That's the way they'll see it. He tells them about Mr Latchley, about Kingsbridge, so you all go off to Kingsbridge ...... What do you find? You find an empty house, no evidence of a pay-off ...... no nothing! Mr Kinsey is yet again the one to cause trouble ...... Mr Latchley laughs it off and you've got nowhere.'

'Unless .....!' I said.

'Unless what?'

'Unless I find where they moved to from Kingsbridge.'

'What good would that do?'

'Written proof .....?'

'Not enough!'

'Legal proof .....?'

'Possibly ...... Possibly. But first you have to find where they went to......and even then, they might not oblige.'

'Any better suggestions?' I asked

He sighed and shook his head.

'In that case,' I concluded. 'Thanks for the coffee ...... I'll head for Kingsbridge and start from there.'

229

I jumped to my feet with the thought of something positive to do at last, but Faversham stayed seated, giving me a puzzled frown.

'Why are you doing this?' he asked. 'Is it something personal between you and Mr Latchley? They haven't exactly welcomed you with open arms ...... the villagers that is ...... yet you've risked your neck for them, and now you're risking it again?'

I scratched my head. 'You'll probably think this is a bit melodramatic: but it's something I've got to do ...... I've got to right a few wrongs! God only knows the damage I've caused in the past; now this is the chance to straighten out a few things. There's Gwenlyn, Jabber .... and even a certain Nicholas Faversham ...... maybe others in the village ...... misled, misunderstood. There's some fools, some idiots of course, but basically decent people. For once, I want to save something, not destroy it. I don't like bullies ...... I don't like Jonathan Latchley ...... what he does, how he does it. I was a bully ...... maybe still am ...... That's ironic isn't it? I don't like bullies, yet I am one ... ... perhaps that implies that I don't even like myself, who knows? Anyway, the time has come for me to do something about it.'

I looked down at him and envied his youth and his innocence. I stuck out a hand and after a moment's hesitation he tentatively shook it, not looking quite so naïve as when we'd first met.

'I must be going,' I said finally. 'Once again, thank you for your help this morning.'

'A pleasure,' he said rising to his feet. 'Any time.'

'By the way,' I added as an afterthought. 'What happened to your predecessor? I meant to ask you before, but never had the chance.'

'Ah! Yes. Mr Latchley mentioned him once, come to think of it. Told me he'd got a bit too inquisitive for his own good. I was to get on with my work and not ask too many questions, otherwise I'd get the sack as well. It never occurred to me that anything funny might be going on. Still, you live and learn, don't you?'

I nodded my agreement. 'One final thing,' I said while looking down at my feet. 'Could I possibly borrow a pair of shoes?'

Five minutes later, I set off for Kingsbridge.

*****

I got a lift in the back of a lorry. It was open topped, and by the time I got to Kingsbridge I was freezing cold. A brisk walk to the house warmed me up but it came as no surprise to find that it was empty.

Over the next hour I spoke to the neighbours, the post office and the agents handling the sale of the property. The neighbours said that they had hardly had any contact and so no friendships had been built up. The post office knew nothing of any forwarding address. Anyone interested in buying the house was to be put in contact with Jonathan Latchley as he was handling the finances of the sale. It had been necessary to tell a different story each time, so I hoped Latchley wouldn't be told anything especially from the agents for the sale. They all eyed me with suspicion, and on looking at my unkempt appearance, it was obvious why.

I had nowhere to go, so I hitched another lift to Windle Bridge. I needed a bath, a shave, more clothes, some food and some money. It was still broad daylight when I got there later in the afternoon, and although I was pleased at the quick travel, I didn't want to just hang around until it was dark so as to creep in unnoticed. In the end I decided to kill some time and go and see Jabber. I gave the village a wide berth and joined the cliff path further south.

It was twilight when I got there but to my dismay, his hut had gone. I looked around, relieved to find that his boat was still there, pulled well up above the new high water mark. There were a few old bits and pieces lying around to show where the hut had once been, but no sign of anything else.

It wasn't until I smelt strong coffee wafting in the wind that I knew he was still there somewhere. I retraced my steps to the path and walked further along and was rewarded to find that the rebuilt, ramshackle, corrugated hut was now nestling on a broad ledge well up from the beach. I worked my way round and found a newly worn path in the undergrowth and without invitation, I poked my head through the door.

The look on Jabber's face was one to be savoured and I was glad he wasn't of weak disposition. I smiled to demonstrate that I wasn't a ghost, then stepped inside to shut out the cold.

'Well I'll be ......!' he exclaimed. 'They've been announcing you dead all day!' He shook his head in disbelief. 'I was thinking to meself ...... that's it, no more Alexander Kinsey ..... Ha! ..... My, but you're a rum'un laddie, that you are!'

I sat down on the pile of old bedding, feeling quite a tramp myself in my messed up clothes. 'And you've moved house, I see?' I commented. 'Literally!'

'What? ..... Oh, yes.' he replied. 'Right farce that was in the fish hall. Wouldn't listen to me, so I thinks, if that young son of mine is carrying on with his dredging, I'd best move house before there's no beach to live on!'

The smile faded from my face. 'Gwenlyn?' I asked. 'Is she ......

upset? Have you seen her or spoken to her? What has she said?'

He rubbed his nose with the back of his hand and looked serious. 'Aye, lad, she's right cut up and all.' Then he smiled, 'But she'll be real glad to be seeing you again.'

I didn't return his smile.

'What's the matter, lad? Surely you'll be wanting to be seeing the lass?'

I nodded my head, then dismissed the thought with a wave of my hand.

'Not quite as easy as that then, lad?' He observed.

I replied sadly, 'No, I wish it were.'

I told him everything that had happened: from my headlong dive into the harbour, Latchley tying me up on the dredger, Nicholas Faversham and finally the wasted trip to Kingsbridge.

He sat and pondered for a while but didn't look too hopeful. 'I'm sorry, lad. I'm partly to blame for getting you in this mess,'

'Don't blame yourself,' I assured him. 'I'll sneak into the house in the dark, grab a few things, and maybe I'll think of something. You never know ....' My voice trailed off.

We talked about harmless things and even shared memories of 'Riding the Wind,' it seemed such a long time ago now. I saw that the old man was getting tired, which I assumed was due to the effort of moving his hut and contents by himself all in the same day. I got up to leave and made for the door.

'One last thing, laddie,' he said carefully. 'I'd be thinking it wise to stay away from Gwenlyn. No knowing what young Latchley will do, so don't get tempted like.'

'Thanks, old timer,' I said affectionately. 'I'll be in touch, I don't know when ..... sometime ...... I'll come back when I've thought of something.'

I closed the door behind me and began the slow walk along the unlit path back to Windle Bridge. It was well into the evening by now and apart from the pubs, I expected the village to be in its usual state of quietness for that time of night. I moved stealthily when I got close. My clothes were dark, but even so, I kept to the shadows.

I was immediately suspicious when I found that the back door was open and even more suspicious when I heard a sound from upstairs. I padded silently across the kitchen floor and looked up the stairs and saw a faint glow of light from the bedroom. Looking around for some sort of weapon I settled on the poker from the kitchen boiler and crept noiselessly up the stairs.

I tested each stair before committing my weight to it, trying to remember which ones creaked and which ones didn't. I was ready to run and disguise my face if necessary, but I also wanted to find out who was prowling around my house.

I stepped onto the landing and raised the poker and while standing well back I peeped round into the lighted room. The door was open and a figure sat on the bed, illuminated by the dim light from the wall. The intruder obviously wanted to be secretive otherwise he or she would have turned on the main lights. The thick curtains were drawn, so very little, if any, light would be seen from the outside.

The figure turned round and looked straight at me and I took a sharp intake of breath. It was as if Gwenlyn was looking right through me. She had a crooked smile on her face and deep shadows were being cast across her cheeks from the light. She stood up and ran her fingers seductively through her hair and rolled her shoulders in a slow, sensual, snake like manner. She was naked to the waist and as she walked towards the door to the landing, shadowy silhouettes danced across her breasts.

I stood rooted to the spot, transfixed by the evil stare in her eyes. I knew that she couldn't see me as I stood in the darkness, but just a few more paces would take her out of the direct glare of the light, and she would probably see the outline of my shape. She stopped, and gave a venomous smile, pouting her lips in a cold indication of carnal desire.

'Is that you, Jonathan, darling?' she whispered in a husky voice, full of innuendo, and I took the opportunity to melt into the darkness beside the bookcase that stood on the landing. All the tender thoughts I'd ever had for Gwenlyn Bardell evaporated in an instant. I felt a surge of anger ...... I also felt sick.

'Jonathan ..... Jonathan darling? ..... Is that you?'

She switched on the main bedroom light and I pressed myself harder against the wall.

'Jonathan, you pig! ..... Are you fooling about?' she snapped, in a much less passionate tone. She looked down the stairs, just within my view but fortunately, she was looking away. She shouted again then gave up and switched the main bedroom light off again and retreated into the more dimly lit room.

I waited a full minute before I dared look, and saw her sitting on the bed again, shoulders pulled back in a gesture of defiance. She was slowly pulling a brush through her hair and I almost let out an audible sigh of relief. It was amazing how similar Charlotte looked to Gwenlyn when her hair was down. I'd only seen Charlotte with her hair up, and the similarity had shaken me badly. I would have to wait and hide until she went, though the prospect of having to wait while she and presumably, Jonathan Latchley, as he was the only Jonathan I had heard

235

of in the village, did whatever it was they were going to do, was not appealing. I felt sorry for Nicholas Faversham. I even felt sorry for Peta Lofgren.

I reached out my hand, and very slowly turned the door knob of the bedroom opposite where Charlotte was. It moved smoothly and silently and I eased open the door and soundlessly slid into the safe haven of the room. I was only just in time because I heard the sound of the back door opening and someone quietly coming in. I had left the bedroom door slightly ajar and I could still see Charlotte on the bed.

She didn't seem to have heard any noise, so she was taken totally by surprise when someone appeared in the doorway. I was equally surprised when I saw that it was Gwenlyn who was the new visitor.

I couldn't catch the opening words of the confrontation as I had had to keep the door almost completely closed to avoid detection, but once Gwenlyn had entered the room, I opened the door wider and could see and hear everything. Charlotte had at some point grabbed her blouse and was hurriedly dressing while Gwenlyn stood waiting impatiently.

'Who was it this time?' Gwenlyn challenged.

Chatlotte was still embarrassed from being caught and hadn't as yet recovered her composure. 'Er ..... I was waiting ......' Her fingers fumbled on the top button. 'For ...... er ...... Peta. Yes, for Peta. He said he'd meet me here.' She looked nervously at the door.

'I saw the light go on and off when I walked past outside,' Gwenlyn announced. 'There's not supposed to be anyone in here ...... and what do I find? My sister waiting for a man! Have you no respect? Alexander dead for a day, and here you are, ready to make love in his bed!'

Charlotte tossed her hair back and tucked her blouse into her skirt.

'So what,' she said casually. 'At least I have my fun ...... By the time you get around to it, you'll be old and grey. I quite liked that Major ... ... a bit of a man; wouldn't have minded him myself.'

'Bitch!' Gwenlyn cried.

'Oh! Names is it now?' Charlotte taunted. 'Well, big sister, I'll sleep with who I like ...... as often as I like ...... and where I like. This isn't your house ...... and how do you know this was the Major's bedroom? My big sister wasn't being naughty was she? No! .....you weren't really ...... you wouldn't know how!'

'Get out!' Gwenlyn ordered. 'Out! How dare you be so ..... so ... .. sick! To even suggest .....!'

Charlotte pushed past Gwenlyn and headed for the door. 'Go on sister, admit it ......you would love to have lain on this bed ...... to feel him stroking your hair ...... your body ...... you'll be a frustrated old spinster and then you'll ......'

There was a noise from downstairs and Charlotte suddenly looked worried.

'Who's that?' Gwenlyn asked Charlotte.

'I ...... well, I suppose it will be ......'

Jonathan Latchley bounded to the top of the stairs and I could just make out the smile on his face as he turned the corner and marched into the bedroom.

'Hello!' he said cheerfully, then stopped abruptly as he saw both sisters there. 'Oh ...... Hello ...... Yes, Gwenlyn my dear ...... I ..... I thought you might be here ...... the light ...... better to investigate. You'll be upset of course. Thought I'd come and cheer you up ... er ... Charlotte ... Gwenlyn will be showing you round? You've probably not been in Tom's place for a while?'

His back was towards me, and his shape filled the doorway but the next thing I knew was Charlotte pushing him to one side and storming down the stairs. He looked after her until she reached the bottom, then walked into the bedroom. Gwenlyn had perched herself on the edge of the bed with her head in her hands.

'Gwenlyn, my dear,' he said to her softly as he, too sat on the bed in my full view. 'This isn't as it may appear.' He touched her shoulder but she pushed him away. 'Look, it was all a mistake. It shouldn't have happened, I'm sorry.'

'A mistake!' she yelled. 'Shouldn't have happened! She was up here waiting for Peta Lofgren! You call that a mistake! You've been kind to her for too long …… and here of all places!'

Relief was etched suddenly all over his face. 'You're so right, my dear.' His emphasis disguising the fact that he had so very nearly been found out. 'So right …… Much too long. I'll have a talk with her. She's young still, she'll learn. I'll talk to Peta as well. It's disgraceful that they should take such liberties!'

He placed a comforting arm around her shoulder and she made no effort to resist as he pulled her towards him. She sobbed quietly as she leaned her head against his chest while he murmured tender endearments to calm her troubled mind.

He released her briefly while he took of his coat, and she used the opportunity to wipe her eyes.

'We need to talk.' He said softly, lifting her chin with his hand. He looked longingly into her eyes and leaned slowly forward until his lips pressed firmly onto hers, then gently pulled her down onto the bed.

Chapter 14

I was already halfway though the door, but stopped quickly when I saw Gwenlyn struggle and push herself away from him. I moved back into the shadows and waited anxiously.

'No, Jonathan! Not here, it wouldn't be right. It wasn't right for Charlotte, so it can't be right for us.'

I was conscious straight away of his anger and disappointment, it was written all over his face, and I thought he was going to grab her, and rape her in front of my very eyes. I was ready to pounce, whatever the consequences. It was with great self control that he forced himself back into a seating position. Gwenlyn got to her feet and wandered to the door, completely oblivious to his frustrations.

'Downstairs ...... we'll talk downstairs ...... not here. He only died yesterday,' she mumbled sadly.

'Was there something between you?' he asked delicately, in a tone that didn't match his face. She wasn't able to see his sour expression, but when she turned to look at him, his demeanour quickly changed.

'I ...... I don't know. Maybe there was, or almost. I'd waited so long for him to come......and you and me, we've been engaged for so many years. Can you understand?'

He nodded his head in a knowing manner giving the impression that he was full of sympathy and compassion. 'I know, my dear. And it is I who must apologise. It's not been easy taking on the business, and I wanted the time to be right …… right for us both.'

She was quiet for a moment then turned back towards the open door. 'Let's talk downstairs. I'm all confused. These last few weeks haven't been easy …… You do understand, don't you?'

'Of course I understand,' he said impatiently. 'But don't forget, I caught you up here that time …… what do you expect me to think? I know I shouldn't have hit you, but I was jealous. You know how it is …… I care for you so much, I just lost my temper.'

She came onto the landing and started downstairs leaving Latchley to give the bed a violent kick before he followed her down. I gave them a few minutes then sneaked into the bedroom. It was no good taking clothes, so I just took the remainder of the money that I'd hidden away. There was about fifty pounds, which wasn't much, but it was all there was. I didn't dare take any of my belongings as it could arouse suspicion, so I had to be content to leave in the ragged clothes I was already wearing, and the small amount of cash.

I headed for the door and noticed, as an afterthought, that Latchely's coat was still on the bed. I thought he might still have the gun, in which case, I would tactfully dispose of it for him, knowing that he wouldn't be able to question anyone as to its whereabouts. But there was no gun; in fact the pockets were empty apart from a bunch of keys. I replaced them, then had second thoughts. I could think of no use for them for myself, but it might cause him a modicum of inconvenience if his car keys were to disappear. A small compensation after what he'd done to me, but nevertheless, better than nothing.

I checked to make sure I had left nothing out of place, then gingerly moved down the stairs. I saw a light under the door of the back room and heard the murmur of quiet voices. There was no keyhole so I couldn't see what Latchley was doing, but when I listened carefully, it sounded as if the intimate part of their conversation was over. They had moved onto safer, more superficial subjects like the present state of the fishing and crabbing.

I left quietly through the back door and dodged from shadow to shadow down to the waterfront. A wave of depression hit me as I recognised that I had nowhere to go. I glanced at the dredger moored in the darkness and felt a shiver of fear as I looked at the vessel which had so nearly taken my life.

On impulse, I walked out of the shadows, across the road and onto the harbour wall. I looked around, but everywhere seemed deserted, so I ran to the far end and untied the dredgers stern moorings, raced back and did the same to the for'ard. Within seconds, I was back across the road and into the shadows and safety. I moved carefully past the two pubs, then cautiously past the remaining few houses and started up the hill which led out of the village.

When I finally reached the bridge I stopped to look back down to the harbour. The tide was on the turn and already the dredger was slowly being dragged out by the receding waves. The stern had moved away from the harbour wall, and soon it began to rise and fall as it drifted into the open sea. I knew it was rash and irresponsible of me, and I pondered briefly on he consequences should the dredger cause any accident to other shipping, I had a faint twinge of regret, but I knew it was too late to do anything about it.

I took one, last look at the village of Windle Bridge wondering if I would ever return, or ever be able to return. I had never really had a home, so here I was, moving on again, travelling away from the only house I had ever owned. I started to run, expressing my anger in the pounding of my legs. I shouted as I ran, voicing my gloom and dejection, venting my despair as I punched the air with my fists.

I pushed myself by running at reckless speed, thundering along the flat stretch of Slapton Ley and pumping my thighs up the hill at the far end. I could feel the pressure building up in my head as I forced myself beyond my limits and eventually, as it always did, the anger subsided and I slowed to a gentle, loping stride. I felt the tiredness of body and mind rapidly taking over so I slowed to a walk while I looked for somewhere to spend the night. I was nearly in Dartmouth, but still in open country, so I moved away from the road side and collapsed into the thick hedging next to a cart track.

My eyes closed in fatigue as I bedded down in the insulating warmth of a thick blanket of autumn leaves and found myself being poked in the side by Jonathan Latchley's keys. I moved them round in my pocket, but their very presence set me thinking.

Latchley would probably be left stranded in Windle Bridge, leaving me with possible access to any secrets that may lay hidden in his office in Dartmouth. It wasn't too far to go, and there was every possibility of one of the keys fitting the office door. With only a moment's hesitation I rose from my crude bed and continued the walk into Dartmouth, and hence to Latchley's office.

The street was dark, and it was difficult selecting the right key, but I found it in the end, and let myself into the outer office usually occupied by the secretary. The connecting door was open, and I risked the use of a small lamp. None of the desk drawers were locked, so I didn't expect anything of importance to be found there, but still looked just in case. I was careful to leave everything exactly as I found it, but there was nothing incriminating to be found anywhere.

I examined the set of keys again and noticed that there was one which was very oddly shaped; certainly not a normal door key. I presumed it to be some sort of security lock, so I set about finding something that it would open. I tried the usual sites behind pictures, in filing cabinets, but there was nothing. I even tried the secretary's office, but again, nothing. I walked up and down the room looking for any clues but quickly came to the conclusion that if he had a safe at all, then he kept it at home.

Amazingly enough, I had never bothered to find out where his home was, so I wouldn't be able to find it if I tried. I thought of trying to find out if he was on the telephone there, but even that was of little help. I stamped my foot in exasperation, and the floorboards creaked in response. I wandered round the room looking everywhere for inspiration, and ended up leaning against the far wall in order to take in one, last overall view of the room before I gave up, then realised that the place I was standing didn't have any creaking floorboards. I stamped my foot, but it was solid.

On the off chance, I knelt and pulled back the carpet to discover a lump of solid concrete set into the floor in the centre of which was a small door, maybe six inches square. I fished out the key, and to my great satisfaction, it fitted. I turned it, and opened up the cleverly concealed safe inside of which was about a cubic foot of space containing a collection of papers and documents. I noted the order in which they were placed and carefully lifted them onto the desk.

There were sums and figures related to the dredging, including expenditure and profit margins. There was also, more interestingly, the details of sale of the six quarries, with the dates of closure of each; the last two being within the last year. Each one had been used to raise capital, but the final two, I noticed, had been sold well below the quoted market value. I soon discovered the reason when I saw an added clause

243

at the foot of the page. Jonathan Latchley had sold at the reduced price, with the proviso that he could repurchase within two years if he so desired.

It was a shrewd arrangement. The new owner of the two quarries had got his hands on a bargain and would get at least two years high profits. Meanwhile, Latchley had managed to raise substantial capital to cover both the pay off for Kingsbridge and leave enough to finance the dredging. I did a few, quick pieces of mental arithmetic and worked out that according to the expected profits; if the dredging was completed, there would be sufficient to cover the repurchase amount of the two quarries, but if the dredging was not completed, there would be a serious shortfall, leaving Latchley pretty well bankrupt.

It was only written proof of what I already knew or had guessed, and sifting through the rest of the papers was of very little help. I carefully rearranged the papers into their correct order and was about to replace them in the safe when I saw a scrap of paper sticking out of one of the documents. The document itself was of no importance but the scrap of paper had an address scribbled on it. I concluded that it had either been placed in the safe by mistake after being scooped up with other papers, or that it was of such importance that it justified the extra security of the safe.

I made a note of the address and replaced it, and everything else, carefully back in the safe, locked it, replaced the carpet and let myself out into the street again. If I had what I thought I had, then I could possibly lay my hands on enough concrete evidence to discredit Jonathan Latchley and possibly prevent any further damage to the harbour and village at Windle Bridge.

I walked with a much lighter step through the night time streets of Dartmouth and ran up the hill out of the town. I was eager to get to the address I had copied, but for that, I needed to get to Bristol, in which case, I would have to wait until morning. I was fortunate to find a hay barn which gave some warmth for the night and I snatched a few hours sleep then set off again at five in the morning.

There was little traffic about but my main concern was that I might catch a lift from someone I knew. On looking down at my filthy attire and feeling my unshaven chin, I appeared every bit a tramp, and would probably be unrecognisable to almost anyone. I got a lift on a lorry going to Torquay and from there I sorted out a rail ticket, and by the afternoon I had arrived at Bristol Temple Meads station.

I walked to the city centre where I bought some new clothes and toiletries then set about finding a hotel for the night, and more importantly, a long, hot bath and a shave. I tried six hotels before I was successful and even then, the room looked as scruffy as I did, but within an hour, I was transformed.

By the time I walked out of the small hotel it was evening and dark. I had bought a map of the city and found the whereabouts of Cotham Brow. It was a couple of miles away so I took a bus which seemed to be going in the right direction. By seven o'clock I had alighted on the Cheltenham Road and was following the map to my destination. It was a long, steep hill and the house I was looking for was almost at the top. I paused for a moment, then apprehensively knocked on the door.

A familiar, and surprised figure opened up and I was asked in, whereupon I spent the next two hours telling my story and explaining what I needed to borrow. I wasn't dealt with very sympathetically, but I explained that it was for the benefit of the villagers, and that I had no wish to interfere directly with any arrangements which may have taken place since the move from Kingsbridge.

I was asked the question about how I had got the address in the first place, and had to further explain about Latchley's attempt to get rid of me permanently, and hence, the clear conscience about letting myself into his office. I didn't think I was believed totally, but I had still told the truth, whether they believed it or not. I was informed that there had been a final pay-off, so with my mental recollection of the figures from the sale, I concluded that Latchley would be in debt unless he finished all of the dredging. Even then, there would barely be enough money to repurchase the two quarries, so it was no wonder he wanted to continue dredging at all costs.

It also made me think again about how he had offered to buy me out, and where he would have got the money to do so. I voiced my thoughts and was greeted with the answer that Jonathan Latchley frequently promised the earth to get himself out of trouble, but with no real intention of paying up. I mentally waved goodbye to what would have been a very useful ten thousand pounds, but commented that I was pleased that at least they had got something out of Latchley.

I said my thank yous and made my way back to the town centre. It was a cold, windy night and I shivered, not so much with the cold, but with the sight of the bomb damage that was left untouched in Bristol. The bed was damp, but I slept until I was rudely awakened by the manager banging on my door to tell me to stop shouting. The sight of the bomb damage had triggered off my own memories of the war, and my skin felt hot and clammy from the unconscious tossing and turning. I didn't sleep again for the rest of the night.

I took a cold bath in the morning, paid my bill to a sleepy manager, and made my way to the station again. It was a sultry, overcast morning with a steady drizzle coming down, which soon left me wet through. Occasional gusts of wind stripped the last, few

246

remaining autumn leaves from the trees, forcing the bare branches to stand naked and exposed in anticipation of the approaching winter.

When I arrived in Dartmouth, the sky was black with cloud, and squalls of drenching rain, driven by blustery wind nearly knocked me off my feet. There was hardly any traffic, so I had to walk most of the way to Windle Bridge. A mixture of salt spray and driving rain stabbed my eyes, so most of the journey was spent head down, with ice-cold hands shielding my face. By the time I reached the turning for the village, the constant buffeting of the wind, and the energy sapping power of the rain had made me feel incredibly tired. Looking out over the sea by the graveyard also left me with a grim foreboding as I saw the build up of a storm from the east. Far off lightning slashed the waves, heralding the distant thunder which rumbled soon afterwards. Clouds gyrated overhead allowing frequent flashes of the moon to spotlight white topped breakers slamming into each other in their race to the shore. Darkness had long ago enveloped the houses as I hastened my step over the bridge and down to the harbour.

There was no need to conceal myself anymore, but I became suspicious when I saw that that there was actually no-one from whom I needed to conceal myself anyway! Both the pubs were closed, and very few lights were burning in the houses nearby. It was usually a quiet village at night anyway, but not this early; it was like a ghost town, with not a soul in sight anywhere!

The dredger was pitching uneasily at its moorings as the waves pounded unchecked into the harbour and with what little light there was available, I thought I detected some damage to the bows. I smiled to myself that I had possibly succeeded in putting a stop to the dredging after all, albeit only temporarily.

I contemplated going first of all to see James Bardell to relate my discoveries, but decided that Peers Lofgren would probably be the best one to confer with initially. I peered up the road anyway, but the Bardell's house next to mine showed no lights.

I doubled back and walked past the fish hall and out of curiosity opened the door a crack and looked inside. To my surprise, the place was packed full with all the villagers, just as it had been for the doomed meeting that Jabber had arranged so recently, resulting in my supposed death. All their attention was being drawn to the front, enabling me to slip in unnoticed out of the wind and rain. One of the bare light bulbs by the door had blown, so I was able to secrete myself behind one of the pillars with little chance of being recognised. I was surrounded by piles of seine nets awaiting repair while on the wall hung a dozen sets of waders which the fishermen used during the long nights in the boats. It all added to the character of the place, uniting with the overpowering smell of fish which permeated everything in the hall.

James Bardell, Peers Lofgren, Jonathan Latchley and Gwenlyn were standing on the concrete platform at the far end. Peers Lofgren was holding sway with a stirring call to unite the village and co-operate until the dredging was done. He outlined plans to give the dredger crew some fishing jobs once the dredging was completed, and now that any bad influences, (presumably myself) had gone, the village could soon return to normal.

There was generous applause from fishing and dredging men alike and Lofgren sat down with a contented smile on his face. James Bardell took the stand and raised his arm for silence.

'Good people of Windle Bridge,' he began, straining his voice so that all could hear. 'We have had some troubled times over the years and none more so than recently.' There were grunts of approval. 'But we have battled on, and have come to a firm agreement, which is why you have been called here together at such short notice.

My good friend, Peers, has already mentioned about the disruption that has been caused by Major Kinsey coming along with falsehoods and lies. We have not seen anything of him since his assault on two of the faithful members of our fishing fleet. One can only presume that he met with the just deserts that his life of violence deserved.'

There was much nodding of heads at this, but I saw a distinct look of sadness on Gwenlyn's face, and I wondered what further lies and rumours had been spread about me.

'Jonathan here assures me that the dredging will be completed in record time, and so remove any further risk to the village.'

I nearly burst out laughing at his short-sightedness. It seemed to be a trait throughout the village; even Gwenlyn had appeared unbelievably naïve on a number of issues, and now I had the opportunity to see where she got it from.

'And so, good people,' he continued. 'To demonstrate the new working relationship in the village, I am proud to announce the wedding in six weeks time, of my daughter, Gwenlyn, to Mr Jonathan Latchley!'

Bardell himself began the applause and the rest of the villagers joined in. I saw Gwenlyn's feeble attempt to smile, whereas Latchley's grin stretched from ear to ear.

'Good people!' Bardell shouted above the clapping, 'I give you Mr Jonathan Latchley!'

Latchley stepped proudly to the front and bowed graciously to the assembled throng. I shook my head in disbelief at the charade being played out, but got grim satisfaction while I awaited my moment.

'Thank you …… thank you!' Latchley chimed, nodding his head

to all corners of the hall in turn. 'This is indeed a very auspicious occasion, and may I personally thank my future father-in-law, and all you good people for the faith you've shown in me.' The room went quiet as Latchley reached into his pocket for his prepared speech. 'As a representative of the dredging interests of the village, it gives me the greatest of pleasure to be able to jointly announce the forthcoming wedding with the lovely Gwenlyn, daughter of James Bardell and representative of the fishing interests of the village. A marriage of two interests as much as two individuals.

You will know, of course, that we have been engaged for a number of years, and many, seeing this beautiful example of God's creation, will be thinking, 'why did he take so long?''

A wave of laughter went around the hall and Latchley smiled in acknowledgement at the appreciation of his mild touch of humour.

'I admit that, though a man of impeccable taste, I have felt woefully inadequate to take the hand of this dear, young lady. The events which have occurred in our community over the last few weeks have made me think how fortunate I have been to attract the affections of such a charming woman, I would be a fool not to capitalise on such attention.

Mention has been made of the late Mr Kinsey, a sad case, but one from which we can all learn a great deal. We can all be victims of circumstance, and although the deceased was, as we know, a man of violent, and ...... dare I say it ...... murderous nature ...... we surely cannot hold that against him now that he is no longer with us. Now is a time for reconciliation and forgiveness ...... a time to rebuild the unity of our village, a time even to rebuild our harbour! I fully intend to carry out my promise of using the dredger to build a temporary breakwater as was discussed at our last gathering here.

Finally .....' he said with a big sigh. 'I am proud to say .....' He took a pace to his right and lifted the hand of a very sad looking Gwenlyn. 'I am proud to say, that this is the happiest day of my life!'

I stepped out from behind the pillar. A shame to spoil the happiest day of someone's life, I thought, but that's how it is.

'Why wait six weeks?' I shouted.

Latchley squinted in my direction, trying to make out who was speaking, but I kept my face in the shadow.

'Six weeks?' he repeated. 'What a strange question to ask! Easy enough ......Convenience! The dredging will be finished ...... or nearly finished ...... Some time to tidy up loose ends with the port authorities in Plymouth ...... No point in any sooner.' He shrugged dismissively, and went to sit down on one of the available chairs.

'Sure there's no other reason?' I shouted back.

'Of course not! Who is this asking, anyway?' he queried.

'Why not five weeks?' I said as I walked out of the shadow and into the brighter light.

There were gasps from the back of the hall as people turned round and recognised me, while the blood drained from Latchley's face. I strolled to the front with the crowd conveniently parting as I walked through. Gwenlyn sat down with a jolt, but I avoided looking at her for as long as I could so as not to miss Latchley's reaction. James Bardell was red in the face and was sharing a rapid conversation with Peers Lofgren.

'You have no right to come here like this!' Bardell boomed.

I looked at him with contempt. 'No right! So you have a right to condone the rock throwing while I was in the water a few days ago! And that's a right is it? A privilege ...... an honour for the occupants

251

of Windle Bridge ….. judge, jury and executioner …… is that it? Do you think you're above the law to be able to mete out your own justice? Too good compared with everyone else in the land, are you?'

I took a step onto the concrete platform and looked at each of them in turn, Latchley, Bardell and then Lofgren …… I still avoided looking at Gwenlyn.

'Mr Bardell is correct!' Lofgren said with indignation. 'You have no right to come here after the things you have done!'

I walked right up to him and stared him straight in the eye from barely six inches. 'I don't think I'm hearing properly,' I said sharply. 'I'm just as much an inhabitant of this village as anyone here, so I have as much right as……' My eyes alighted on Gwenlyn with a mixture of relief and fear written on her face. I wiped the back of my hand across my mouth while I looked at the villagers. '…..Here's what I am going to do. All I ask is the right to speak …… That's all! I'll say what I have to say …… if you don't believe me, or if you don't accept what I say, then I'll go! I'll empty my house and be gone, and on my word of honour, I will never come back.'

'What honour?' someone shouted, but I didn't get the chance to reply before Lofgren stepped up to speak.

'It is a mark of this country as it is in my own, that a man may speak. I do not like this man anymore than you do, but if he must speak, then let him speak and be done with it.'

'Thank-you,' I said courteously. 'A gentleman …… and my word stands ….. You listen and if you don't approve, then I will leave; is that acceptable?'

There were some half-hearted nods of heads and a few shakes. It was a tough, uncompromising assembly, moulded, male and female alike, by livelihoods dictated by the sea. Impassive, weather beaten faces telling their own individual stories of hardship and adversity. In many ways it was no surprise that they handled their grievances in such an intransigent manner.

'Fair enough,' I continued. 'I know many of you by sight, some by name ...... you all either know each other, or are related to each other: brothers, sisters, cousins, aunts, uncles; but you don't know me, do you? ..... You know what's been said about me, about my past. Well, I don't deny it. The bare facts of what you heard are true, but we all have a past, even those of you who are closely related, closely associated with others, you have a past! ..... And don't deny it; there are areas of that past that you wouldn't want other people to know about. We all have chapters of our lives we would like to re-write, but sadly, no matter how much we regret it and no matter how hard we try, we can't do it, It's imposiible!'

None of them even flinched; stone hard faces like granite statues, but I wasn't put off. Human nature is the same the world over.

'My past shows me to be a bully! A perfectionist with a paranoid fear of failure, such that while in the army I would drive my men to their limits and beyond ...... some of them cracked ...... some of them didn't survive. And I knew that eventually ...... one day ...... I would crack too. I knew that I would fail, make a mistake ...... a bad one ... ... and I did. I killed a room full of children and the nuns who were looking after them.'

Expressions of horror spread over many of their faces, and one woman whom I recognised as someone I had met in one of the shops, began crying. I waited while someone comforted her, and until the hall became still and quiet again.

'And that's not all! The rest of my unit was massacred

immediately afterwards! Only two of us survived, and the other is a cripple. I'm not proud ...... I'm bitterly ...... bitterly ashamed! Since that time I have been tortured day and night by that memory. Not only that, but we failed to destroy our target, which was an enemy command post which coordinated the communications around the Salerno beaches in Italy. Thousands were slaughtered on those very same beaches on that very same day! I have to live with that ...... Don't you see? I have to live with that day and night ...... Every bloody day, and every bloody night!'

I stopped as my voice broke and took some deep breaths before I was able to continue. 'I spent six months in a psychiatric wing and then I joined the church! ..... Yes! ..... Some of you look surprised! It's not Major Kinsey, it's the Reverend Kinsey! I was curate in a country parish with a kind, gentle old man and his wife. I only came down here when I discovered who I really was ...... the son of Thomas Bradbury. I was welcomed ...... at first ...... But for reasons which I shall make very clear, Jonathan Latchley wanted me out of the way. He found out about my past and spread rumours ...... And the result? You all know because you've been part of it, so it's very plain for you all to see. I'm ostracized, driven out ...... supposedly drowned ...... and all because of this man! And yet you believe everything he says!'

I stepped off the platform and walked across the front of the hall, mingling with the people. 'What do you see from down here?' I asked, then I pointed at Latchley who glared back angrily. 'You see a businessman. Not like us down here; us common fisher folk. He wears a tie; has an office, a car, speaks well. We admire him, respect him, envy him, envy his money, his power, his influence. So when he says something, we believe it. When he says that an ex-soldier has come here to cause trouble; we believe him, do exactly as he says ......

exactly as he wants.

We lose half a harbour wall, but do we listen to the murdering ex-soldier? ..... Do we listen to this man's father even? No, we don't ...... but I tell you that the man to whom you so willingly bow down.....' And I pointed an accusing finger at the fuming Jonathan Latchley. 'I tell you that the very roots of this man's life are founded on deceit!'

I stopped my pacing up and down and looked long and hard at Gwenlyn, who eventually and embarrassingly, met my gaze. 'Good people of Windle Bridge ......all speeches in here start with the words 'good people'..... perhaps you are good ...... I've seen little evidence from most of you! Only two people accepted me for what I was ...... for what I am, Old Jabber ...... a tramp ...... a hermit ...... and a gentleman ...... and Miss Gwenlyn Bardell.

I stepped onto the platform again, my eyes never leaving hers. 'A life of deceit!' I repeated for all to hear. 'His whole life has been one of deceit and it now threatens this whole village. Six weeks? ..... Why did I ask six weeks? ..... Why not four? why not five? The Reverend Kinsey could officiate at the wedding of this charming couple, but the Reverend Kinsey could only do that in six weeks' time. The Reverend Kinsey could not do it in five weeks' time, because, until then, Mr Jonathan Latchley is still married to somebody else!'

Chapter 15

'That's a damn lie!' Latchley yelled in outrage. 'You can't believe such an absurdity ...... not from someone like him!'

I kept completely calm, reaching into my pocket and withdrawing some papers. Latchley lunged at them but I side-stepped smartly, and he lost his balance, knocking into James Bardell. I waved the papers in the air for all to see.

'The wedding took place eight years ago in London, of Mr Jonathan Latchley and Miss Jane Louise Finchley who gave birth five months later to a son, Edward Charles Latchley.'

There were shouts from the villagers and I had some difficulty in restoring order.

'The proof is here ...... but that's not the whole story! You forget that he'd got engaged the year before to Gwenlyn here, but on being called to London for a contract, believe it or not, to provide sand bags for the war effort, he had a brief romance with Miss Finchley. On finding out that she was pregnant, rather than face public disgrace, he married her, hoping to keep it secret and eventually find some way to divorce her at a later date.'

Latchley looked at me with fire in his eyes. Any credibility he once had was now destroyed, but the villagers still needed to know the extent of the likely damage he had caused.

'But ......' I continued, 'he underestimated the woman, who loved him passionately. She threatened to expose his secret unless he acknowledged her. He refused, so she began to extort money out of him to keep her quiet. He paid up, and the new Mrs Latchley purchased a house in Kingsbridge so that she could be near her husband, and so he could see his son. The amount of money paid to keep her silent rose more and more until he had to sell off six quarries one by one.'

I looked around the enthralled audience, and saw Peta Lofgren standing impassive halfway back. I would need to be careful what I said, and how I said it.

'The last quarry closed less than a year ago, but fortunately for Mr Latchley here, a big contract came up for dredging one million tons of shingle off the coast of Windle Bridge to be removed to Plymouth. He offered his wife a final settlement if she would go away for good, to which she agreed. The problem was that he needed every ounce of that shingle to cover the expense of the pay-off and also have a surplus to repurchase just two of the quarries so as to start all over again. But he didn't reckon on the effect the removal of the shingle would have on the harbour and the village.'

'He's going to rebuild the harbour!' came a shout from one of the dredger crew.

I shook my head. 'By the time he's finished dredging, there may well be no harbour! ..... There may well be no village either!'

'Ludicrous!' Came the cry from Latchley again, and one or two others joined in.

I shouted above the noise. 'A few days ago, I had the misfortune to be hounded out of this same hall, and my only means of escape was to dive into the water in the harbour. Now have any of you given any thought as to where I hid?'

There was some shrugging of shoulders and shaking of heads and a silence fell on the hall.

'All right …… I'll tell you ……I hid underneath the harbour wall.'

They looked puzzled, so I explained about trying to avoid the rocks that were being thrown at me, and ultimately, trying to hide in the shadow by the harbour wall adjacent to the road, and finding myself, in fact, underneath it. I also explained about being forced aboard the dredger and Latchley's attempt to kill me. When I had finished, the hall remained quiet and I stood back to await their decision. Latchley stood stock still, dazed with shock.

'People of Windle Bridge,' Peers Lofgren began. 'We now have to decide whether or not to believe this man, and what to do next?'

Dan Bredan immediately raised his hand. 'I reckons I believe him, even if he is a murdering son of a bitch!'

There were murmurs of agreement all round, and I began to relax with relief.

'Very well, Mr Kinsey,' Lofgren said again, taking charge. 'What do you suggest?'

'Suggest?' I said. 'Now …… I'm no weatherman, but all of you here; you're fishermen and women …… sailors …… you know the sea. When I came in here, there was heavy rain and strong winds coming in from the east. There was thunder and lightning in the distance so is that a storm coming this way or not?'

'Aye ……' Bredan shouted again. 'Glass has been falling for nigh on two days now, so yes, there's a storm brewing, we all knows it.'

'In that case,' I replied. 'I suggest we don't take any chances, and

259

that we evacuate the village ...... starting with those closest to the sea. Move everyone up the hill towards the bridge and the cemetery. Nothing may happen, but if it's a bad storm, as you say, then people will be out of danger ..... Take waterproofs, some warm clothes ...... children first. I'll say it again, let's take no chances; if nothing collapses there'll be a chance to strengthen the harbour wall before the next storm, but it's much too late for this one.'

I forgot about Latchley in the urgency of the situation and was just about to issue some final orders when Lofgren interrupted me.

'One thing, Mr Kinsey, before we do anything. There is one hole in your story. For what reason was Mr Latchley here granted a divorce? He had been trying for many years, or so you say ...... and suddenly he is successful. The pay-off, as you call it, cannot be that much larger than that which the lady has been getting previously, yet suddenly, she changes her mind.'

I sensed Latchley stiffen. He had been accused of a fair number of things, including attempted murder, but Lofgren asked the one question I dreaded, and I think, the one question Latchley himself dreaded more than anything else as well. An accusation of attempted murder was his word against mine, but Lofgren's question had much greater implications.

'It's not that important.' I said, dismissing the subject.

'Well I am thinking it is!' Lofgren stressed fiercely.

I hesitated, but couldn't envisage of any other way round it, so I took a deep breath. 'What are most divorces granted for? Latchley here wanted to marry Gwenlyn ...... his wife wouldn't let him, no matter how much he paid her so he had to prove to his wife that he had been having an adulterous affair, she would then feel obliged to divorce him.'

'Who, Mr Kinsey?' Lofgren asked softly so that no one else but those close could hear.

'It's really not important,' I said avoiding his question.

He shouted this time. 'Who?'

He knew ...... of course he knew ...... I caught him looking at Peta, his son out of the corner of his eye. 'Very well ...... It was Charlotte Bardell.'

I had underestimated the speed at which Peta Lofgren could move. Within seconds he had mounted the concrete platform and had his fingers around Latchley's throat. In the confusion that followed I caught the words Peers Lofgren was shouting into his son's ear as he tried to separate the two of them.

'You would not listen! I tell you all the time she is a bad girl! Now will you believe me?'

We pulled Peta away from Latchley and it was only then that I remembered James Bardell. He was slumped down on the edge of the platform with Gwenlyn's arms around him, a broken man. I started over to try and show comfort in some way, but Peers Lofgren, still holding his son, stopped me.

'No!' He ordered. 'Continue ...... You must tell it all!'

I looked at him reluctantly, then faced the bewildered villagers who were becoming more restless by the minute. 'I'm sorry ...... I didn't want it to come to this. Nicholas Faversham, when I talked to him, told me how he had met up with Charlotte in Dartmouth and Plymouth ...... but it was a cover up. Faversham had been told by Latchley here that Charlotte wanted to see him, but it was just an excuse for Latchley to be with Charlotte so that Charlotte could be taken to Kingsbridge and paraded in front of Mrs Jane Latchley. If anyone had discovered that Charlotte was missing from the village, Faversham would get the blame. And that's it; Jane Latchley consented to a pay-off and divorce, and I was the only one left who could prove anything, so Latchley tried to dispose of me as well.'

I had only just finished speaking when there was a loud crash from outside, like an explosion of some sort. The whole building shook and the lights flickered off causing pandemonium in the hall. The front door flew open and a violent gust of salt spray burst through.

There was screaming and shouting in the frenzy following the sudden blackness, with cries of pain as bodies were crushed in the panic which followed, and the walls quivered as if being struck by an earthquake.

'It's the harbour wall!' yelled a voice from near the door and then the lights came on again.

I heard a scuffling sound behind me and whirled round to find Latchley backing away towards the exit doors where the fish was usually loaded onto trucks. He had his left arm pinned firmly round Gwenlyn's waist and was pointing his gun at her head.

'Nobody move!' he barked above the commotion in the hall. As he reached the doors he kicked them ajar with one foot and stood poised in the opening. 'If anyone follows, she'll get hurt ...... Understand?'

Gwenlyn cried out, but he merely squeezed her tighter, stifling her breath.

There was another crack from outside and he took the opportunity to disappear with Gwenlyn into the darkness. I was about to give chase when the floor vibrated as if it was about to give way.

'Everyone out!' I commanded above the din. 'Through the exit doors here! Collect any children, especially those in the houses closest to the harbour!'

The lights went out again and stayed out this time, and there were shrieks of alarm as more spray rifled through the door. I raised my voice and repeated the order and moved aside to let people through.

'Peers Lofgren ...... where are you?' I yelled in the darkness.

'I am here!' came the reply not far away.

'Meet me at the harbour end of the hall ...... as quick as you can ...... we must see what's happened outside!'

I moved to one side of the hall and worked my way round in the pitch black, avoiding the people who were scrambling madly to get through the small back doors away from the harbour. The wind was blowing like a hurricane and when I got close to the door, I could barely stand on my feet. Lofgren was already there, and together we peered out into the blackness.

The side harbour wall had disappeared and the road outside had cracked in the middle and was slowly tilting away from us. The storm had built up while we had been engrossed in our meeting inside, and it had hit with a sudden, incredible ferocity.

'It is not good, Mr Kinsey,' Lofgren shouted over the din. 'There is no protection for the village now!'

The dredger, loose from its moorings now that the harbour wall had collapsed, was being driven in by the giant waves and was acting like a battering ram on the disintegrating road. It was being lifted like a toy and hammered down again, destroying everything in its path. I dragged Lofgren back into the hall, shouting as loud as I could to make myself heard.

'Can you get some good men? ..... We'll need to check every

house along the front. Go in through back doors or windows ......
Smash your way in if necessary! Make sure everyone is out ...... use
the back street ...... get them up the hill ...... the bottom of the hill is
vulnerable, it's too close to the harbour, so have some strong men there;
with ropes, torches ...... anything you can lay your hands on which
may be useful ...... and then we'll check on the houses progressively
working back from the harbour! We'll need to be quick, we don't know
how badly the foundations of the village have been undermined!'

Lofgren vanished into the darkness of the hall, and I heard him
barking orders and asking the whereabouts of certain, trustworthy men.
There was another deep rumble and some plasterwork fell from the
ceiling onto my head. I peered out of the door again to see more of the
road plummet into the raging waters. It wouldn't be long before the
first building fell. I looked along the road to my left and espied a
moving shadow thirty or forty yards away.

I half closed my eyes against the force of the wind and spray and
struggled along the outside wall of the fish hall. A wave crashed down
and the water washed a foot deep round my ankles, pulling at my legs,
enticing me into the depths. I grabbed onto a drainpipe and clung on
for dear life as another wave hit. I ran the next twenty yards while the
water receded until I reached the figure.

The owner of the shop where I had been refused service, was
trying to save some of his stock which was rapidly being destroyed as
water poured through the broken windows.

'There's no time for that!' I yelled.

'But it's mine!' He sobbed back. 'It's all I've got!'

'It's too late to save it now!' But he carried on regardless. 'Look!
..... It's too, late!' I said again grabbing him by the arm as another wave
hit. We both fell and the backwash sucked us towards the sea. I twisted

round and thrust my legs out, pushing them against the surface of the road. It was enough to stop the pull into the sea as I dragged him to his feet and struck him hard across the cheek.

'What's you name?' I bellowed.

'Edward ...... Edward Ramsden ......Sir!' he replied, cowering back with fright.

'Well, Mr Ramsden, I want you at the bottom of the hill. I want you guiding people across the bottom piece of road and directing them up the hill, away from danger ...... Is that understood?'

He was a portly little man, bereft of hair, and under normal circumstances his reply of 'Yes, Sir! ..... Right away. Sir!' would have amused me.

I watched him scutter the rest of the way to the foot of the hill before I retraced my steps to the fish hall. I went in through the main door and worked my way around the stone tables inside.

'Is everyone out?' I shouted again and again, with no reply, but in trying to find my way, I tripped over a soft bundle on the floor. I bent down and found the unconscious form of a woman, probably trampled in the rush to escape. I lifted her up and carried her out of the rear doors. There were people outside heading for the hill out of the village and I spotted Peers Lofgren giving a group of six men hurried instructions about evacuation.

'Lofgren! Over here!' I shouted.

He looked up and saw me emerging from the hall and marched over quickly with his men. I recognised three of them as dredger crew and the others as fishermen. Lofgren looked down at the woman I was carrying.

'Mrs Tredditch,' he said and spoke to the man next to him.

'Benjamin; take Mrs Tredditch ...... I do not know where her husband is ...... take her to the hill.'

'Edward Ramsden's there.' I interrupted.

'Good ...... Benjamin, let Edward look after her, then come back here, we must clear the rest of the houses.'

I handed her over into the strong arms of Benjamin, then gestured towards the dark interior of the fish hall. 'She was in there, unconscious on the floor. There may be others, but it's pitch black inside ...... someone will need to check with a torch.'

Lofgren gave instructions to one of the dredger crew who had a torch and told him where to rendezvous once he had checked thoroughly.

'Six men are checking all the houses,' Lofgren confirmed. 'Others are making sure that whole families are accounted for.'

I looked up and down the street, feeling the tremor of crumbling foundations under my feet. 'Gwenlyn?' I asked tentatively. 'Latchley, or Gwenlyn ...... any sign at all?'

He shook his head, 'I am sorry ...... I have seen nothing. He will be hiding. We will have to find him later.' He made as if to go then hesitated. 'I am owing you an apology, Mr Kinsey. I should have listened to you. Us Norwegians can be very stubborn!'

'Huh! ...... Never mind,' I replied. 'What's done is done ...... Let's just get these people out safely. We've all made our mistakes, but life goes on.'

His face broke into a faint smile and we briefly shook hands before getting on with our respective jobs.

'The road by the hill?' I commented as we parted.

'Four men with ropes ...... on their way ...... probably in position by now.'

I nodded my head in approval then set off to supervise the stragglers who were struggling to get out of the village.

Within an hour, all the villagers who could be found had congregated above the bridge. There was no transport available and telephone lines were down so it was decided to send someone to Torcross. It was possible that they were in need of assistance as well, but unlikely as they had no harbour as such and were further north from where the beaches had been affected. There would hopefully be transport there to carry some of the older inhabitants and the children, who were all now wet and cold, to safety.

Lofgren organised a head count, and apart from Gwenlyn and Latchley, everyone was accounted for. I looked further up the road and saw James Bardell and Charlotte arguing fiercely, but they were too far away for me to catch what they were saying. Charlotte had not been at the meeting and although I was deaf to Bardell's words, I could guess what was being said. I turned my attention to Lofgren who was happier now that the whole village was out of danger.

I pulled him to one side and spoke to him. 'I must go and look for Gwenlyn.'

'Jonathan Latchley is a dangerous man,' he cautioned.

'I know,' I said with some trepidation.

'But you still go?'

'I must ...... I don't know what he might do to her.'

'In the same circumstances, I would go too. Be careful, Mr Kinsey.'

I left them all there, huddled together for warmth and security, with Lofgren shepherding the flock.

On reaching the bottom of the hill, the road had all but vanished, leaving a two foot wide strip which I had to negotiate to gain access to the village through some of the back streets. Someone had thoughtfully tied a rope as a hand rail around the most precarious part, and I was able to find my way into the deserted village without too much trouble.

Some of the houses closest to the harbour had already succumbed to the force of the waves. The dredger itself was now on its side smashing its way into the fish hall like some giant monster eating away at the masonry, There was a continuous barrage of collapsing brickwork as foundations crumbled and fell prey to the clawing fingers of the sea.

I had no idea where to look, and wondered for a moment if he would possibly head towards Jabber's hut. I hoped Jabber would be all right and was glad that he had moved further back from the sea and consequently, further away from trouble. I decided to search the village first before trying down the coast, knowing that Latchley could be hiding anywhere.

I proceeded cautiously as I expected him to be waiting for me, knowing I would come, especially now the villagers were clear. I kept close into the walls of the houses, glancing all around me for any movement. I span round at one point with the eerie sensation of being followed; the hunter being hunted. I saw nothing in the gloom so I headed up the road to my house and that of James Bardell.

I went into the Bardell's home first, and crept silently from room to room, but there was no sign of any occupation. With my heart thumping, I moved across to my house and entered in through the back door. I padded through the kitchen and inspected the downstairs rooms then moved on up the stairs to the first floor landing. The door to my bedroom was closed, but I saw a faint glow of light under the door. I flattened myself against the wall and gripped the door handle turning it slowly until I felt the door start to open.

I pushed hard and flung myself through the door rolling in a bundle across the floor. I cannoned into the bed which stopped my momentum and I raised my head, but the room was empty. A single candle burned on the dressing table and I cursed myself for falling for the ruse. I had made my presence known with the noise, so Latchley would now know where I was.

I tip-toed out of the bedroom and squeezed myself between cupboard and wall as I had done when I had hidden from Charlotte. From this relatively safe position I proceeded to gently lever open the door of the room opposite mine, where I had hidden on the previous occasion. I released the doorknob and continued opening the door with my foot.

With the utmost caution, I leaned forward and looked into the room. At first I saw nothing, as the only light was from the candle burning back in my room. I had debated whether or not to leave it alight but had decided that I preferred to see where my attacker was coming from, bearing in mind that he had a firearm, and I didn't.

There was a dark outline on the bed and as the door opened wider, I saw Gwenlyn's frightened eyes staring at me. Neither moving or blinking, they focused far beyond me and I thought she was dead, but then her mouth opened in silent warning. I kicked the door hard and was rewarded with a loud cry of distress from behind it.

I darted through the doorway, intent on immobilising Latchley before he harmed Gwenlyn. I saw the dark silhouette of his shape so without hesitation, I launched myself on him. I hit out hard for his face while at the same time landing my knee in his groin. He let out a loud cry so I struck out with straight fingers at his throat, and he went limp

269

under me. I lifted his immobile arms and felt for the gun, but it was nowhere to be found, probably dropped when I kicked the door.

'It's all right, my love!' I said reassuringly to Gwenlyn on the bed. 'He's out cold! ..... he'll not trouble us anymore.'

She began crying and shaking her head and I got up to go over to her.

'It's all right,' I said again. 'It's all over now.'

'Not quite!' came the voice from the far corner of the room, followed by the striking of a match. Latchley lit the candle on the bedside table allowing me to look down at the unconscious form of Peta Lofgren.

'That's were I was standing when the young man came in.' Latchley commented. 'I'm glad I moved! ..... He was not as cautious as you so I made him stand there while we waited. What kept you? I expected you earlier.'

I made no reply as I looked at Gwenlyn on the bed. She had been beaten horribly and her clothes were dirty and torn. Latchley caught me looking at her and laughed sadistically.

'I told you, didn't I, Kinsey? ..... If you came back, I said she'd get hurt ...... And what did you do? ...... You came back! ..... Now that was foolish of you, Kinsey! I also said that if I can't have her, then neither can you ...... Most convenient of you taking care of Lofgren like that; he's too young and headstrong, and a bullet would have been too noisy, even in this storm.'

I gritted my teeth. 'What now? ..... You've got us both where you want us ...... Peta's unconscious ...... What comes next? A bullet each I suppose?'

He laughed again. 'Ooooh ...... no! ..... Much to messy! I'd never stand a chance if I got caught! I can talk my way out of that episode on the dredger ..... very clever of you to escape by the way. But in a court of law, would they really believe you? ..... No! ..... So no bullets; unless of course you get foolish ...... no, we'll let nature do it's job. Failing that ...... yes, a bullet, but much neater without! Now, no more talk, help her off the bed and get her downstairs. One move and she gets it first. I'll look after Lofgren later.'

I took Gwenlyn's hands and lifted her gently off the bed, Latchley had beaten her badly, and she could barely stand. She put an arm round my neck and I put one of my arms round her waist to hold her up and together we hobbled out of the door.

'I'm sorry,' she whispered. 'I was ..... I was so glad to see you still alive ...... And now this.'

'Ssssh.' I said gently and more or less carried her onto the landing. There was no chance of making a break for it as I was fully preoccupied purely by supporting Gwenlyn. Latchley followed at a safe distance while we struggled down the stairs.

We went out of the back door and into torrential rain that stung the skin like myriads of tiny needles. The wind whistled up the street, forcing us back but Latchley drove us on, pushing us down the hill towards where the harbour used to be. Gwenlyn clung to me despairingly, burying her head into my shoulder, sobbing uncontrollably, and together we began our march to where Latchley planned to dispose of us.

I looked at her battered and bruised face with her soaking wet hair flattened across her cheeks and neck. 'The most beautiful woman I had ever set eyes on,' were my thoughts when I first saw her, and my opinion had not changed, despite what Latchley had done to her. I gently caressed her face and ran my fingers through her matted hair, pulling her close to me.

We arrived behind the fish hall and Latchley directed us along and past the door which led out of the hall into the street. The roof had caved in and the dredger had smashed its way through, meanwhile the building next to it had been completely demolished.

'Through here!' he ordered, kicking me on the back of the legs, forcing me to climb over the brickwork of the once proud building. Already, the waves were pounding at our feet as they hammered what was left of the building into oblivion. We reached the front and looked directly out onto where the road and harbour had once been,

Of the harbour there was no trace and only a thin band of road, hardly two foot wide reached towards the bottom of the hill. Most of the front buildings had at least partly fallen down, littering what was left of the road with obstacles which the sea washed off with each wave.

'Stop here!' Latchley yelled against the deafening sound of the waves thundering by us. We stopped, waiting for his push over the drop into the churning water.

'Let her go!' he snapped and I braced myself ready to take him, but he had timed his move well and a wave hit me just as I let Gwenlyn go. He grabbed her while I fell over the brink into the gulf that was left briefly between each swell. I swung round, clutching with my fingertips, hanging crazily to the edge of the road as my legs were pulled down. He stepped back, taking pleasure in my struggles but looking disappointed when I levered myself back up onto the narrow band of road again.

'A pity, Kinsey!' he spat. 'It would have been easier. Now start walking!'

I stood and faced him, not moving, so he took a pace closer to the edge and held Gwenlyn over the drop.

272

'Walk!'

So I walked ...... backwards, grabbing onto whatever hand supports I could, as the waves alternately tore at my feet then receded with the backwash, revealing the deep drop down to the ocean where the road had once been. I looked longingly at Gwenlyn as we got further and further apart. She began screaming, but every time I as much as slowed down, Latchley made as if to throw her to the mercy of the waves.

I clambered about twenty yards along the precarious edge before I noticed what was happening to the dredger which had lain stranded behind Latchley. An extra pull of the undertow was tilting the prow clear of where it had become lodged in the ruins of the fish hall. A gigantic wave followed, which lifted the whole ship and smashed it down like a giant sledge hammer. The piece of road on which Latchley and Gwenlyn was standing completely gave way while the force of the wave sucked them backwards.

At the last moment, in order to save himself, Latchley let go of Gwenlyn and toppled back towards the gap between road and dredger. He steadied himself, but Gwenlyn was free to move.

'Run!' I screamed at the top of my voice. But she was too weak. She took two tottering steps and fell onto her knees, her legs devoid of the strength needed to carry her. Behind her, Latchley tried to balance himself, but the dredger rose again and the next wave dragged him down pulling legs and body beneath the vessel which crashed down on top of him, crushing him to a bloody pulp.

I ran back as far as I could towards Gwenlyn, but with a mighty roar, the road tumbled in to the sea opening an uncrossable chasm between us. She raised her head and looked at me as the ground under her crumbled away.

'No! ..... Please God, No! ..... No! ..... No!'

I watched, helpless as she slid sideways, her pathetic eyes pleading with mine. One leg went first and although she tried to hold on, she had nothing left with which to fight. She looked longingly at me all the time, searching deep into my very soul, and even as the sea took her, she never stopped looking.

'No! .....' I cried uncontrollably. 'Damn you, God ..... Damn you!'

I fell to my knees, stunned with shock, looking at the void where she had once been. Too dazed to move, I shouted and screamed until my voice was too hoarse to utter another sound, then I cried, and cried, until no more tears would come.

Chapter 16

More and more houses tumbled around about me as the onslaught of the waves continued unabated. It was as if an underground channel had been bored by the sea, digging under the bedrock of the village, which, in turn, disintegrated as the fragile foundations gave way. The noise was ear piercing in its intensity as the mighty waters battered the defeated buildings unmercifully, grinding them to destruction, then drawing them with an irresistible force into the dark depths.

I finally pulled myself to my feet, still horror struck at what had happened. I struggled to maintain my footing as I scaled the mountain of rubble which had once been noble and majestic buildings. The waves and the wind tugged at my body, tempting me to give up the fight, taunting me into submission, willing me to follow Gwenlyn into a watery grave.

I slipped and fell, slithering down until the waters were pounding my back like a huge whip, flogging me until I gave in. Each wave was a lashing for the deaths I had caused; the dead children; the remains of my unit and the beaches littered with the corpses of the invasion troops. As each massive wall of water hit me, I dug my feet and hands into the debris, fighting against the powers that were trying to pull me under. I screamed with agony at each crushing blow, but they were not cries of mercy for myself, instead, I saw the faces of those who had loved the ones I'd killed. I saw their grief ...... I felt it ...... I sensed their loss, their emptiness, their futility.

In the mayhem, I no linger felt pity for myself, I simply mourned for the families who had died because of my stupidity and selfishness ...... and I mourned for Gwenlyn also. I felt the pain and guilt cut deeper than any knife, allowing it to slice into my thoughts and emotions, tearing me apart. I yelled out again and again, the oppression becoming unbearable as the wind whistled its scorn, and the waves crashed with their accusations.

Eventually, I lifted my head and clawed my way up and over the ruins. Inch by inch I pulled against the shattered stones, dragging myself against the force of the water. More than once I slithered back, only to drive myself onwards, until I reached the relative security of higher ground. I stood up shakily, then wandered for a while through the deserted streets, dodging slates and bricks as the houses fell apart. Massive cracks had appeared in the streets and twice I was nearly swallowed up by the gaping openings.

I ended up at my house where I had to kick the back door open as it had jammed in its now distorted frame. Large cracks had formed in the walls, but I showed scant regard for the fact that it was no longer safe to be there anymore. Peta Lofgren had gone. He had obviously regained consciousness, and if he was sensible, made his way to safety. I went into my room where the candle was still burning, though the flame flickered erratically with the movement of the building and with the wind that penetrated through the broken windows. I threw myself on the bed and stared at the ceiling, watching, mesmerised as the plaster split open along uneven, unsteady lines as if sketched by some crazy, invisible artist.

My eyes were red and sore and as the candle flame faded out, I closed them and lay still. I experienced an overwhelming sense of grief, anger and helplessness as I thought of Gwenlyn and such a waste of life. I wanted to cry out about the injustice of it all; how unfair it was that the one who was least to blame should be the one to die. I gained no consolation from the fact that Latchley had also died. I merely felt sorry for him and others like him, who lived lives dictated by greed and deceit.

*****

I lay there with my mind in turmoil, struggling to think rationally, but finding it almost impossible; so much so, that for a while, I doubted my sanity. The one recurring thought, however, was the inclination to get away, to remove myself from the scene of the nightmare. The loud crash of falling masonry outside finally convinced me and I climbed off the bed and gathered together what few possessions were worth taking with me. I came across the photograph album containing the pictures of my father and Gwenlyn and hurriedly tore out a few pages and placed them in a small suitcase with the rest of my belongings.

Minutes later, I stepped out again into the pitch darkness and carefully made my way to the edge of the village to where the road had once led up the hill away from habitation. I could faintly make out the shape of people standing there, the rest having probably been taken to Torcross or to Dartmouth. I was about to negotiate the narrow section where the rope was still in place when a thought suddenly flashed through my mind, and I retreated into the shadows again.

As I had not returned, and as they would find Latchley's body in the morning, I could easily, also be presumed dead. No-one would be any the wiser. I would be able to disappear; start a new life somewhere,

277

and with no guilty past to haunt me.

I conveniently rejected any immediate doubts as to whether it was possible or not, instead, I concentrated on finding another way out of the village. I knew there was no other road, but after some judicious searching I managed to climb over some rocks, scramble up a steep slope and appear on a hill a hundred yards above where the last remaining people were standing.

A vehicle's headlights pierced the night but there was plenty of time to conceal myself. I continued on my way after it had passed me by, and once at the top of the hill, I turned south. The road was deserted so I was able to walk uninterrupted for a number of miles. I was soaking wet so I didn't dare stop until I found somewhere dry and warm.

The rain slackened to a drizzle, though the wind was still high and I was beginning to despair of finding anywhere to rest. Finally, I stumbled on a deserted cottage with an overgrown garden and only half a roof, but it was ideal for my requirements. There wasn't much there, but it was good enough for me to change out of my wet clothes and leave them out to dry a little. There was on old, iron bedstead so I manufactured a makeshift mattress from some damp, feather pillows which I discovered in a cupboard. I didn't have the luxury of a blanket, so I rolled myself up in a piece of carpet; even so, it wasn't long before I began to shiver, but more with delayed shock than with the cold.

I stayed there for the rest of the night and the whole of the next day, and it was well into the following evening when the pangs of hunger forced me to move on. Apart from the obligatory calls of nature, I had remained almost immobile for twenty four hours, and my limbs felt stiff and sore.

I had no real plans, so I walked aimlessly for miles, eventually ending up in a small village where I found a room for the rest of the night above the local public house. In the morning, I hitched a lift to Plymouth where I took board and lodgings for a week and nearly ran out of money.

I knew that I was desperately in need of help. I was wallowing in a fit of depression which had left me at an all time low, yet I could think of no-one to turn to, then I walked past a church and thought of Father John and Isobella.

*****

It was quite late that night when I arrived at their door. The whole house was in darkness and despite repeatedly ringing and knocking, there was no answer. I broke a side window, lifted the catch and climbed in. There was a bright moon, so I avoided turning on the lights so as not to attract attention. There was some fruit and vegetables in the pantry so I helped myself as I'd hardly eaten all day. My old room had not been touched since I had left, so I crept under the bedclothes and slept.

I stayed for three days, never daring to go out in case I was seen. I still had the idea of finding a new identity, consequently I had nearly two weeks growth of beard. I settled into bed early on the third night with the intention of leaving before dawn. I had just dozed off when the light came on and I woke with a start to find Isobella standing in the doorway.

I don't know who was more surprised, but she recovered first, running over and throwing her arms round me in a tight embrace. Father John, on hearing the commotion, appeared soon afterwards and greeted me with the same enthusiasm as his wife had done. He was clearly overcome and it was a while before he was able to speak.

'Alexander! ...... Alexander, my boy! ..... my dear, dear boy!' he kept muttering under his breath while continually shaking his head in disbelief.

When Isobella finally released her grip on me, I noticed her glance at the pictures of Gwenlyn which I had placed on the bedside table. The initial joy of their welcome vanished instantly.

She reached out and picked one of them up, hesitating before she spoke. 'She's ..... she's very beautiful.'

All I managed was a brief nod of my head while the memories of my short stay in Windle Bridge came flooding back.

'Was! ..... She was very beautiful!' I stammered.

'No!' Isobella said firmly. 'She is beautiful!'

I sighed deeply. 'Yes, I suppose in my memories she'll always be beautiful, but you don't know what happened......You don't know what happened between us......What happened at the end.'

Father John sat down on the bed. 'Alexander, my dear boy, we've just spent ten days in Dartmouth, we know everything that happened. As soon as we heard the news, we went straight down. It was the headlines in all the papers. They mentioned that you had disappeared, probably drowned, but we couldn't just stay here and wait, we had to go and find out for ourselves, and here you were, all the time!'

'Not all the time,' I corrected, feeling ashamed. 'I came here as a last resort because I couldn't think of anywhere else to go. I decided that with Gwenlyn dead, and no-one else having seen me, I would be able to escape and start a new life somewhere ...... start afresh ...... new name, that sort of thing. I knew they'd probably presume me drowned, so I saw it as my chance; my one, last chance to break away from my past forever. But I lost my nerve, I had to tell someone, so I ended up back here. I was going to leave first thing tomorrow and you just happened to come back tonight.'

They both looked puzzled, 'But haven't you read a newspaper or listened to a wireless?' Father John asked.

'No,' I said, shaking my head.

'Then you don't even know!' Isobella exclaimed.

'Know what?'

'The night of the storm.'

'What about the night of the storm?'

She looked across at Father John. 'John, dear ...... he doesn't know!'

I pulled myself up quickly, urging them to tell me whatever it was that I didn't know about.

Isobella's expression darkened into a frown. 'When I came up the stairs and first saw you in your room here just now, I thought ...... I thought you knew, but that you couldn't face going back. Alexander, she's ...... she's ......'

She couldn't finish the sentence. Father John sat immobile while she ran from the room.

'What happened, John?' I whispered in the sudden quietness of the room.

Father John kept peering down at the bedclothes, picking off bits of fluff to hide his nervousness. He spoke softly. 'We heard you'd gone back into the village. A young boy called Peta told us how you barged into the room where Jonathan Latchley was holding Gwenlyn. We don't know quite what happened after that. Latchley's body was found

281

in the morning.

Gwenlyn was found further down the coast, swept onto the beach by the tide. The old hermit, Jabber found her, and seeing signs of life, he carried her back to his hut.'

'Then she's alive!' I shouted, leaping off the bed, but Father John's tone didn't lighten.

'You must remember, my boy, that she'd been in the water for goodness knows how long, and then even longer cold and wet on the beach. Jonathan Latchley had done his worst to her and she was weak long before she even went in the water ...... her lungs are badly damaged, she's still unconscious, and they don't expect her to live.

*****

I drove through the night in Father John's Austin, only to be told on my arrival that she was weakening fast. I stayed by her side day and night, talking to her and stroking her hair. Her face was bruised and battered and her eyes sunk deep into their sockets. Many times during those long nights I wondered whether or not it would be better just to let her go.

It was three o'clock one morning when she touched me; the faintest of movements, as in the moonlight, I watched her fingers intertwine with mine. I lifted her hand gently to my lips and held it there ...... and in the stillness, I found peace.

Epilogue

It was too risky for my mother to ever bear her own children as she was too frail so that's how I came to be adopted when I was a few weeks old. I remember her shuffling around the kitchen at the vicarage as if she was floating; she somehow always reminded me of an angel. She passed away when I was only fifteen and even though I missed her dearly, in some strange and inexplicable way it wasn't a sad affair. Dad went on much longer and even managed nine holes of golf just a few weeks before he died!

I knew a little about the events all those years ago, but it wasn't until I asked Dad one evening about the marks on his neck that he told me the whole story. I have written it down pretty well word for word as he described it, with the occasional visit to the newspaper archives to check the odd detail.

There's not much more to add really as the story tells it all, but as I sit here in the garden with my own children and with the first grandchild on the way, just one thought stays with me.... he was the best Dad in the world!

Tom Kinsey 2005